Heartbeat

ALI PIERCE

For my parents
who have shared over
forty-seven years of heartbeats

ALSO BY ALI PIERCE

Fractured Promises

Dirty Blind Date (Novella)

PROLOGUE

I prop open the car door and feel the frigid air of the interior rush over my arms as I'm pelted in the face by the stifling heat of the August morning. I throw an arm across my forehead trying, without success, to shield my eyes from the sun's brightness while simultaneously gasping for breath as my lungs become accustomed to the weight of the humidity. I've always wanted to visit this place, but I'm quickly rethinking my wish, considering its unwelcome embrace.

"Ugh, I'm totally questioning our visit today. It's hot as Hell out there." My mother clears her throat, her universal sign for 'watch your mouth,' as she sits in the front seat slathering sunscreen all over her pale arms.

My brother, Marshall, stands outside my door, baseball cap pulled down tight, with a wicked grin plastered across his face. "Look at the bright side. Splash Mountain will be open. Girls in wet t-shirts. Buck up, buttercup. The day is bound to be full of wet boobs."

Marshall turned fourteen at the beginning of the summer, and it's like he was gifted with girl radar. Girls are all he talks about. He's annoying, and I know I'll never be crazy about girls. Ever.

Dad's shadow falls across my door. "Are you going to sit in the car all day?"

He's bouncing on the balls of his feet like he's preparing to sprint across the parking lot and forget us all in his quest to ride every attraction he can cram his six-foot, five-inch body into. I feel sorry for my mom who'll be forced to stand in line for every ride but never actually step on one because of her motion sickness. She's a saint, especially in this heat, but I think she's secretly looking forward to catching up on some reading while not getting razzed by Dad for bringing books on vacation.

Dad steps back and glances at his watch as Mom slides from the front seat. My body has finally started to acclimate to the heat, so I slowly stretch and climb out of the back seat. I'm not as tall as Dad or Marshall, but I'm not short. Within a few more years, my five-foot, six-inch frame isn't going to fit so comfortably in the back seat.

Marshall slaps me on the back, "Try to keep up with us, will 'ya?" Then he turns and matches dad's stride as they race each other across the parking lot.

I hang back with Mom who's walking as fast as her five-foot frame allows her to travel.

She pats the side of her shorts and pulls a sly grin. "They won't get far. I have their tickets in my pocket." She holds out her fist, and I bump my knuckles to hers.

———

I TWIST my arm around and pinch the back of my shirt, pulling it away from my spine where sweat has pooled at my waistband. We've been stopped near a water fountain, with a statue of a big dude holding a barrel under each arm, long enough for my mom to slide her book from her backpack and dive between the pages. Bored, hungry, and uncomfortable, I lean my chin on my mom's shoulder and start reading her book until I see the word *penis* and quickly avert my eyes. *What the hell is mom reading? Is that even legal to put in a book?*

Marshall lifts his cap and wipes the sweat from his brow. "Whoever thought it was a good idea to visit this place in August should be tied up and tickled until they pee their pants."

Mom shoots a finger in my dad's direction and continues reading while Dad stands next to her, oblivious of the conversation, as he studies the park map while running a finger across its shiny surface. "Not sure who that could have been. Any ideas, Matthew?"

My dad's head pops up at the call of his name. "Huh?"

"Marshall wants to know who decided we should come here in August."

"Oh, that was me. I like the heat."

He drops his head and continues his perusal of the map like he didn't just inform his family that we're all sweating through our shorts because he *enjoys* wringing sweat out of his briefs at the end of the night.

"I'll be over there." I point to a vacant bench on the other side of the carousel. "Come get me when Dad figures out our next stop."

I stalk over and slump down on the seat, pissed off that I'm more focused on my leaking bodily fluids than enjoying my day at the happiest place on Earth. Tilting my head toward the ground to keep the sun from scorching my eyeballs, I catch a glint of silver peeking from under an overturned, empty paper cup. It's probably just a dime which isn't really worth the effort today. My curiosity finally wins and forces me to lean over and flip the cup.

My brain takes a moment to compute what my eyes are

seeing. I reach down and pick up a gold chain. I allow it to dangle it in front of my face as I examine it. I'm no jewelry expert, but it looks delicate and expensive. It twirls in the sunlight as rays reflect off the heart hanging in the center of the chain. I flatten my hand and place the necklace across my palm noticing, for the first time, the heart has a musical note made of sparkling gems with the word "hope" engraved beneath the stones. The way it reflects the sun throws sparkles across my hand. *Why couldn't I have found a rare baseball card or a twenty-dollar bill instead of a useless piece of stupid jewelry?*

I close my fingers around my pointless treasure and stare at people as they pass. A family of seven, wearing identical blue shirts with a silhouette of a mouse, marches by with determined steps. Each family member files by in a straight line, with looks of purpose, as they cross under the archway to the castle.

Thank heavens my mom didn't present us each with matching t-shirts this morning. Even though I *could* have gotten on board with matching cooling neck bandanas. I would have looked totally stupid wearing it, but I would have sacrificed any number of "cool" points if it meant feeling more comfortable and avoided the sweat train currently trickling down my back.

An older woman, maybe a little older than my mom, catches my eye. More accurately, I'm drawn to the bright orange flag that's suspended two feet above her head and secured to a thin pole she's holding in her right hand. My gaze shifts down the pole to her black, curly hair that nearly camouflages a plastic sun visor which is a perfect match to the orange of her flag. The woman stands ramrod straight even though she's sporting a sizable backpack that appears to be pulling at her shoulders. She also has a smaller pack with a first aid symbol strapped around her waist.

I thought I was uncomfortable. This woman looks like she's

leading a pilgrimage out of Hades. I'd feel sorry for her if I still had the energy which evidently left my body hours ago.

With her wrinkled brown shorts and her sweat-dotted yellow polo, she looks ten times more miserable than me. But, she's on her feet and walking which is more than I can say for myself at this point. Actually, she's coming straight at me with no indication of stopping. *What the heck?*

An instant before I jump from my seat concerned she's going to walk across my lap and continue over the back of the bench, the woman stops and abruptly turns giving me an up-close and very personal view of her backside. Patches of wetness show through her clothing in places no boy should ever be caught staring at.

She puts her left hand in her pocket and pulls out a stack of notecards before turning sideways allowing me to see half of her face as well as a small group of students standing around her who look to be close to my age. She starts reading names from each notecard, lifting her chin to watch until a student raises a hand, before she flips to the next notecard and repeats the process. It's at this point, I realize the students must be on a class trip of some kind and she is the poor soul tasked with keeping track of all of them. Suddenly the orange flag and bright yellow shirt make more sense. Heck, the woman has my attention, and I'm not even one of the students on her field trip. She finishes reading names and gives her students instructions that they are free to use the restrooms as well as get something to eat or drink and meet back at the bench—my bench—in thirty minutes.

I'm pretty sure I hear a kid mutter, "Finally," before turning and pulling three other boys toward the nearest popsicle stand. The students waste no time as they peel off in small groups of two and three students. All the students, as well as the frazzled chaperone, scurry away except for a petite blond in a purple dress and shiny shoes. Her dress reminds me of what most of the girls are wearing when my mom drags us to church on Christmas Eve. Even to my twelve-year-old eyes, those clothes look like a terrible choice for a trek around the park.

She approaches the bench, her steps light, but purposeful. Without looking at me or asking if the seat is taken, she steals the empty space on the bench next to me. A sigh filters through her lips as she folds her hands, placing them in her lap, and stares at the people. I try to sneak another glance at her without turning, but I'm only able to see her lower half from my peripheral vantage point. The longer we sit, silence hanging between us, I worry if my deodorant is making good on its promise to keep me odor-free, no matter the exercise. I'll be honest, I've never cared how I smelled until this girl sat down next to me. She's so close that our legs, our very sticky, sweaty limbs, are nearly touching.

Clearing my throat and pitching my voice so it doesn't crack, I tilt my head sideways toward her. "I think that guy in the yellow shirt over there is a lemon salesman. It's the only explanation for his sour face."

I feel her shoulders shift as her eyes look for the man in question. The one with the yellow shirt stretched across his protruding belly and the tilted toupee in danger of falling from his head. A snort, like a baby pig's, escapes from her lips, and she immediately lifts her hand to stifle it. I fully turn to look at her and find blue eyes staring at me from the cutest beet red face I've ever seen.

She drops her eyes as I give her shoulder the smallest of nudges. "Sorry I startled you, but it's totally true."

She lifts her sky-blue gaze to my face and drops her hand. The red of her face has faded to a natural pink hue. "How do you do that?" Her voice is soft, like a feather floating across my ear.

"Do what?" My eyebrows crinkle, confused by her statement.

"Make up stories about random strangers."

"They just come to me. Beats being bored."

Her eyes scan the area, landing on someone for a few seconds before moving to the next. "True. I can see how it would pass the time."

I turn my head and pick another stranger from the crowd. "See that lady over there." I raise my finger just enough to direct her attention.

She sits up straighter to see around another woman who's pushing a two-seater stroller. "The one with the floppy, curly hair?"

"Yep. She owns a poodle named Mopsie. They share everything, including haircuts."

Entertained by the game and prepared for my ridiculous lines, her reaction is a laugh instead of a snort. The giggle is low pitched and kind of cute.

I hold my hand out like I'm serving her. "Your turn."

She's silent for a few minutes as she looks across the crowd, her eyes stopping for a few seconds before moving to someone else. "The little boy wearing the Goofy hat sitting in the stroller."

I nod my head, then realize she's not looking at me and missed my response. "Yeah."

"He's a super baby. Massively intelligent. Used mind control to tell his parents he wanted that hat."

I give her a nudge with my elbow. "Not bad for your first time."

She turns back to look at me, and her hair whips me in the face. I bat it out of my mouth. "Watch it! That's a weapon of destruction you've got there."

"Oh, gosh, I'm so sorry."

"Hey, meathead!" Marshall's voice floats over to us.

I turn my head and see him waving me over to where he is lounging with my parents. My dad stands, scanning the crowd, the park map now stowed in the side pocket of his cargo shorts. The weird book my mom was reading has disappeared which means we're ready to seek out our next thrill. I lift my hand and hold up one finger, to indicate I'll be right there, before I turn back to the girl and open my hand revealing the necklace.

I push it toward her and move to stand up. "Here, why don't you have this."

Her eyes widen as she looks down to see what I'm trying to give her. "Um, that looks really expensive. Why are you giving it to me?"

I lift my shoulders and let them fall as I bite my lip and organize my words. Something from a book I've read slides through my memory. "Hope is the music of life. It can take you anywhere." I give her a big smile and push my hand closer to hers. "Take it."

She hesitates, then lifts it from my palm. "Hope. Music. Life. Thank you." She nods her head to emphasize each word.

I give her a final smile before walking toward my family. Dad takes off, and we all follow as he burns through the crowd. My feet try to keep up as my mind swirls through the conversation with the cute blond girl. We reach the spinning teacups, and I step into the queue behind my brother. The sun blazes down on my head as I mentally curse my dad's love of temperatures that rival the surface of the sun. Water droplets slide down my spine, and I realize I didn't think about sweat once in the past half hour.

PART I

You don't stop living because bad things happen. You keep going.
Gina Neely

1
―――――

HOPE

"Yes! Just like that. Faster. Harder. Yes!"

A loud bang startles me as I slap blindly for my phone trying to recall when I changed my alarm tone.

"You've got more than enough. Use it. Now!"

The demands filter through my haze of sleep as I slowly realize those words can't be silenced with the flick of a button. Pulling my pillow over my head, I protect my ears from the naked aerobics on the other side of the wall. *Damn. When do they sleep? Eat? Work?* If Guinness had a world record for the longest run of continuous sex, my two neighbors had blown through it sometime last week and had yet to be told they'd clinched the title.

Finishing my neuroanatomy project and crawling into bed at three a.m., I'd banked on at least four hours of sleep. I check my phone. It looks like I've missed my estimation by an hour. Any chance of falling asleep again is gone with "Nock'em" and "Bang'em" practically moving *my* bed with their vigorous workout.

I stretch my arms above my head and stare at the ceiling.

Just a couple more months and I'll be in my last year. The finish line is on the horizon and finally close enough to see. I'll buy some earplugs and keep on rolling.

I flip the covers from my body and pad to the bathroom, the only door in my apartment other than the one at the threshold adorned with two deadbolts. I might not live in the safest area of town, but this place is mine. I can overlook its shortcomings knowing I found it and paid for it on my own.

I cruise through my morning routine and leave my apartment, bagel in hand. My shift at Rise and Grind, a busy coffee shop in Evanston, doesn't start for thirty minutes, but I crave the hustle of its atmosphere this morning.

Two hours later, I stand at the counter staring at a tall, suit-clad man who looks a bit like my freshman sociology professor. "That's one gluten-free muffin and two black coffees. Can I get you anything else?"

A smile spreads across my face even though my brain still feels like I'm walking through a thick fog. Professor Look-Alike shakes his head, hands me a twenty-dollar bill and walks away. I make the change and throw his overpayment in the tip jar.

My stereotype of college students, poor and frugal to a fault, was blown to smithereens during my first week of work three years ago. The Northwestern clientele repeatedly fills the container to the brim more than three times a day, and it bolsters my desire to recognize the good in people.

Since Professor had been my last customer in line, I grab a wet cloth and give the front counter a quick rub down. A shadow falls over my hand, and I look up with a smile ready to greet the next patron. My expression doesn't waver even though my heart rate takes off at a gallop. Warm brown eyes, set behind a pair of black-rimmed glasses, arrest my vision. "Java Joe," the name I've dubbed the object of my crush, stands before me. Dressed in a white t-shirt, relaxed jeans, and an expensive-looking dark blazer, he towers over my five-foot frame. A Cheshire Cat grin sits nestled in the short scruff of his jaw.

"Hi. Do you have that sweet, Columbian blend you guys had last week?" His raised brows snap me from my daydream of what he looks like under the soft shirt.

"Oh, um, excuse m—?" A cough lodges in my throat cutting off my words. I pound my chest as I pull air into my lungs. "S-sorry. What did you say?" Heat blankets my cheeks as concern coats his face.

"Are you okay?" He steps forward and extends his arm intending to slap me between my shoulder blades. I move back and blindly reach for my drink under the counter.

"F-f-fine. What can I get you?"

He studies me as my breathing gradually returns to a normal rhythm. I grasp my drink and take a long pull. I swallow and plaster a smile on my face hoping the floor will open up and reveal a hole I can leap into.

He pulls out his wallet and lowers his eyes while looking through it. "I'd love a cup of your Columbian blend."

"I'm sorry we don't have that flavor this week. The owner likes to change it up. Rotate flavors. Makes it exciting. Keeps the patrons coming back." Gah. Words pour from my mouth like I've pressed the trigger on a machine gun.

"Hmmm." I zero in on his thin pink lips. "I guess I'll take today's house blend."

I stand stock-still, my ears five steps behind his words. His chuckle forces my action.

"Coming right up. Um, anything else for you today?"

He scratches his cheek while still holding his wallet. He smiles, and my heart melts. Java Joe's teeth are perfect, like always. "Nope. Just a to-go cup, please."

I ring his order, pour his coffee, and place it on the counter in front of him. My brain screams at me to say something to this hunk who's been coming into the shop every week for the past three months.

His brown eyes fall to my name tag as he hands me a twenty-dollar bill. *It's now or never.* I look down and give a surprised laugh. His eyes meet mine, his forehead scrunched in confusion. "Something wrong, Hope?" His low, steady voice stops me mid-laugh.

"The serial number on your twenty ends in a seven. Everyone who pays with a bill that has a seven is registered in a raffle, provided they leave their name with me." My tongue is bolder than my heart which pounds in my ears. I give him a toothy smile and slide the pen and pad of paper I keep next to the register over in front of him.

"Is that so?" He reaches for the pen, and I glue my eyes to his hand. I'm practically jumping out of my skin unable to believe he's going to comply with my bogus request. "Tell me. What do I win if I add my phone number as well?" I look up, and he winks before scrawling his name and number on the small pad. "I'm looking forward to hearing if I won. Something tells me I have a pretty good shot." He tosses the pen down and picks up his coffee, taking a sip while eying me over the rim. "My compliments to the owner. Today's blend will most definitely have me returning for more." He double taps the counter between us, turns, and walks out the door.

My heart is beating so hard I feel it in my fingertips. I cannot believe I did that. Java Joe just gave me his name and number. Satisfaction washes through me as I stare at the paper, proud of myself for being assertive and making something happen. I think I like this bold version of myself. I need more of her.

I look around to see everyone drinking their coffees and occupied with their laptops, phones, and tablets. I run my fingertips over the counter, pulling the sacred pad of paper closer for inspection. My eyes roam over his name, and a strangled laugh leaves my mouth. Joseph Roberts is written in deep, confident strokes over ten precise, neatly written digits. Looks like Java Joe fits him just fine.

2

HOPE

"I CAN'T BELIEVE WE'RE IN THE SAME FIELD."

I raise my glass and take a sip of water, pausing a moment to fill my eyes with the deliciousness that is Joe Roberts. His gaze is focused on me as his hands busy themselves with the silverware, glass, and bread plate in front of him. At first glance, he looks shy and nervous. Yet, as I take another drink, I notice he's arranged his personal space in perfect, symmetrical order. This brown-haired hottie isn't anxious; he's a neat freak. My lips stall halfway to a smile worried he'll think I'm engaging in an inside joke at his expense.

Joe's intense, chocolate brown stare holds my attention. "Medicine has been my passion since I lost my mom to cancer in high school. Helping care for her and watching her suffer devastated me. It was humbling and frustrating. I wanted to take away her pain, but I was powerless against the poison spreading throughout her body." His breath catches as his gaze drops away. After a moment, eyes glazed with wetness meet mine before he sighs and runs a hand through his short, chestnut hair. "When she passed, I vowed to spend my life helping others like her. I never wanted their families to feel the same pain as my dad and I did." He raises a hand and rubs the back of his neck. His embarrassment for sharing such a personal story is evident in the pink hue of his cheeks and half-smile he forces across his lips.

I reach across our small table and glide my fingers across the back of his hand. I want to stand and wrap my arms around him, but I'm conflicted. Would that be appropriate just two hours into our first *official* date?

I'm adamant about not counting the times Joe has stopped by Rise and Grind over the last month. A five-minute conversation at the register while I filled his order does not qualify as a date. Tonight's dinner had been a month in the making. After I'd asked Joe for his number, it had taken me another two days of internal pep talks before I called and asked him to dinner. We'd instantly hit it off over the phone, but due to our busy schedules, tonight was the first time we'd shared more than ten minutes of uninterrupted conversation.

Which brings me to why I'm sitting across from this gorgeous doctor looking the way I do. Wrapped in a form-fitting dress, blond hair coaxed into soft waves, and legs shaved (one can never be too prepared), I'm a bucket of nervous energy.

Joe looks at our hands before lifting his eyes to mine. I give him a smile and a quick squeeze before withdrawing my fingers and placing my hands in my lap.

"So, do you have any plans for declaring a specialty?"

Giving myself a moment to collect my words, I take a sip of my water. I'm unsure how he'll react to my desire to specialize in a traditionally male-dominated area. "I haven't officially decided, but I'm fairly certain I want to specialize in orthopedic surgery with an emphasis in pediatrics. I have a passionate desire to help and take care of others, especially children."

I watch his face, trying to gauge his reaction to my words.

If I hadn't been paying attention, I could have mistaken his smile for encouragement instead of the condescension I encounter nearly every time I respond to that question.

Joe takes a sip of his wine, rubs his lips together, and replaces his glass on the table at a perfect ninety-degree angle to his knife. "Your choice is commendable, and I applaud your goal to enter such a difficult specialty."

His response has me questioning the derision I thought I'd glimpsed a moment before. Maybe my cynicism, fueled by past comments, has clouded my ability to decipher support versus sarcasm.

We trade conversation throughout dinner, which ends with a shared piece of chocolate volcano cake, before the server places the bill on the edge of the table. I stare at the check, wishing I could rewind this night and repeat the ease and comfort I've felt sitting across from Joe. This has been an amazing first date, and the thought of it ending dampens my spirits. I'm not ready to return to my empty, lonely apartment. Call it a result of being an only child in a single-parent home where I'd spent hours alone wishing I had a friend, a neighbor, or anyone with whom I could interact. Don't misunderstand, my mom did a phenomenal job as a single parent, but her jobs kept us apart when I really needed someone to talk to.

Joe pulls out his credit card and places it next to the bill. Our eyes share a silent conversation while we wait for the server to collect the payment and return with the receipt. Joe's gaze holds a simmering heat, telling me he doesn't want the night to end any more than I do. The server slides the receipt and a pen onto the corner of our table before moving on to her next customer.

My eyes trace the movements of his long fingers as he fills in a sizable tip before scrawling his name across the bottom of the receipt. I fight a grin when I glimpse his name. Yep, he's totally nailed the doctor signature.

He stands, pulls out my chair, and helps me to my feet. Joe is one of a dying breed of gentlemen, and I take a second to indulge in my romantic, white-horse fantasies. He places his strong palm at the base of my spine and holds out his other hand indicating I should proceed ahead of him. My feet move at a languid pace allowing the warmth from his hand to caress my back through my dress. My body tingles as I wind through the restaurant, his chest so close I feel goosebumps rise across my neck. I exit through the front door and stop on the sidewalk, unsure where we go from here. His hand snakes around my hip as he turns me toward him.

"This has been one hell of a first date. Who would have thought we'd be standing here a month ago?" His face lights with mischief as he refers to the day he gave me his number in the coffee shop.

"I'd have to say, tonight firmly falls within my top three first dates of all time."

His eyebrows fly to his hairline as he pulls his hand to his chest feigning injury. "I'm aggrieved. I hate to be anything less than number one."

I pull my phone from my purse, glancing at the time, before curling my lips in what I hope is a seductive tilt. "Well, I still have a few hours before my dress turns to tatters and my car turns into a pumpkin. Care to try and crack my number one date spot?"

He tilts his head toward mine as he drops his hands on either side of my hips and gives them a playful squeeze. His lips skim my cheek as he leans in to whisper in my ear. "Challenge accepted."

His words send shivers throughout my body as my imagination takes off at an Olympic sprint. Guilt tries to slink into my consciousness, but I push that bitch back and slap some duct tape across her mouth for good measure.

For as long as I can remember, I've focused on nothing

more than school. The overuse of my brain has starved my libido leaving it parched and begging for action. Joe is like a desert oasis, and all my girly parts are seeking permission to come out and play. I need this. I'm wearing a dress and make-up for crying out loud, and I deserve the release this night may bring.

Joe slides his mouth across my jaw stopping to hover over my lips. Heat prickles across my skin at the delicious tickle of his short scruff. Warm air escapes his lips sending silent promises straight to my heated core.

I lift my chin as the pull of the moment makes me bold. "Is your place available?"

He exhales a heavy breath before his lips flutter across mine. "Are you sure?" His words are tinted with concern as he releases them against my lips.

I swallow the sudden nervousness coursing through my body. He pulls back, and his eyes search mine as he wraps my hands in his and waits for my response. I bite my lip and shift my eyes to the side as I debate my true answer. I'm afraid he'll sense my indecision and throw on the brakes about continuing on to his place.

This man is more than I'd hoped. Smart, polite, sensitive, gorgeous. He's what I want, and I'm not letting this chance melt into the sidewalk. "Yes, I'm sure. Nervous, a little out of my element, but sure."

His smile is blinding and slightly crooked as he leans forward and pulls me flush against his chest lifting my feet from the ground in the process. He dips his chin, whispering words meant only for me. "I'm so glad my bill had a seven."

My tongue darts out to wet my bottom lip, and, quick as lightning, he leans forward and licks an identical path across my mouth.

"Mmmm. Chocolate covered Hope. Delectable."

He releases me, and I slide down his front until my feet are firmly planted on the ground. Grabbing my hand, he gives it a squeeze and slowly walks down the sidewalk pulling me toward the parking lot.

It's been forever since I've felt this quickening of my heart and the heat of desire coursing through my body. I'm hungry. Starved for intimacy and yearning for a connection, I'm ready to reward myself with what I want. Tonight is the closest I've felt to someone in years, and I won't apologize for taking what I need.

3

———

HOPE

MY PHONE BUZZES, AND MY EYES LAND ON JOE'S NAME AS THE text notification brightens the screen. I drop my tablet to my lap and pick up my phone, greedy for his words.

Joe: Pizza tonight? My place?

I grin, knowing the opportunity for more than pizza is available if we're hanging at his apartment. While my place is available, it's barely more than a closet with a toilet. It's serviceable for me but totally lacks a romantic vibe when my mattress, which sits on the floor, does triple duty as the table, couch, and bed.

Joe's place is a two-bedroom unit he shares, though I have yet to meet his roommate—the elusive EJ. According to Joe, they've lived together since undergrad and are quite the inseparable pair when their schedules are not completely opposite. Joe speculates EJ may be seeing someone because in his words, "No one's schedule is hectic enough to ghost an apartment for over a month."

Growing our relationship hasn't been easy. Between Joe's resident hours and my schooling, we've had difficulty finding times when we're both available *and* awake. Most of our time together has been stolen minutes here and there. Lunch in the hospital cafeteria. Sharing a coffee at five a.m. before my shift at Rise and Grind. A fifteen-minute goodnight kiss outside the emergency room entrance before Joe's twelve-hour shift.

My mom's been hounding me to set up a dinner between the three of us, and, in this case, I've been thankful for our intermittent schedules. I know I can't shield him from her intrusive inquiries forever, but I plan to gradually ease him (in small controlled doses) into the whirlwind who is Julia Murphy. When I'm comfortable he can't be scared off, we'll all go out, and she can work him over as I die of humiliation. Until then, I'm greedily hoarding his time, keeping him to myself, and tucking him into my heart. My brain may not be ready for a serious label, but the beat of my heart is gradually synching with his.

I snap out of my thoughts and return my attention to my phone. In the ten minutes I've been daydreaming, Joe has texted again.

Joe: Are you there? Did I catch you at a bad time?

I smile and clear my visions from my mind.

Me: Here. Would that pizza have mushrooms on it?

His response is instant. He must be on a break, or it's really slow at the hospital today.

Joe: Uhhh. Maybe, sausage?

I'm not the biggest fan of sausage, but I can eat it. Judging by his response, he isn't too fond of my mushroom suggestion.

Me: Sure.

Joe: Great. Meet at my place at 9?

Me: OK

I look at the time and realize I need a snack to hold me over until pizza which is still three hours away.

With the heat in my apartment on the fritz again and knowing my mom is working, I've spent most of the day studying at her house. As long as I don't leave evidence of my stay, I can escape without her questioning why I visited but didn't stay to see her.

I wander to the pantry and let my eyes roam sparse shelves. Mom must be working double shifts. It would explain why I've received sporadic texts from her this week.

A handful of granola bars (expiration date one year ago), a cereal box, and a jar of something of unknown origin stare back at me from the shelves. I grab a stool to search the upper shelf and score an unopened roll of crackers pushed into the corner against the wall. I rip the package open on my way to the living room while making a mental note to drop off some groceries later this week. I don't want my mom to starve because she doesn't have time to make a grocery run.

I drop to the couch and pick up my tablet. After staring at the diagram of the vagus nerve for another ten minutes, I fling the device to my right where it lands upside down in the crook between the cushion and the armrest. Tenth cranial nerve be damned. It has nothing on Joe and the fantasies swirling through my mind.

While Joe is typically easy-going when we're together, he's

commanding, yet gentle, when we cross the threshold to his bedroom. He's vocal with his requests and loves it when I reciprocate, though I fail miserably at the task considering my lack of experience.

All of my previous sexual encounters had been riddled with misguided groping and silent rooting in the darkness of a college dorm room and ended within five minutes after they'd begun. Not my finest decisions, but they'd gained me the ability to collect some of the sexual experience I'd previously lacked.

While sex with Joe is significantly superior to my previous experiences, it isn't over the top exceptional. It's the intimacy afterward that is a symphony to my heart and the reason I've overlooked any misgivings I've had about the sex. The words he pours into my ears are water to my thirsty soul and endear me to him more than physical intimacy ever will. He holds me, listens to me, and validates me.

My mind drifts back to the present, and I realize I've been reliving my intimacy infatuation for nearly an hour. I look down at my shirt and see scattered crumbs from the crackers I've consumed, and the empty sleeve lies crushed beneath my left leg. I carefully sit up, walk to the kitchen garbage, and brush all crumbs directly into the can so I don't leave any trace I was here without seeing Mom.

I grab my keys and head home to take a leisurely shower and make sure my body is shaved, buffed, and polished for tonight's anticipated activities. It may not be earth-shattering, but "Afterglow Joe" is so worth anything I may be missing on the front end.

———

MY FINGER HITS Joe's buzzer as I fidget with the hem of my sweatshirt feeling shy and uncomfortable since this is the first time I've driven to his apartment. The other times I've been here, he's picked me up.

I've overestimated the drive time which puts me in his visitor's parking lot ten minutes earlier than planned. I hope he's home so I can avoid sitting on his doorstep like a stray dog until he arrives.

As I stand waiting, my eyes drift across the building's mailboxes wondering if each person's name fits what I imagine they look like. It's a silly game I haven't made time to play in years. To stave off boredom, I'd pass a stranger on the street and imagine what his family, what he liked to eat, or what his house looked like.

My mind jumps to the nameless stranger who'd given me the promise of hope before he walked out of my life. No matter how diligently I'd looked or how often, I'd never found him, and the reality stifled my hope. Ultimately, it was the reason I'd closed the door on the game.

The intercom buzzes and Joe's voice trickles through the static. "You're early." The flat resonance tickles my nerves and gives me a strange feeling in my gut. *Is he annoyed that I'm early?*

"Yeah. Is that OK?" The question skitters across my tongue as I fail to quiet my pulse.

A pause, long enough to make me uncomfortable, crackles through the air. "Of course, I just got out of the shower, and I'm dripping water across my carpet."

"Oh. Uh, sorry."

"Come on up. I'll throw on some clothes, but I hold you responsible for any wrinkles or mismatched clothing."

"Very funny. You always look good. I'll wear a blindfold all night if it makes you feel better."

A strong breath catches the intercom like he's pulling air through his nose. Hardness tints his lowered voice, "Be careful what you offer, Miss Murphy. I may just take you up on it."

He disconnects, and the door gives a loud beep. His words wipe every thought from my brain. Damn. I think I just summoned an alternate-universe Joe.

I take a deep breath, open his building's door, and ascend two flights of stairs on weak legs. I reach his apartment and raise my fist to knock, but before I do, the door is forcefully pulled inward. I can't stop my reaction, and my eyes widen scanning the man who stands on the other side of the threshold. Low slung jeans, unbuttoned flannel shirt draped across his shoulders, naked chest, and bare feet. If this is how he greets me when he's not ready, I'll set an alarm to arrive early for the rest of my life.

He reaches through the open doorway and pulls me forward by my hips until I'm flush to his chest. Soap and Joe's musky deodorant fills my senses as he squeezes my ass before running his hands up my back, stopping at the base of my low ponytail. He growls and pulls my hair, tilting my head toward his downturned face. "I've missed you."

His whispered words fill me with warmth as his mouth fuses with mine. His tongue hits my lips, forcing them open before he delves in possessing my mouth like he's a death row inmate and I'm his last supper. Without warning, he pulls my top lip into his mouth and bites down hard. I release a startled squeal. Shit. That hurt. I gasp for air as I lift my palms to his pecs and push him backward with the full force of my angry five-foot frame. *What the hell is happening right now? Where has he been hiding this aggression?*

He releases me, surprise painted across his face, as I glare at him while dabbing my tongue across my stinging lip.

"What was that?" I wipe the back of my forearm across my mouth, a small smear of blood catching my eye before I lower my arm. I swallow, and the iron tang of blood slides down my throat. "I'm bleeding."

Joe blinks. I watch his face for an explanation and observe the moment his expression changes. It's like a cage has been thrown shut, and the beast has retreated into the darkness. He steps forward and falls to his knees, pressing his head against my breasts as he wraps his arms around my waist.

"I'm so sorry. Work was shit. Then you were here and offering to be blindfolded. Then I saw you, and I just lost control. It won't happen again." He lifts his head and looks up at me, regret seeping from his eyes as he begs forgiveness. "I'm such a bastard." He lifts his hand, cups my face, and swipes his thumb across my lip to caress the tender skin. "I made you bleed. I'm a damn doctor. I'm supposed to stop bleeding, not cause it!"

I raise my hands and feather them through his hair, allowing the soft strands to tickle my fingers as they slide across my skin. I take a deep breath, trapping the air in my lungs before releasing it. This is Joe. The one who listens to me and holds me close. The man who's already managed to capture a piece of my heart.

His day had been crap, and I hadn't even recognized it. He had needed to let go, bury his emotions, and erase the stress of his day. I know, better than most, how a hospital shift can break a doctor. I'm the one Joe had called to help him forget, and I've rejected him. Maybe I'm the one who should be apologizing for not recognizing his needs. His passion for his profession, colleagues, and patients is a gift to be celebrated, not denied.

"Hey, your greeting took me by surprise. I've never seen this side of you before, and I'm not sure how to react. I love how devoted you are to your patients. I don't blame you for bringing your stress home. I get it, but maybe give me a warning next time, yeah?"

He closes his eyes, turns his cheek, and rests his ear directly above my heart. His strong arms squeeze my waist in a firm hug. "I'm so damn thankful I have you. I'm sorry. I'll do my best to leave my stress at work in the future."

I lean into his embrace. This. Strong arms. Skin to skin contact. This is *my* Joe.

4

HOPE

M y hand shoots out from under the covers blindly grabbing for my phone before the buzzing wakes Joe. Totally a morning person, Joe leaves his blinds cracked so the morning light wakes him up instead of using an alarm. His room is pitch black which signals it's still the middle of the night. My hand connects with my phone, and I pull it to my face. My eyes involuntarily squint as I'm blinded by the brightness of the screen.

Unknown caller.

I silence the buzz as I consider if I should answer. My answer is made when *missed call* flashes across my screen. I reach over, deposit my phone on the edge of the nightstand, and snuggle into my pillow.

My eyes drift shut, and my screen lights again. The brightness against the room's backdrop of darkness seeps through my closed eyelids. Even in my sleepy haze, I know it can't be the hospital. I don't have to be there until tomorrow night. Correction, later tonight. I run my hands over my face and sit up, careful not to wake Joe. I slide from the bed snatching my phone up as I quickly pad to the bathroom. I shut the door and opt to use the nightlight instead of blinding myself by turning on the overhead bulb.

I look at my phone, the unknown number causing dread to creep up my spine. I slide my thumb across the screen. "Hello."

"Hope Murphy?" The direct, no-nonsense female voice steals my breath and puts me on edge.

"Yes. This is Hope."

"I'm sorry." What stranger starts a phone call with *I'm sorry?*

"Who is this?"

"I'm sorry, Ms. Murphy." The formality raises the hairs on my arms. Something's wrong and this woman's meager "sorry" is upsetting me more each time I hear it. She has bad news. I want to scream at her to spit out what she has to say, but my tongue lies silent behind my teeth. "This is Denise Jones calling from Our Saviors Hospital in Geneva. Are you the daughter of Julia Murphy?"

Perspiration gathers at my temple. At my whispered, "Yes." Dorothy? Diane? Denise? continues with information that sounds more like a press release than a phone call. Nothing she says confirms what my gut is telling me, but I know. Nearly three years of medical school has exposed me to these conversations. I've always been on the other side, and I find my brain putting words to my ears before this stranger's mouth utters the sounds.

"There's been an accident. Your mom was brought in about an hour ago. From what I've been told, she was involved in a one-car accident on I-39. I need to ask you to come to Our Saviors as soon as possible. We are located in Geneva. Do you need directions?"

Need directions? I am less than two miles away. My mom is

lying hurt, broken, and alone in a hospital bed within damn walking distance.

"Is she OK?" I switch to doctor mode, shoving my feelings into a lockbox while I gather information.

Silence blankets the line as Denise takes a moment before carefully choosing her words. "Hospital privacy guidelines do not allow me to give a medical status. Do you have anyone that can come with you? I can meet you in the lobby when you arrive." She rattles off instructions, though I don't make an effort to commit the information to memory.

"I'll be there within ten minutes. Thank you." My mom's constant chiding about minding my manners causes the polite words to burn my lips as they leave my mouth. Never will I be thankful to Denise for changing the course of my life with her phone call.

———

JOE BREEZES through the sliding doors of Our Saviors with authority and purpose that only an attending doctor can exude. Immediately switching to work mode, he finds Denise Jones and demands a full medical report of my mom's injuries. I stand next to him, my mouth silent, and my mind as blank as a brand-new whiteboard. Denise defers his request to the attending physician and leads us to the ER where Micah Stahl, a well-respected medical colleague of Joe's, is speaking on the phone at the nurse's station.

"...severe brain bleed...inoperable internal trauma...automobile accident." Dr. Stahl isn't speaking to someone, he's dictating his medical report. His words pelt me like a police officer's billy club, necessary in a situation, yet harsh and unforgiving.

Micah makes eye contract with Joe as we approach. His

eyes flare for a moment before he turns his chair, showing us the back of his lab coat. I'm not sure if he's protecting us from the severity of his words or shielding us from the information he has yet to share.

Joe flags down a familiar nurse; her name skirts the recesses of my mind. They both step into an empty triage room, and I choose to wander down the hall staring at the familiar walls of the hospital I've called home for the past year.

I need to allow myself this alone time. I don't need to hear what my heart already knows. My mom is gone. Brain bleeds and internal trauma are not injuries indicative of a full recovery after a few days of rest. They are a death sentence to even the youngest and healthiest of humans.

My thoughts supply information of their own accord. The accident was on I-39. My mom was no doubt returning home from work. She works so many damn hours. I've tried to convince her to slow down, take some time for herself now that I'm out of the house and not such a financial hardship. She tells me to hush up whenever I refer to myself as a burden. She has no problem telling me she'll continue to take care of me until the day she dies.

Dies.

Dead.

My mom is dead, maybe not in the physical sense, but I know it's imminent if it hasn't already pulled her away. The woman who made me soup when I was sick, worked double shifts so she could send me to expensive summer camps, and saved for six months so I'd have a prom dress that rivaled those of my classmates, has left me without even saying goodbye. She hates to say "goodbye," says it's an oxymoron since there's nothing good about it. She prefers "until next time" because it gives the person the goal to return. She loves quotes and little sayings. They are the only extravagance she willingly allows herself, if you can call a coffee mug that says *When life gives you a frown, turn it upside down* an extravagance.

I spot a plastic chair shoved into a corner and drop into it. Before my butt hits the seat, my vision turns blurry, and I lift my fingers to my face and wipe away the sudden tears. I've been so lost in my thoughts I didn't recognize I'd loosened the lock on my emotions and allowed an onslaught of wetness to coat my cheeks.

A sudden uncontrollable desire to have Joe's arms around me pulls me from my chair and moves my feet down the hallway toward the triage room where I'd last seen him. I round a corner and see him walking toward me. His eyes find mine, and I stop. My legs go weak, and I place a hand on the nearest wall to keep me upright. He takes off at a run, his feet bringing him to me in less than twenty paces. His arms wrap around my shoulders, and I let go. My legs release my weight as my body attempts to slide to the floor. The muscles of Joe's arms tighten as he keeps me upright while dropping his cheek to mine.

"Give it to me. Let go. I've got you. I'm here for you." Words, coated in affection, wash over me as tears run down my face. Joe holds me until my tears start to subside. My body shakes from the aftermath of my breakdown.

I pull back, gripping Joe's biceps as I search his eyes. He's waiting for me to voice the question he sees in the anguish on my face. "My mom. They couldn't save her?"

His lips thin as he stares directly into my eyes. His focus grounds me as he refuses to look away. He's lending me the strength I need to hear the words I'm forcing him to say. "No. They tried, but she didn't make it to the hospital."

My heart stutters. My mom is dead. Never again will I see her face, hear her words, or feel her touch. My grandparents are no longer living. I have no siblings. In a way, I've spent much of my life by myself, but until this very moment, I've never felt truly and utterly alone.

Sensing my thoughts, Joe leans down and brushes a chaste kiss across my wet lips. "I've got you. You're not alone. I'm here."

5

HOPE

My mind concentrates on the squelch of the mud as it sucks at the pointed heels of my shoes with each step. Suck, pull, suck, pull. Morbidly, I imagine my entire body being pulled into the mud. Cold, wet, suffocating darkness. I'm positive it would be no different than how I feel today.

I pick my way through the grass, my arm tucked into Joe's. My eyes stay focused on the ground as I approach the plot. Joe stops, and I halt my forward steps as I raise my gaze to the light oak casket sitting atop metal rails. Sprays of flowers in yellows and white adorn the surface like fragrant protectors of the woman who eternally sleeps beneath them. The wood of the casket gleams in the sunlight mocking the darkness that has taken root in my heart. My mom's lifeless body is trapped inside the box I'd been forced to choose.

Three days ago, I'd sat frozen and mute at the mortuary while the funeral director pointed out features like I was shopping for a new car. The satin interior, the hidden seam construction, the solid oak body. My mind had clouded, and I'd wanted to vomit. I didn't give a damn about the construction. My mom was dead, and no top of the line casket was going to miraculously bring her back to me. I'd become hysterical, screaming at the man with the quiet demeanor and kind eyes who was asking too much of me.

Joe had ushered me outside, dropping to his butt and pulling me into his lap beneath a giant oak tree behind the funeral home. The warmth of his embrace was my lifeline as I released the tears I'd fought since leaving the hospital three days ago. He held me, allowing his strength to seep through my skin, without uttering one word. He'd stroked my hair, and I'd cried harder since it reminded me of the times my mom had done the same thing when I was upset. Time slipped by, but Joe's arms never loosened as my heart broke. Not only would she be absent from my medical school graduation, my wedding, the birth of my children, but I would be forced to endure those experiences without her by my side.

The minutes bled into an hour before Joe had asked if I wanted him to make the rest of the arrangements. I'd stared into his caramel-brown gaze and realized I wasn't alone. He was there holding my hand, making sure I ate, and pulling me out of bed when my desire laid dormant at my feet. I'd shaken my head, and he'd risen and pulled me to my feet allowing his body to shelter mine beneath the leaves of the great oak. A breeze had lifted the hairs at the nape of my neck, and I'd felt her. Goosebumps pebbled my skin as the wind died as fast as it had arrived. My mom was there, her whispers brought to my heart on the wings of the air. She was telling me this man would be my sounding board, my confidant, and my rock since she no longer could.

Love had shown in the warmth of his smile as I'd looked at him and returned the gesture. We'd walked back into the funeral home, Joe's hand gripping mine until the last detail was decided.

The clearing of a throat jolts me back to the present. The pastor from my mom's church stands at the head of the casket.

When I'd gone back into the funeral home after my outburst, I'd chosen an oak casket convinced my mom had been the calming effect I'd felt under the giant oak tree.

I stare at the pastor, mesmerized by the movement of his lips while the drum of my own heartbeat silences his words. My ears pulse as memories slide through my brain accompanied by the song of my heart. Peace fills me as I feel my mom's love pumping through my body. Joe takes my hand and squeezes it. My mom is here, and she trusts Joe to be my protector when she can no longer do it herself.

Goosebumps rise across my arms as I feel a faint whisper against my cheek.

Until next time, my love.

6

HOPE

It feels like I'm moving through quicksand as I stumble across the employee parking lot on the way to my car. I drop my eyes to my tennis shoes to make sure the laces aren't made of lead. Fatigue filters through my bones. It's been a week since my mom's funeral, and I'm running on energy reserves stored in my pinkie at this point.

My final assignment of the term had been emailed this morning to Dr. Smyth, who generously gave me a three-day extension due to my circumstances.

It figures, the hospital had been crazy busy on my final twelve-hour rotation as a third-year medical student. In the entirety of medical school, I don't think I've seen the number of stitches that I assisted with today. Check the phase of the moon people, and don't use any sharp objects for the next twenty-four hours.

I stop at my car and dig through my purse for my elusive keys. My fingers slide across cool metal, and a bittersweet smile touches my lips as I pull them out attached to my favorite keychain—*Did you just pick your nose?* It had been a gift from my mom following a debate we'd had about how hungry a person would have to be to eat boogers.

I click the locks and open my door, but a note on the front of my windshield catches my eye. I reach out and snatch it from the glass before sagging into the driver's seat.

My place after work. Love you, J

As tired as my body is, the hairs across my arms raise in excitement. He'd told me he wouldn't be available until this weekend, which is still three days away.

My lips curl into a grin. I crave being cared for by this man.

A second wind breezes through my body as I start my car and head in the direction of his apartment.

———

My EYES WIDEN, and I forget to breathe as I look between him and the open box sitting in his palm. I blink, thinking maybe I put too much stock in my second wind, and I'm actually dreaming.

Joe's eyes sparkle up at me from his kneeling position on the floor. "Hope? Will you?"

A diamond, bigger than I've ever seen in person, glitters from its slit between the black cushioning of the ring box.

I take a deep breath, belatedly realizing my lungs are screaming for air. "B-b-but we haven't known each other very long."

He sets the box next to my knee on the couch and reaches for both of my hands. "Hope, I wouldn't ask you if I wasn't sure." He lifts a hand to smooth the wisps of my hair that have fallen from my ponytail.

After the stress of today's shift, I'm surprised I still have hair and haven't torn it all out.

Joe's smile is wide as his eyes search my face, and I see a trace of nervousness as he waits for my answer.

"What about medical school? I've accomplished too much to leave with only two semesters left."

He shifts his eyes to the side as he bites his bottom lip. His worry becomes more pronounced as I watch him. The way his eyes bounce, I sense he's choosing his words carefully, unsure how I'll react. "You know I've received the oncology position in Boulder?" His question sounds more like a statement, but I nod.

He received word right before my mom's funeral, but we haven't talked about it since he read me the letter. I figured he was still weighing his options before he spoke to me about it.

"Hear me out. I've looked into Northwestern's policies and made some calls. Under certain circumstances, you can apply to defer completion for emergency situations. Some medical schools will consider a transfer under special circumstances, too."

I didn't know deferral during medical school was even an option. *Could I do it? Would I forget everything I'd learned?*

"When I spoke with the Human Resources Coordinator at Trinity General, she volunteered to help in any way she can." Joe squeezes my hands and tightens his fingers around mine. His skin is soft and warm, and I dwell on the sensations as they travel up my arms. "With this new position, I can afford to buy us a place. Once you get acclimated and settle in, you can decide what you want to do. I want to take care of you. I just need you to say the word."

My fatigued brain works to process the overload of information. Three months ago, Joe and I hadn't even gone on our first date, and my mom was still alive. A lifetime has been lived in those ninety days. Now I'm sitting here contemplating if I should quit medical school. Transfer. Defer. Whatever.

An unforeseen incident. An accident. A fluke. The black and white difference a phone call can make is staggering.

Joe gives my hands another squeeze. The hope shining from his eyes is contagious. I drop our connected fingers and take his face in my hands. I lean forward and place my lips against his, giving his mouth a chance to feel and hear my answer. "Yes. My heart wants nothing more than to be your wife."

Joe's arms encircle me as his mouth slants across mine. Excitement, tinged by possession, fuels his tongue as he sweeps any reservations from my thoughts. *Nothing in this world is free.* My mom's voice flares down my spine before I can extinguish its heat.

———

I GIVE the judge's clerk a small smile while I pull my phone from my purse and drop my hair over my pink ears. I shift uncomfortably in my long white dress as I check for a notification that isn't there. Joe promised he'd meet me at noon, and it's twelve fifteen. I debate texting, but I fear he may tell me he can't get away from the hospital.

We've been in Colorado less than a month, and his working hours have been relentless. Needless to say, we've spent less time together in Colorado than we did in Illinois. I've brought up my frustrations on the rare occasions I've seen him, but guilt follows on the heels of my questioning.

He apologizes and begs me to stick it out through the first year, after which he'll be able to slow down at the hospital. When we are together, he's always attentive and affectionate, and I feel guilty for wasting our precious time by voicing my annoyances.

Joe's working to make a name for himself as well as provide for us. I'm the one who's struggling. I've lacked the desire and initiative to look into my medical school options, and Joe hasn't pushed me or asked about it at all. I need to focus on my personal goals instead of finding fault with Joe's.

The office door opens, and Joe strides in looking handsome in his Armani suit and red power tie. I tuck my phone into my purse and stand up, flashing him a bright, if a bit forced, smile.

He leans forward, placing a quick kiss on my lips before pulling away and running his eyes down the length of my body. "You look gorgeous, and I'm sorry I'm late. Ready to be Mrs. Roberts?" His eyes twinkle with excitement as he links his hand with mine.

I smooth my free hand down the front of my dress and give him a quick nod.

The judge's clerk winks at us. "Knock on the door, he's expecting you."

Fifteen minutes later, we exit the office as Dr. and Mrs. Roberts. We stop on the steps of the courthouse and Joe gives me a searing kiss. I grasp the lapels of his suit coat and pull him toward me in an attempt to deepen the kiss, but he lifts his hands to my shoulders and sets me away from him.

"I would give anything to drive home and start celebrating with my wife, but I have to be back at the hospital in fifteen minutes."

I can't keep the disappointment from my face, and he reacts with an exaggerated wince.

"I know. I'm sorry. A new patient was admitted this morning, and I don't feel comfortable leaving her since I'm not on call tomorrow."

I bite back a sarcastic comment about leaving his wife on her wedding day and nod my head instead.

He leans in for a final, quick peck. "Celebrating starts the minute I walk in the house. See you soon."

My dress, one my mom bought me for a medical school

banquet last year, billows around my legs as I watch him walk away until he turns the corner and steps out of sight.

I cross the street and walk to the parking garage while contemplating my wedding day. I'd arrived at the courthouse, single and alone. Thirty-five minutes later, I'm married, but I'm still leaving alone.

Before I'd jumped in and said, "I do," I should have formulated ideas and weighed my options. Created Plans A thru G and examined my alternatives. But I stupidly chose to do none of those. For if I had, I might have saved myself from the poisonous bite of the snake, otherwise known as life.

7
____

HOPE

I GLANCE AT THE GPS FOR THE THIRD TIME BEFORE I SIGNAL and shoot around a Toyota Prius out for a Sunday drive. Don't send a lynch mob after me. I have no ill will toward Sunday drivers unless it is a Monday morning and I'm running five minutes late to a job interview. Which happens to be my current predicament as I cut back into the right lane making the Toyota quickly disappear in my rearview mirror.

"Just had to do it, didn't you?" I toss the question into the cabin of my car like it can volley an answer of agreement back to my ears.

Joe had worked eighty-two hours at the hospital this week, and he'd walked in the door while I'd been running around in my bra, attempting to zip my skirt, put on heels, and brush my teeth all at the same time. He'd taken one look at me not fully dressed and stalked the ten steps to arrive in front of me. He'd scooped me up, carried me into the family room, and bent me over the arm of the leather couch without saying a single word. He'd slid my skirt and panties down my legs and proceeded to eat his breakfast on his knees. I'd been so turned on, I'd come on his tongue less than three minutes later. As soon as my legs were strong enough to hold my weight, I'd pulled on my shirt and skirt, slid the foot needing a shoe into the waiting high heel in the kitchen, and scooted out the door.

Considering what I'd accomplished in those few minutes, I should be pleased with my task management skills. However, I now find myself speeding toward my interview in my Lexus 330 desperately trying to twist my hair into some form of an updo and cursing my stupidity for forgetting to pull on panties in my haste to get out the door.

I don't hold Joe responsible considering his sleep-deprived brain had probably forgotten about my interview today. We'd been in Colorado for six months, and I had yet to gain the desire to go back to school.

While I'm working through my grief with a psychiatrist, progress has been slow. Dr. Johansen has encouraged me to seek out a job or volunteer opportunity relating to medicine, hoping it will help me work through my repressed reasons for not finishing school. Dr. Johansen believes my guilt, irrational as it is, stems from not being able to save my mom. I've resisted her claims, though in my heart, I'm beginning to see the kernels of truth in her theory.

It has been three months of twice-a-week sessions, and I still have troubling days, but I'm progressing toward healthier outlets for dealing with my emotions. I've signed up for a baking class and applied for a job as an EMT which is why I'm currently trying to beat the time GPS says I'm going to arrive at the interview.

I spy the green exit sign about a mile up the road and step on the gas. I signal for the exit and take the first left at the light at the bottom of the ramp. Two more blocks and I'm pulling into a visitor's parking spot at the Boulder County Fire Station #251. I kill the engine and jump out making sure to grab my purse and the folder with my resume and credentials.

I ring the bell next to the massive garage door and wait.

Less than ten seconds later, a handsome guy, about my age and dressed in a uniform of blue button-down short-sleeve shirt and black pants, opens the door and waves me in.

He holds out a strong, tanned hand. "I'm Shawn McNair. You must be Hope Roberts."

I reach out and shake his hand before I slide a stray piece of blond hair behind my ear. "Guilty as charged. Nice to meet you."

"Glad you weren't on time. We just got back from a call, and you would have been waiting a few minutes."

I stare at his face looking for censure. Instead, I see openness and warmth. While I was racing to be on time, he was saving a life. I don't know how, but he confirms he can read minds with his next statement.

"Not a life-threatening call. Mr. Hayward forgot where he put his hearing aid again. We popped over to help him find it."

He points to an open door at the end of the hall. "Chief Matthews will be conducting the interview, but he's asked me to sit in."

His deep, jovial voice calms my nervousness. I follow McNair down the hall and into a small office. I'm greeted by a large man standing behind a desk that looks child-sized compared to his stature. I accept the seat he indicates and place my hands in my lap. His appearance reflects an uncanny resemblance to a bearded Chris Hemsworth. He smiles and points to his face.

"Before you ask, I'm not the guy who plays Thor, though I'm not embarrassed to admit I let my wife believe that the night I met her." He ends his statement with a wink, and a laugh bursts from my lungs. He looks at McNair, and they both nod.

The interview consists of run of the mill questions about my schooling, my certifications, and what type of hours I'm looking for. After fifteen minutes, Chief Matthews grabs a file from the corner of his desk, opens it, and pulls a single sheet of paper from inside.

"I'm going to be honest. The job has been posted for over three weeks, and we've had no qualified applicants apply. Provided you can show up to work on time, don't faint at the sight of blood, and continue to get along with McNair, I think we'll all get along just fine."

I look at McNair and a smile ghosts across his face. They both knew my hire was in the bag before I walked in the station, yet they led me to believe there was a chance I wouldn't get the position. I won't say anything now, but just wait until I've worked here for a bit. They'll soon find out; I can joke just as well as the next guy.

8

HOPE

"Thanks, Martha. I appreciate the special treatment."

"Anything for you, Sugar."

I tap the counter twice with my fist before picking up the two coffees and making my way to the door. I turn and push it open with my backside as her smile follows me across the threshold of Martha's Sips and Nibbles. A retired bus driver from Mississippi, Martha is a southern lady through and through.

McNair pulls up to the curb and leans across the cab to open my door.

"One vanilla bean latte with an extra shot of caramel for you, and one black as the Devil's soul for me."

McNair wrinkles his nose as I blow on my dark brew. "I don't know how you drink that stuff straight. It's more bitter than a four-time divorcee."

I chuckle and take a sip, careful not to burn my tongue. "It's a habit I picked up in medical school. Sugar makes me crash an hour after drinking it. Not a great reaction halfway through a twelve-hour shift."

"Shit. You couldn't pay me to drink that sludge, sugar crash or not." He shakes his head and takes a drink from his cup. "Ahhh, that's some good shit right there."

I raise an eyebrow. "You do you, Sugar Daddy, and I'll do me."

McNair coughs, spraying coffee across the dashboard.

I lift my shoulder and pull a face. "That sounded way worse out loud than it did in my head."

McNair burns me with his stare as he dabs at the steering wheel with a crumpled napkin. "A little warning next time, yeah?"

I reach across the console and tap him on the shoulder. "Hey, it's not my fault your brain lives in the gutter."

Static from our radio wipes the smiles from our faces. "Bus 201? We have a report of a slip and fall at Wesley Willows nursing home. Male, age eighty-nine, conscious. His right hip may be broken."

I reach forward and tap the button to pull up the text from dispatch. Ten seconds later, the map and coordinates appear on the computer screen, and I radio the operator. "Copy. We are en route. Estimated time of arrival 4 minutes."

I place my coffee in the cupholder as McNair reaches forward and flips on the lights and siren. We've been on for less than twenty minutes, and we're already on our way to the first call. It looks like today is going to be a busy one.

———

I HIT the button to open the garage door as I pull into our drive. A little thrill runs through me when my lights illuminate the back of Joe's Chevy Tahoe. Joe's hospital hours, combined with my new work schedule, make racking up face time with each other nothing short of impossible. It's been three days since I've seen him. Even then, we'd only had enough time for a scorching hot kiss as we passed each other in the kitchen. He'd been on his way to work, and I'd just arrived home.

I desperately need a few days to re-charge and re-connect with him. My heart speeds up at the thought that maybe he's craving the same urgency to be here with me. Whatever the reasons, this time is a gift, and I can't contain my excitement in seeing him at home.

I pull in, cut the ignition, and jump out before the garage door even finishes closing. I walk through the door and into an oasis for my romance starved brain. The kitchen lights are set to low, and a pair of lit candles flicker at me from their position in the middle of the dining room table. The smell of roasted tomato sauce hangs in the air, and my favorite Neil Diamond song, *Sweet Caroline*, drifts from the speakers in the great room.

My eyes scan the room and stop on the sexy male specimen that is my husband. He's sitting on the couch, feet propped on the coffee table, in all his shirtless glory. He's engrossed in a book and doesn't know that I'm home. I quietly toe off my shoes and set my keys on the side table. Padding over, I approach him from behind leaning over the back of the couch and planting a soft kiss below his ear.

He moves faster than a lightning bolt reaching out and pulling me over the back of the couch. Like a well-choreographed move, I land with my butt cradled squarely in his lap, and my legs resting to one side. I'm being held like one would hold a baby, but Joe's eyes hold a bold desire no child should ever witness.

"Welcome home, wife." His growl vibrates through his chest, and my skin warms as the sound travels down my arm that's trapped between his body and mine. He nuzzles my neck placing warm, fleeting kisses down the column of my exposed skin.

Melting into his embrace, I turn my head and brush my mouth across his. I do it again then pause allowing the heat of his breath to mingle with mine. "What are you doing home?" I release the words into his mouth on an exhale, losing my thoughts as he pulls my uniform shirt from my pants and his fingers delve under the fabric.

He leans forward and captures my mouth. His tongue dives in, and he devours me like a starved man. He licks and sucks. Advancing and retreating as his fingers inch up my torso kneading my flesh until his hand grasps a heavy breast. My satisfied moan fills the space before his free hand gives my other breast a firm twist. My spine arches as I lift my chest pushing my tits toward his fingers in a wordless plea for more.

Needing to meld my skin to his, I tear at my shirt. The size of the buttons slows my progress, and I nearly scream with impatience. "Get this off. I need your mouth."

My pleas are answered when he rips his lips from mine and pulls his two hands from under my shirt. He undoes the bottom two buttons with the precision and speed of a surgeon as I struggle with the last two roadblocks. He bats my fingers away and takes the fabric between his two hands tearing it apart and exposing the scalloped edges of my lace bra.

"Red? My favorite color." He bares his teeth in a wolfish grin, and I wonder if he's imagining me in a little red cape with a basket on my arm. He lifts his hands and roughly pulls down both cups exposing my dusty, pink nipples and full breasts. Glittering pools of onyx drink their fill before he leans forward and traps a hardened nipple between his lips.

I hook an arm behind his head pulling him closer in a silent request. He opens his jaw and allows my hardened nub to fall from his lips before he moves to my other breast and starts the process over. He shifts his body, leaning into me, until my back falls on the couch before he follows me down and pins me beneath him.

Rising on his elbows, he stares at me memorizing each little nuance like he's never seen my face. The frenzied pace of the past few minutes slows to a blue flame. Slower, more controlled, but a million times hotter. I wiggle beneath him hoping to spur him back into the pace we'd established, but my movements are impotent in nudging his lean, yet strong, frame.

"I know your mom's death, this move, and our marriage was sudden, but I love you, Hope. With every beat of my heart, I love you more. Don't ever doubt that." He lowers his head and takes my mouth in a kiss that rivals every previous kiss. It's sensual, unhurried, and dripping with unbridled passion.

———

Two HOURS and a round of sex later, I set my fork down and study Joe as I pat my napkin across my lips. He's antsy tonight like an underlying current is running just below the surface of his skin.

While I'm overjoyed to be sitting across from him, I can't deny my curiosity for his unplanned night off. It's been six weeks since he's given himself an evening away from the hospital. I can't help the negative tangent burrowing through my mind that maybe his out of character appearance is indicative of some problem he has yet to share with me. *Is it work? Is it us? What am I sensing that I cannot see?*

While he's not verbalized any worries, his anxiousness may have been magnified by him being in the house alone before I returned from my shift. While I grew up in an environment where I was often left alone, Joe didn't. He'd told me he didn't remember being alone while growing up because his mom was always there and available to him. Whether after school, as a chaperone on a field trip, or sitting in the stands at his little league games, he'd said his mom had always been present. It gave me insight as to why he seemed unable to tolerate unstructured time bathed in silence.

My scrutiny garners his attention, and we share an unspoken look before his brow crinkles, and he returns his focus to his plate.

"So, I don't think you ever answered my question from earlier."

He picks up his glass and takes a sip letting the water slide down his throat before answering. "Do I need a reason other than I miss my wife and wanted to have a relaxing evening at home?"

While I don't entirely believe his reasoning, my heart flutters in response to his words which tells me maybe he recognizes the distance between us. Perhaps tonight is the first step for us in addressing our floundering emotional and physical connections. I've wanted to do something to bridge our gap, but I've failed to develop any lasting solutions besides relying on the hope that our relationship will improve on its own.

"Fair enough." I lift my shoulders in a shrug not indicating I smell bullshit in his response. I switch tactics. "How was your day?"

I study his face and catch the nearly imperceptible tightening of his jaw as he takes another drink. "Same hospital. Same work. Different patients."

"I haven't thought to ask about Mrs. Andrews lately. How's she doing?"

His eyes shift to the side and go vacant, but not in a bad way. A ghost of a smile shadows his face, and I know he's recalling a pleasant memory.

"She's doing well. I was able to call her last Tuesday and tell her she's officially in remission. Best damn phone call I've ever made."

I jump from my chair and throw my arms around his neck. Wetness gathers at the corner of my eyes. Mrs. Andrews has been a special patient for Joe as she reminds him so much of his mom who lost her battle to cancer around the same age. Joe is emotionally invested and determined to help her beat this horrible disease. I pull back and flash him a huge smile. "That's incredible. You're incredible. We need to celebrate."

He brings his hands to my waist and gives me a quick squeeze while his dark eyes arrest mine and turn predatory. I think I may have woken the lion who is hungry for his lamb. "That interlude on the couch was just the appetizer, little one. I can celebrate all night long."

9

HOPE

My eyelids flutter as a faint tickle runs across the base of my spine. The remnants of sleep pull at my brain as I nuzzle my cheek into my pillow. Awareness nips at my consciousness as a cool breeze slides across the middle of my back to the top of my thighs. My naked backside. My eyes snap open as I bring my elbows under my torso and push up on the bed. I blink to clear the final haze of sleep and turn my head. Molten heat stares back at me, and Joe's smirk sets me on fire. I think his grin could charm the pants off the Devil himself. I drop my head and take inventory of my body realizing I'm completely naked. It appears his smile succeeded in charming the pants off someone other than the Devil.

Joe lies on his side facing me with his elbow cocked and hand cradling his head. My gaze drifts down his body and stops at his firm cock which happens to be pointing straight at me like a divining rod looking for water. By the heat coming from his eyes, I believe I'm the cool drink set to quench his thirst.

I look between his dick and his smolder and raise an eyebrow. "Is there a reason I'm naked? I distinctly remember going to sleep with panties, black ones to be exact, covering my lady bits. I also remember going to sleep *alone.*" I lift the lilt of my voice in a tease hoping to keep my disappointment for going to bed by myself from peeking through.

He raises an eyebrow in challenge. "Oh, did you now?"

I roll to my side and hook a leg across his thighs effectively pushing him to his back as I slide my arm across his bare chest in a half-hearted act of pinning him to the bed. "Yes, Dr. Roberts, I went to sleep alone in this big bed, and I was wearing black panties. Are you trying to tell me I've taken to sleep stripping?"

He chuckles, and the vibration tickles my fingertips where they rest on his warm skin. "If you take to sleep stripping, the world of medicine is in trouble because I'll refuse to ever sleep again."

I tap him on the chest. "Very funny. Now quit avoiding my question."

He lifts my hand from his chest and entwines our fingers before turning his head in my direction and cocking it to the side. "You don't remember?"

I widen my eyes at him and shake my head.

"I got home an hour ago. I planned to take a quick shower in the guest bathroom then crawl into bed with you and catch a few hours of shut-eye before you got up. I walked into our bedroom to grab a pair of boxers, and there you were. On your stomach in the dead center of our bed surrounded by pillows, sheets kicked to the end of the bed, arms pulled up under your chest, and your butt pointing toward the ceiling and covered in my favorite lace boy shorts. I tried to walk away, honey. But your ass and those panties. A guy's only got so much control when he's staring at his wife sprawled out like a damn porn star." He looks at me with puppy dog eyes.

My stare bores into at him, and I circle my hand in a gesture for him to continue the story.

"I walked over and lightly stroked your back. I may have slid my fingertips under the waistband of lace, and I may have caressed the crack of your ass a few times. And then…" His eyes turn semi-guilty like a kid who stole two pieces of candy but ate one before fessing to his crime.

"And then you just slid my panties down my legs and walked away?" A quick mental inventory indicates I'm not sore or sticky, so I am sure he's been truthful so far.

"Yes." His eyes widen. "I mean I would have if you hadn't lifted your butt higher in what I thought was an invitation."

I scrunch my brows and wrinkle my nose. "Invitation?"

He disengages from my fingers and palms his face as his ears redden. "Honey, are you telling me you don't remember any of this?"

I shake my head, and he continues.

"You lifted your butt, and I thought you'd woken up and wanted to play. So, I slid my fingers in either side of your panties and pulled them down to your ankles. You even used your feet to kick them the rest of the way off. Imagine my surprise when I continued to caress your backside, but you remained stock still. I thought you were messing with me until I kissed your sweet spot on your neck, and I got nothing. No movement, no groan of excitement. Nada." He removes his hand and looks down at his semi-erect dick before looking back at me. "Damn. Talk about letting the air out of my sails. I felt like some kind of idiot. Needless to say, I've been watching you sleep for the past twenty minutes waiting for you to pop open your eyes and blurt 'Gotcha.'"

My abs contract as I stifle a giggle.

It's been nearly three years, his hours haven't gotten any better, and my frustrations with our relationship have multiplied. I keep hoping for a change, but he never slows down. It's like work is his addiction, but I'd be a hypocrite if I threw all the blame on his shoulders. I could demand he takes fewer hours or threaten to leave him, but in doing so, I would knowingly kill my hidden obsession. The one Dr. Johansen is worried will destroy my ability to experience a healthy, loving relationship. And I'm not ready or willing to do that just yet.

Just like Joe craves the high he gets from helping others, I covet our intimacy. Though these are the most words spoken between us in over two weeks, I find myself melting into his words, his looks, and his touch and convincing myself snapshots of my husband are better than nothing.

"Well, I'm up now. And…I'm not wearing any panties. Even though your story seems like a bit of a stretch." Really it isn't considering my mom told me I used to engage in coherent conversations while asleep. I'm not ready to let Joe in on that tidbit though. I'd let him sweat being a creeper before filling him in later. "I'm also fully rested. Though I can't say the same for you."

Shifting my body, I sit up on my knees and position them on either side of his hips. I run my hand through his hair while holding his gaze. His face harbors shadows beneath his eyes. Lack of sleep is the first indicator of his stress, and his current nocturnal patterns tell me he's climbing to dangerous levels.

His smile is blinding as he catches the back of my head in his hand and brings my mouth to his for a kiss. His lips touch mine and ignite a banked inferno within me that had sparked to life during his talk of touching and caressing me while I slept. *What kind of strange bird am I that I'm turned on by that?*

I part my lips, and he sweeps in taking possession of my mouth and capturing my breath as he drags the tip of his tongue along the roof of my mouth. I gasp as heat and desire race through my blood. The bundle of nerves between my legs flares and screams for his touch.

He pulls my bottom lip into his mouth and playfully takes a bite before soothing it with his tongue.

"This. You." I breathe the words hoping my desires snake through him without having to voice the words.

He licks my shoulder, and I feel slick wetness seep from the lips between my legs. The tendrils of my impending orgasm start to build as he slides his palm down my spine. The pressure of his hand pulls me into him, trapping my nipples against his pecs. I rock on my knees, and he responds by running his palm up and down my back in strong, slow strokes. Our combined movements force my sensitive nipples against the coarse hairs of his chest sending prickling heat to my core. I arch my back as my body attempts to give instructions my mouth refuses to make.

I rock on my knees and tighten my muscles searching for the sensations that lie just out of reach. The lips of my pussy connect with his smooth, hard cock. I roll my hips, grinding against him as the heat of his dick slides across my wet folds.

"Just like that." His words escape on a groan as he laces his fingers under the flesh of my ass and pulls my body flush with his. My clit throbs as my juices drip from my opening and coat his shaft with every thrust. Our eyes meet before traveling down to watch as we rock against each other.

I feather my lips across his with a softness that belies the hunger inside me. "Please." The single word is my prayer for release.

He leans up and swipes a waiting condom off the night-stand and hands it to me. Our gaze connects as he feeds me a silent question. I tear the wrapper, pulling the disk out and sliding it on him while averting my eyes to the disappointment as it washes across his face. Even if I have no idea how to solve our marital distance, I'm certain bringing a baby into our relationship is not the answer. I love Joe, but I don't love where we are.

I lean forward and press my lips to his, "I've missed you." My words have barely filled the room before he flips me to my back and settles his body between my legs. He hovers above me, one arm braced next to my ear as his other hand glides down the center of my chest stopping to rest on my sensitive clit. "I've wanted you since the day I slid my phone number across the counter at Rise and Grind." He lowers his hand gathering wetness on his thumb and forefinger before capturing my clit.

I lift my hips offering myself to his explorations.

He circles and pinches, and I buck my body twisting the sheets in my hands as I race toward my release.

"You are so beautiful, Hope."

His words tumble from his mouth, and I explode. My breath comes in gasps as a thousand pinpricks of pleasure detonate throughout my body. It takes me a second to realize I'm chanting Joe's name as the touch of his hands slowly recedes.

I'm on the cusp of awareness when Joe lifts my hips and plunges into me with one strong thrust. He stills, letting me adjust to his size, before he slowly withdraws then pushes back in. His thrusts establish a rhythm that hurtles him toward orgasm. His movements are strong and deep while he pins his eyes to the joining of our bodies. I focus on the flare of fire in his expression as he watches himself continually plunge into the heat of my core.

Without slowing, he lifts his head and hits me with a devilish smirk under his heated stare. His grin is salacious as he grabs my ankle and throws it over his shoulder before repeating the motion with my other leg. My eyes widen, and he returns the silly expression before he slams into me, the burn riding the line between pleasure and pain, and a hiss escapes my lips.

"That's right, baby, suck me in with your wet cunt."

My eyes cut to his. His words making me cringe. His laser gaze, his clenched jaw, his bared teeth. My husband has vanished, replaced by a ferocious untamed beast.

My breathing escalates as he pounds into me, looking but not seeing me as he tears into my body. I want to pull away, scared by this change, yet my body responds and ignores my mind's fear. Searing heat slithers through my core, tightening the walls of my pussy.

"Joe, Joe, Joe."

His ears are deaf to my chants as he reaches forward and clamps his fingers around my clit triggering an orgasm that pulls the vision from my eyes. Cloaked in semi-darkness, I soar and ride the intensity as he continues his punishing thrusts. His hands circle my ankles pushing them over his head as he slams into me one more time before throwing his head back and groaning through his release.

I stare at the ceiling waiting for my breath to return to normal, as Joe places a trail of chaste kisses across my chest and whispers, "I love you, Hope."

The chaos in my head roars with how suddenly his demeanor flips from an animal back to my husband. He nuzzles my neck before pulling out and walking to the bathroom leaving me flat on my back and ignorantly unaware of the tears coating my lashes.

How long has my husband been hiding this animal lurking inside? My thoughts flip back to another time I caught a glimpse. He'd bitten me and drawn blood, scaring me in his uncontrolled frenzy. He'd claimed to be under a huge amount of stress, and he'd apologized immediately.

Does he realize what just happened? I know he's been working an extreme number of hours, but until today I had no idea the effects of his stress and what he'd kept hidden.

Does he not trust me to share his burdens? Has our distance spiraled us into a marriage of two strangers? Questions race through my mind, and while I'm unsure what's going on, I can no longer *hope* things will change. Joe's pushed me over the cliff, and I'm finally ready to act before the tendrils of our marriage snap.

My eyes drift shut. I want a full marriage. One where each partner puts the other first. Where dreams and goals are discussed, and burdens are shared. One with emotional and physical connections happening daily, not every other week or month.

Joe and I need time to destress, re-connect, re-charge, and discuss our future, but we can't do that here. We need to do it away from the hospital, our home, and our colleagues. An idea skates through my thoughts, and my lips turn up in a small grin. I'll start making arrangements today because I refuse to embrace this animal Joe's brought into our bed.

10

HOPE

I HEAR THE SPRAY OF THE SHOWER SHUT OFF AS I OPEN MY EYES and blink away sleep. The sheer curtains on the floor to ceiling windows across from our bed flutter in the slight breeze as it filters through the cracked sliding door. Sunlight slashes across the bed, and I slip my foot from beneath the covers to absorb the warmth of the rays.

Last night's activities and my decisions flash through my head as I glance at the clock on the bedside table. The red numbers tell me it's a little past seven. I can either sleep another hour, or I can get out of bed and catch a rare, coveted glimpse of my husband before he slips out the door. Remembering my decision to put us first, I opt for the latter swinging my legs over the bed before padding into the bathroom. I'm hoping for a peek at my husband's sculpted body before he ruins my view with a button-down and dress pants.

A towel sits low on his waist and another covers his head as he vigorously rubs the wetness from his hair. Water droplets hit my face as I sneak up behind him and wrap my arms around his waist. Not expecting a bathroom visitor, he tenses before dropping the towel to his shoulders and pulling me around in front of him. Caught between the marble countertop and his hard body, I face the mirror and watch as he bends his head. His eyes never leave our reflection as he lays a path of kisses from my ear to my collar bone.

His breath tickles my neck as he whispers, "Good morning," before he turns away to pull on a pair of boxer briefs. My eyes feast on the roundness of his tight ass as he pulls the material up his hard thighs. The glance he shoots me over his shoulder tells me he knows exactly what his little tease does to me.

He steps over and turns me around to face him. "I'm sorry. I was a little off last night. Yesterday wasn't the best day at work, and I ended up bringing some of the negativity home with me."

"You know you can always talk to me, right?" I squeeze his forearm so he can't physically retreat even though I can't keep his mind from doing so.

"Yeah, I know. I just don't like to pull you into my problems."

"We're a team. That's what I'm here for. Please don't shut me out."

We stare at each other as war rages behind his eyes. My stomach sinks. He thinks I'm not strong enough to help shoulder his burdens. I've been so caught within my own head; I've missed the needs he's kept hidden.

After a pregnant pause, he gives me a forced smile and kisses the end of my nose. "It's nothing I can't handle."

My breath leaves me like a deflating balloon, but I nod, and he leaves to finish getting dressed before he walks out the door at seven-thirty.

I hope the trip I'm planning doesn't end up being a case of too little, too late.

———

I'M WALKING through the door at the station as my phone pings. Balancing my bribe in one hand, I pull my cell from my pocket with the other before rolling my eyes over the screen.

Joe: I forgot to tell you EJ is in town. Care if we grab a beer before I come home? You're welcome to join us.

I forget he can't see the shake of my head. EJ has been Joe's friend for years, and while I'm often invited to hang with them, I'll be the first to admit I've never been able to appreciate their inside jokes or understand their special bond. While we've been polite to each other during the few occasions we've spent together, we amicably tolerate each other. Honestly, I'd rather sit at home with a good book than listen to those two reminisce about their college-day shenanigans.

Me: I'm working the night shift. Do your thing. I'll see you tomorrow. Tell EJ I said hi. Love you.

Joe: Okay. Be safe tonight.

Me: You too.

I slide my phone in my back pocket and walk to my locker to drop off my purse before heading to the kitchen. I place the Tupperware container of chocolatey goodness in the center of the counter, pull off the lid, and wait. I haven't seen a single person since I walked in, but I know they're here because I saw the rig and the truck both parked in the garage bay on my way in.

Two minutes later, Chief Matthews comes around the corner at a good clip with his eyes focused and nose twitching.

My honey—caramel double chocolate brownies—has caught the proverbial queen bee on the first pass.

I step in front of the container and look up at Chief, who is, and always will be, Thor in my mind. He raises his eyebrows and attempts to peer around me, confident his nose has brought him to the scene of sugary oblivion.

"Is that chocolate I smell?"

I sidestep, blocking his view as best I can with my small frame, and take an exaggerated sniff as I shake my head. "I don't smell anything. Wait." I inhale again. "Did McNair burn his tamales again?" I widen my eyes giving him a look of pure innocence.

His chuckle is rough as he shakes his head. "What do you think? He knows how to make two things: charcoal and dirty dishes. If he wasn't my best EMT, no disrespect intended, I would have fired him years ago for purposely trying to smoke us out of the station. Now, do I, or do I not, smell one of your baking masterpieces?"

I dip my chin in a nod. "Yep. New recipe. Caramel chocolate brownies. Would you like to try one?"

He gives me a confused look like I just asked him if he wanted to mud wrestle with me this weekend. "Do I want to try them? Heck, yes. I do. As long as you didn't char them to a crisp and douse them in lighter fluid, and even then, I'd probably just dunk 'em in milk to water down the aftertaste of the kerosene."

He steps around me, swipes a large square from the container, and takes a hearty bite.

I watch, hyper-focused on his reaction, looking for signs of food rapture. I need him to love these, or my plan will be in jeopardy of failure. His lids drop as he chews. By all visual accounts, I've just served my boss a slice of food porn. My suspicion is confirmed moments later when a moan escapes his lips along with a couple of dark crumbs.

He pops the rest of the delicacy in his mouth before giving his praise.

"Roberts, you are a taste bud master. Anything you want? Name it. It's yours."

I give myself a mental fist bump as a giggle floats across my tongue and into the space between us. I spy a big piece of chocolate stuck to his bottom tooth.

"You've got something right there, Chief." Opening my mouth, I circle my index finger around my bottom teeth.

His brows raise to his hairline and his cheeks pink in embarrassment as he tries to use his tongue to dislodge it. I attempt to contain my laughter, but it sneaks out when he shows me his teeth, silently asking if the piece is gone. Not only is it not gone, but he's managed to smear chocolate across the front of his bottom four teeth. I give him a thumbs-up, and he nods his head, satisfied, even though he has no idea what a goof he looks like.

I smile as the day of the interview rushes through my mind. I figure chocolate-coated teeth are an even trade considering I endured an entire interview only to be told at the end I was the sole qualified candidate.

I tap my index finger to my bottom lip and cock my head to one side. "You know Chief, there is one little favor you could grant me."

His lips twist up at the corners, and he turns folding his arms across his chest as he leans a hip against the counter. He drops his chin and shakes his head berating himself under his breath. Something about being a sucker for women and baked goods.

"Something tells me those treats weren't a spontaneous gift. Out with it."

"Joe and I never had a honeymoon. I need a week off at the end of the month so I can surprise him with a trip to New York City."

My request leaves my mouth on a single breath of air. We need this trip, especially after our conversation this morning and the debacle of last night. Joe needs to trust me with his problems and not shut me out, and I need to show him what the hospital is stealing from our marriage.

Chief strokes his jaw as he looks at me with an unreadable, flat expression. After what seems like an hour of silence, he nods his head. "Done. As long as you can get Grimes to cover for you and McNair is okay with it, you're good to go."

I step forward and embrace him in a quick hug while trying to contain my giddiness. "Thanks. I'll talk to the guys right away."

I take off down the hall toward the game room where I'm sure I'll find both of the guys parked in front of the enormous TV playing that ridiculous game where people shoot each other and have a dance-off to celebrate.

As I step around the corner, I wave at Gill, our newest member of the fire crew. He lifts his chin and continues into the kitchen.

His loud snort and snarky comment hit me two seconds later. "Chief, what the hell do you have on your teeth? If I didn't know better, I'd say you were literally talking shit again."

His continued whoops of laughter push me down the hall, and I cannot stifle my grin knowing I just played my boss, got a week off, and completed phase one of my plan all at the same time. Thank heavens for my accomplices: caramel and chocolate.

11

HOPE

MY KNEE BOUNCES OUT A SONGLESS RHYTHM AS I STARE AT THE planes taking off in the distance. Joe's boss at the hospital had been surprisingly supportive of my request that Joe take a week off so I could surprise him with a belated honeymoon. He'd even offered to speak with Joe's colleagues to work out a plan to cover his cases in his absence.

The hardest sell for this whole trip was Joe himself. At first, he'd downright refused claiming he couldn't be away from his patients for any length of time. Then he'd claimed the hospital wasn't prepared for his absence. I'd let him work himself into a lather then countered with the ace I'd kept in my back pocket which was the schedule his colleagues had created. He'd finally relented but adamantly stressed we are gone no more than seven days. He'd also insisted the hospital call him with any changes in patient status. He'd also informed me he'd be checking in twice a day for patient updates. While I'd not been a fan of his requirements, I considered him agreeing to go was enough of a win in my book.

I turn my gaze to where he sits across from me drinking a coffee and reading an old *Sports Illustrated* magazine like he doesn't have one care in the world. I'm secretly jealous of his devil-may-care attitude when it comes to flying.

With this being the second time in my life that I've flown, I'm a nervous wreck. I'm not an anxious person by nature, but the thought of hurtling down a runway and lifting off into the sky at a forty-five-degree angle has me literally sweating through my shirt. *What if I get sick? What if I can't get to the lavatory fast enough? What if other people see me get sick?* These irrational worries play on a continuous loop in my head to the point of giving me a massive headache. This trip is supposed to be fun and romantic, and I'm going to faint before it even has a chance to start.

I stand up and move to the seat next to Joe. I've tried to remain calm. The only outward appearance that I'm freaking out is my bouncing leg and deer-in-the-headlights stare. I lean my head against his shoulder and close my eyes trying to talk myself off the ledge of anxiety I'm currently teetering on.

"What if the plane crashes?" My voice is so quiet; my own ears have difficulty registering my question.

Joe turns his strong jaw in my direction, and I raise my head meeting his questioning gaze. "Huh?" His blank expression indicates he hasn't clued into the chaos running through my mind.

I take a deep breath and release it in an attempt to cleanse my mind of its wayward thoughts. "Never mind."

"Good morning, passengers. We, on behalf of United Airlines, would like to thank you for choosing United for your travel in the sky today. We would now like to begin boarding all first-class passengers for flight 205 direct from Denver to LaGuardia. All first-class passengers are asked to proceed to the boarding area for priority boarding."

Joe looks over and smiles. "Ready?"

My smile isn't very convincing as I nod my head. "I think so."

He brings my hand to his lips and kisses the backs of my fingers. "I know I've been a hardass about this trip. In case I forget to tell you later, our honeymoon was epic. I'm glad we did it."

I roll my eyes. "We haven't even arrived yet, and you're already telling me how epic the trip was?"

"Call me optimistic, but something tells me this trip will be one we'll never forget. Not to mention, I'm banking on having lots of sex, and sex is *always* epic."

He waggles his eyebrows and stands, pulling me up with him in the process. I laugh at his silliness. Like a ghost from the past, this is old Joe. Calm, funny, passionate. It's easy to forget he has a wicked sense of humor hiding under his serious-doctor persona.

He places his hand on the small of my back, and we proceed through the gate and down the jet bridge. This trip is going to be epic.

———

"How much farther do you think it is?" I slow my steps hoping to gain some relief from the horrible pinching sensation in the toes of my stilettos.

Leave it to me to volunteer to walk to the venue while wearing a pair of four-inch high, toe-crunching—totally awesome looking—stilettos. The heated desire in Joe's eyes when I stepped out of the bathroom before we'd left had been worth it. That had been before I'd clocked ten thousand steps. It currently feels like every one of my toes is bleeding.

Joe looks up from his phone and walks a few steps before turning around in a circle. The street is dotted with fixtures made to look like old gas lights. The bulbs flicker and dance, bathing the street in an ethereal glow.

"Are you looking for a street sign or performing a rain dance?"

He smirks in my direction before bending down and hauling me into his arms. He gives me a sidelong glance as he crosses the street, purposely avoiding an answer to my sarcastic question. "It should be on this block. Keep your eyes peeled for a red door."

I turn my head and scan the facades of the passing buildings. Most are nondescript and fairly plain so a red door shouldn't be difficult to spot.

Ten minutes later, we've walked the same two blocks three times. "We need to stop. Put me down for a second, please."

He stops abruptly, releasing his hold around my legs and allowing me to slide down the front of his suit-clad body. He'd been pouring over the screen of his phone when I'd walked out of the bathroom this morning. When I'd asked him what he was up to, he simply said, "It's a surprise I'm saving for later." Seeing the excitement in his eyes, I'd relented, determined to drop the subject and let him have his secret.

"Hope, I'm sorry. I thought this would be a unique spot to visit. From what I read, this place is a secret, so it's not easy to find unless you know what you're looking for. I didn't figure it would be this difficult. Are you ready to catch a cab back to the hotel?"

His eyes are shadowed, and his shoulders slump as he confesses his failure. My heart stutters, and I vow we're going to find this secret spot even if I have to rip off my shoes and walk barefoot through the streets of New York.

"Nope. I'm not ready to give up."

He smiles and takes my hand, and we start walking back the way we came. I scrutinize each building, knowing we've probably passed the place five times. A small brass nameplate next to a wooden door catches my eye.

E. Arden. *Why does that name sound familiar?*

"Joe, search E. Arden on your phone."

He looks at me with a confused glance but does as I ask.

"E. Arden is short for Elizabeth Arden, an American businesswoman who founded a cosmetics empire." He bends his head and continues scanning the rest of the information. A broad smile appears before he looks up. "Says here. She founded the Red Door Salon in New York in 1910." He turns his head and scans the street again before approaching the wooden door. "This has to be the place."

His excitement is contagious, and my heart rate picks up as he lifts his finger and pushes the ornate, antique-looking bell to the left of the door. Less than a minute later, the door is answered by a guy about my age who looks like he stepped out of a 1930's history book. His dark hair is slicked back, and he's dressed in a three-piece pinstriped suit.

"Welcome to the Red Door. My name is William. I'll be your bar guide this evening."

Joe takes my hand and tucks it into the crook of his arm escorting me inside.

The dark hallway is dimly lit by wall sconces that throw flickering shadows across the papered wall. I feel like I've stepped through a magical portal back in time. William stops at a set of wooden double doors and turns to us.

"May you have a wonderful night here at the Red Door. Please call upon me once you've determined your drink selections." He opens the doors and steps back.

My eyes go wide as I take in the room. Stairs along the wall lead to multiple levels featuring small private balconies. A gleaming wooden bar covers the left wall where I count three bartenders, all dressed like William, pouring drinks and passing them to waiting patrons. Smoke and the sweet smell of cigars permeate the room giving it a cloud-like atmosphere. Patrons are dressed formally in everything from modern styles to vintage flapper costumes. A wooden dance floor, sunken into the middle of the room, is covered with dozens of people flying across the space in perfect time to the swing music pumping through the establishment.

I pull Joe's arm and step up on my toes so I can speak directly into his ear. "I would walk another ten thousand steps in my heels if I knew this place was my reward. Thank you!"

He smiles and wraps an arm around my waist pulling me into his side before leaning down to kiss my neck just below my ear. "Best wife ever. I love you."

Goosebumps raise across my arms, I've wanted to see his enthusiasm and feel this connection for so long, but fear creeps into my chest. I'm not sure if a week is enough time to repair the damage that's already been done.

12

HOPE

My eyes pop open as I'm startled awake. Blinking away the sleep and peering into the darkness, I push down the sudden nausea churning in my stomach.

I scan the art on the walls, the fireplace across from the bed, and the position of the furniture as my heartbeat speeds to alarming levels. Momentary amnesia clouds my senses before I remember I'm in a hotel room in New York. I sit up. The sheet falls away and exposes my naked breasts as I run a palm across the bedsheets finding them warm, but empty.

A shaft of light glows beneath the door that leads into the suite's sitting room.

I slip out of bed snagging Joe's discarded shirt from the floor and throwing it on while padding to the door. The creek of the handle sounds like a cannon shooting through the quiet space.

Joe turns, cell phone to his ear. For a split second, his eyes meet mine, and I register the blind panic bleeding from their depths. He shifts, presenting me with his naked back before resuming his phone call.

Beads of perspiration prickle my neck. This isn't a normal call. Something's happened, and Joe is scared.

I pace to his side, taking calming breaths to quell the chaos of emotions clogging my brain. I place a hand on his back and goosebumps rise across his skin as my fingertips slide up his spine. His skin is clammy, and his muscles are bunched and ready for flight. He lifts his free hand and runs it through his hair.

His voice, which has been absent until this moment, bursts from his mouth. "This can't be happening. Those levels have been stable for months. Tell me this is a fucking m-mistake." His anguish pours through the crack in his voice. "I trust your judgment, but I feel like I should be there." He pulls at his hair as he listens. "No, don't do that yet. Let me think about it. I'll call you back in a couple of hours." He pulls the phone from his ear and stabs the screen to end the call.

He drops his chin to his chest. The rasp of our breaths is the only sound in the otherwise silent room.

"Joe, what is it? Is it your dad?" I wrap my arms around his waist and rest my cheek against the softness of his smooth back. His chest shudders before he says,

"My dad's fine. It's Mrs. Andrews. She was re-admitted about four hours ago. Chest pains. Trouble breathing." He pauses, and I feel another shudder rock through his body. I tighten my hold at his waist. "A chest x-ray showed a shadow on her aorta. The MRI confirmed a mass the size of a pea. It doesn't look good."

I slide around to his front making sure to keep him locked in my embrace as I move. He's near shattering, and I'm prepared to catch him when the dam finally breaks.

I raise my arms and thread my hands through the short hair on either side of his stricken face. "She's a fighter. She can beat this. I'll call the airline and switch our tickets. I'll make sure we're there by morning." I raise on my toes and brush his lips with my whisper, "You're not alone. I've got you."

He stands, frozen in his fear. His eyes scan my face looking for strength in the promise of my words. His lids close in a long blink before he cuts me with his statement. "I want you to stay here. We still have four more days. I want you to complete our list so you can tell our kids someday."

A denial sits poised on the tip of my tongue before he's done speaking. "No! I'm going with you."

He lifts his hands to my shoulders, and the gentleness he reserves for when he wants to win a fight paints his face. I can see him mentally digging his heels in, and I ready my argument.

"Hope, please, do this for me. I need you to do this." His face hardens, and I see the moment he shutters my choice and makes the decision for me. He's retreated and refuses to let me shoulder his pain.

I take a seat on the couch buying time as I organize the words he needs to hear even though my acceptance feels like poison coating my tongue. "If I do this, I need something from you."

His jaw tightens, and his head moves in a nearly imperceptible nod, yet he remains silent waiting for me to start negotiations.

"If I do this, you'll answer my calls and give me updates each day?"

His answer is clipped, but instant. "Yes."

"You *promise* you won't shut me out?" Knowing this is my one non-negotiable, he swallows and looks away before he slowly nods his agreement. "Okay. I'll stay."

I walk straight into the bathroom, turning on the shower and allowing the warmth of the spray to fill the air with wisps of steam. The warmth of his shirtless body engulfs mine from behind. I drop my head back to his firm chest, and his arms come around me in an intimate embrace. I love this man, and he loves me, but I'm not convinced love alone will be able to save us.

He releases me, steps back, and lifts his borrowed shirt from my body. Nudging me, he walks us forward allowing the heated water to rain over our intertwined bodies.

My heart bleeds for him, for me, for the life I thought we'd have. In refusing my support, Joe has severed nearly every fragile thread left holding us together. Knowing I risk emotional devastation, I offer him the only comfort I know he'll willingly accept.

I grasp his hands and place them over my heart making a final plea. "Open your heart and let me take care of you."

His mouth ghosts across mine. His voice is barely a whisper, and I strain to decipher his words as droplets of water slide down my face. "My heart beats for you. Only you."

Had I known what would await me when I returned to Boulder, I would have wrapped my arms around him, put my ear to his chest, and memorized the song of his heart.

13

HOPE

I EXIT THE DRESSING ROOM ON THE SECOND FLOOR OF Nordstrom and power walk to the nearest women's restroom, which appears to be tucked into a corner near the kitchen wares. Excellent for me since I'd planned to stop here after I'd finished trying on the numerous outfits I'd found on the clearance racks in the women's department.

I push open the bathroom door and stand in awe, straining bladder momentarily forgotten, as I stare at the opulence of the powder/sitting room. Ornate silver mirrors cover one wall above a waist-high marble counter lined with four small stools topped with forest green velvet. I lift my eyes to the high, coffered ceiling and gawk at the crystal chandelier. This sitting room is a design masterpiece, and it's by far the swankiest I've ever seen.

My screaming bladder reminds me of my reason for the visit, and I hurry to the other side of the room pushing through the door. I don't know why I'm surprised by the continued opulence bleeding over into the actual restroom. Each stool is hidden behind its own carved wooden door. I take it all in with wide eyes before hurrying into an unoccupied stall and locking the door. I hang my purse and shopping bag on a small hook and bend to do my business.

A metallic sound immediately followed by a shallow plunk hits my ears seconds before I remember that I'd put my cell phone in my back pocket after checking it for messages while I was in the dressing room. I cringe. I already know, without looking, that my cell phone is lying at the bottom of the toilet bowl under a gallon of water.

I pop to my feet, my underwear still hanging at my knees, and turn around. "Shit. I cannot believe this." My ears get hot as I continue to curse my stupidity. I stare at the water wondering how often Nordstrom has their cleaning crew scrub the toilets. After some mental encouragement, I reach in, grab the phone, and pull my hand out. I've never been so upset and grossed out at the same time.

Needing to use the toilet before my bladder explodes, I place my wet phone on the floor and finish the reason for my visit. I exit the little room with my items, including my water-logged phone, stopping at the sink to wash my hands before I grab some paper towels and frantically blot the water off of my phone. After removing as much water as possible, I say a little prayer, push the power button, and wait.

Nothing happens. No blinking notification light, no white piece of fruit. I continue to stare at the lifeless, black screen. Maybe it's going through a diagnostic check before it turns back on.

Five minutes later, I'm still staring at nothingness, and fear sets in. I'm alone in a strange city, in a different state, without a way to communicate. Damn. This is not happening. I rack my brain, but the only number I can recall is the one for the house I grew up in. And the only reason I remember it is because I couldn't graduate kindergarten until I could recite my home phone number.

I don't know Joe's number. It's a cell phone, so it's not like I can look up his number. My feet pace the black and white tiles of the sitting area while I struggle with a plan. It's not like I'm returning home today. I'll be here for another four days. *How do I contact Joe? Do I go buy another phone?*

After another ten minutes pass, I'm no closer to a plan. No longer able to hide out in the bathroom, I make my way to the exit. Thirty minutes ago, I was debating the merits of a misplaced button on a clearance dress and now I'm contemplating how I'm going to communicate with a waterlogged and ruined phone.

My heart flutters, and my skin prickles as I realize the significance of how one accident obliterates my plans. I am an independent woman, yet I'm cut off at the knees by the most trivial hiccup.

I leave Nordstrom, a small bag of lingerie hanging from my wrist. Thank goodness, I'd visited that department first so my shopping trip wasn't a total loss.

I walk toward the hotel considering options as they materialize. My eyes snag on a store's signage as I'm about to pass by. A small coffee shop, Sip and Send, offers *coffee with an electronic twist.* The slogan is designed to catch travelers and locals looking to surf the Internet while enjoying a caffeinated beverage.

I wait to cut across the sidewalk, noticing for the first time how many people crowd the small space. I wonder where their feet will take them today. *Are they tourists? Born and bred New Yorkers?*

As I ponder the lives of the surrounding strangers, my eyes land on the small girl passing in front of me. She's maybe seven-years-old by my estimation. She holds the hand of a woman not much older than myself.

Dismissing her caregiver, my attention is drawn back to the girl. Dressed in a white button-down Oxford shirt, tights, and green plaid skirt, her hands flutter at her thighs. Her tights are falling, and she's trying to pull them up without drawing notice to her movements.

A grin passes my lips as I remember my own struggles with wearing tights as well as the arguments I used to have with my mother about wearing them. While her hair is red, not blond like my own, I see the ghost of my childhood in the braids she wears. They bounce along her back with each stuttered step, and I can almost feel the tickle of hair across my own back as my mind rewinds. She's going on a field trip. One she doesn't want to attend. She'll be different and the other kids will ignore her, but she's afraid to speak her mind. The red head's toes skid across the pavement as she hurries to keep pace with the woman who's paying no heed to the young girl's struggles as they cross the street. They step down the sidewalk and disappear from view.

I shake my head falling out of the reverie that has taken hold of my thoughts. It's been years since I've returned to the game—the one where I create a world of hope through a stranger's eyes. My hand lifts to my neck searching for the piece of jewelry from my green-eyed hero. Broken and thrown into the back of my jewelry box, it's been a stretch of time since I've thought about the necklace's significance. The boy had given me a gift more priceless than gold. He'd shown me how to exercise my mind and seek hope in difficult situations.

The stress of today brings him to the forefront of my mind, and I steel myself to grasp my pieced-together plan.

I open the door and walk into Sip and Send. The walls are covered with eclectic, bright-colored artwork and cozy, high-back armchairs and side tables dot the floor in little patterns. A bank of computers sits on a table that stretches across the back wall.

The barista greets me with a smile, and the relaxing smell of coffee pulls me forward.

"Good afternoon, I'm Melody. What can I get for you?" Her blue eyes sparkle with warmth as she waits for my order.

"Hi." My gaze bounces from the sign above her head to her calm face. "Uh, I'll have your small house blend. Black."

"Absolutely. Coming right up." I watch as she turns and makes my drink with an efficiency that speaks to her bubbly nature. She pushes the paper cup across the counter. "That'll be $5.62."

I glance at the computers along the wall as I hand her my debit card. "I need to use a computer. Can I pay for that as well?"

She swipes my card before handing it back to me. "Your coffee is your ticket. Computers are free for paying customers provided you're not here to watch porn."

She gives me a wink, and I feel my neck heat with embarrassment as my eyes widen. "I would never." My words get caught in my throat, and I push them out around a cough. "Do people do that?"

Her white teeth brighten her wide smile. "Only the pervs. My gut tells me you're not a skeeze, so I think we're safe."

I clear my throat, still reeling from her words. "I just need to send an email."

She holds out her hand indicating the row of electronics. "You'll need to sign in with your own email address, but feel free to knock yourself out."

"Thanks." I slide my card back in my wallet and drop it into my oversized purse before picking up my coffee and making my way to the nearest computer.

My account loads and a plethora of useless emails hit my inbox. I hit compose and type in Joe's email address hoping today will be the random day he opens his personal email. The only time he seems to make an effort to check it is when he's expecting contact from his dad. I have no other way to reach him outside of calling the hospital when I get back to the hotel and leaving him a message or having him paged. I'll use the hospital as plan **B** if I don't hear from him by tomorrow. I'd rather not scare him by calling the hospital if I can help it.

Joe,
I've made a stupid blunder. I accidentally dropped my phone in the toilet while I was shopping. My phone is ruined. Please call the hotel, and leave me a message when you get this. I don't want to buy another phone without your help since you know I stink at anything to do with technology. I'll see you soon.
Love,
Hope

I send the message and log off of my account before standing up and making my way to the door with my drink in hand. I send a mouthed "thank you" to Melody, catching her eye while she's filling a customer's order.

She raises her free hand and sends me a wave. "Thank you for stopping. I hope you got what you needed."

I nod my head and step into the warmth of the afternoon sun. I continue down the sidewalk, dodging people who look like they're on a mission. I smile as I watch the strangers. I'm without a phone, without a method of communication until I return to the hotel, but I'm oddly content. I feel like a child who's been given permission to play outside until dinnertime. I'm in an amazing city, my time is my own, and I am beholden to no one. Maybe I'll even cross off an item on *The Honeymoon To-Do List* before I head back to the hotel.

14

HOPE

THE PINK AND ORANGE HORIZON DIPS AND RISES WITH THE SWAY of the boat. I lean both forearms on the railing and marvel at the beauty as the sun gives a final majestic bow before disappearing into the water.

I recall the message waiting for me, at the front desk, when I got back to the hotel last night.

> *Hope,*
> *Glad I checked my email tonight! Something told me I needed the distraction from my racing thoughts, so I logged on.*
> *I'm sorry about your phone. You can buy a replacement in New York, or we can get you one as soon as you get back. Call the hospital and have me paged if you need me. I hope you're putting big check marks on our bucket list.*
> *Love,*
> *Joe*

His words, written in a female hand, had been a comfort, but also a thorn. I'm homesick for him, but apprehension clogs my mind for the conversation we'll need to have when I return.

I want to be his partner and his confidant, but the longer I'm away, the more I question if Joe will ever see me in those roles.

The Statue of Liberty and Ellis Island had been the last item on my list, and my visit allows me to put a big red "X" through the name. My skin tingles with excitement for the rich history of this pinnacle of freedom. The number of people who have spent a lifetime of savings to catch a glimpse of her as their boat glided across the harbor is astounding and amazing.

Today's visit had been exhilarating to my soul. A closet history buff, I greedily gulped the information the tour directors had offered. The magic from years of bright dreams whispered through my ears and lifted the hairs at the nape of my neck. More than once, I'd turned around to share something with Joe before remembering I was alone.

I pull my jacket tighter against the crisp breeze, no longer warmed by the rays of the sun. My mind drifts like the push and pull of the waves before me.

For three years, I've bobbed within the sea of uncertainty choosing to bury my goals when I assumed the role of Joe's wife. Before my mother died, I'd been hell-bent on becoming a pediatric orthopedist. Straight as an arrow, I'd made a goal, laid the path, and taken off at a sprint toward the finish line. After my mom's death, I'd lost sight of myself and veered off track, attaching myself to Joe's coattails, content to live with intermittent scraps of his time and affection.

I look across the dark water and catch sight of a bird's shadow as it dives beneath a wave. It emerges without a fish, climbs into the air, and returns for another try. I'm mesmerized, unable to look away as the bird continues to fail. Yet, his hope in catching a fish urges him to continue to try.

Diving and climbing.

Rising and falling.

Goosebumps raise across my arms. Without words, this

bird is sharing a secret. Never lose hope. *Defeat lies in the failure of doing nothing and never moving forward. It doesn't matter if you walk the same path or veer onto a different one. Keep moving, and never give up.* Dr. Johansen's words flit through my mind as I continue to watch the perseverance of this bird. I remember how I'd scoffed at Dr. Johansen's words the day she shared them with me. I'd been suffocating under the uncertainty of what I wanted from myself and my relationships with others. Her words had burrowed below the surface of my skin lying dormant until this moment when my heart and mind were ready to accept their truth.

My eyes water as my epiphany hits me. I've placed my expectation of happiness at someone else's feet. I've been waiting for Joe to change and neglected to recognize *my* discontent resides within *me.* I'm stuck in mediocrity because I've failed to act on my own behalf. Two major aspects of my life— my marriage and my schooling—are unraveling because I've subconsciously surrendered hope, and *I've* failed to move forward.

Dr. Johansen had tried to open my eyes to this breakthrough, but I'd been too lost in my expectations of others to see the value of her words. It has taken three years, countless hours of self-reflection, and one determined bird to help me understand that I am the person responsible for creating *my* happiness. I'm capable of standing on my own because I've finally regained my hope.

The deep baritone of the boat's horn rattles through my chest. My mind is clear, and my heart is light as we motor through the harbor. The dock awaits, and I'm giddy with anticipation for tomorrow. My eyes are open, and I'm ready to continue the race. A happy marriage and a successful medical practice await me at the finish line.

15

HOPE

Bored, yet anxious, my thumb plays across my platinum wedding set as I scan the crowded terminal. I've spent the better part of the last fifteen minutes playing with the prisms cast across the blue carpeted boarding area by my diamond. Being stranded within the confines of O'Hare Airport for an unplanned six-hour layover is enough to steal the patience of a guard at Kensington Palace.

Granted, I've spent a good chunk of my time lunching on grilled salmon and chasing it with a glass of white wine while perusing the latest issue of *Architecture Digest* in the peaceful atmosphere of the first-class lounge, but I am ready to be home —yesterday. My fingers drum across the shiny surface of the magazine that lies ignored in the middle of my lap. The separation from Joe is making me jittery. Add to that the unfortunate phone incident, and I'm a mess.

It kills me my contact with Joe has been reduced to one message. Finishing this trip had felt like an albatross around my neck, but I'd made a promise, and I'd kept it for the sole purpose of bringing a little joy to the bleakness of Joe's week.

A noise pulls my vision to the ticket counter in time to

glimpse a subtle grimace from the buxom-blond agent, as she listens to a petite, gray-haired woman whose stooped posture and animated hand gestures belie the strength of her vocal cords and the diverse color of her vocabulary.

I'm too far removed to vouch for the shade of the agent's lipstick, but I'm close enough to hear the full impact of Granny's wrath.

"Excuse me?! What do you mean Fluffy can't ride in my purse? She *needs* me. She'll be scared shitless if you put her in the cargo bay! There ain't no damned way I'll do that. If your manager isn't here in five minutes, I'll be forced to pull Fluffy out and put her right here on your counter. *You* can explain it to her. Pftt. You think I'm mad? I'm a tame pussy cat compared to an upset Fluffy."

The agent's eyes dart right and left like she's expecting a band of animal control officers to materialize out of the empty seats. I feel bad for her. I'm sure she's just doing her job.

Completely engrossed in Granny's verbal tirade, I miss the appearance of a man who steps up to the counter in an attempt to gain the agent's attention. I see the moment Agent Goldilocks's gaze meets his. She leans forward, eyes widening as her tongue darts out to wet her bottom lip.

My attention is riveted to the play of his crisp, white Oxford shirt as it pulls across the broad expanse of his back. He bends, placing a leather briefcase on the floor next to his feet, before putting a large hand on Granny's shoulder as he speaks into her gray hair. She lets out a laugh and turns her head to glance at him over her shoulder. He side-steps, situating his body so they can continue their exchange, and my jaw drops to my chest.

Gorgeous, beautiful, dazzling, handsome. Nope. Not one of those conveys his magnificence. He smiles while talking to Granny, and I realize no words in any language will do this man justice. He's ruined people watching for the rest of my life since no one will ever compare to him.

A loud hiss pulls me from my mental tangent as I return my eyes to the ticket counter. Oh shit. Granny's made good on her promise. Fluffy's purse/carrier is perched on the ticket counter, dangerously close to sliding to the floor. Suddenly, a furry head, full of piss and vinegar, pops out. Even from the safety of my vantage point, I'm scared. Hair raised across her head, Fluffy takes a swipe at Goldilocks's face. Her face pales as she jumps back while demanding the older woman remove Fluffy from the counter.

Granny shoots her a glare, but reaches out and scoops Fluffy off the counter. The man—aka Kitty Whisperer—leans in and speaks directly to Fluffy before petting the cat on its head. I kid you not, Fluffy moves toward him and places her paw on his arm seeking more attention. If I didn't witness it, I wouldn't believe it. The man continues to pet Fluffy as he engages in a conversation with both Granny and Goldilocks. Goldilocks listens while tapping her fingers across her keyboard as Whisperer and Granny wait. She looks up and smiles before handing a white ticket to the man and a yellow ticket to Granny.

Whisperer bends down to retrieve his briefcase before grabbing Granny's purse and guiding her, and Fluffy, to a bank of seating near the boarding area.

I study them as they talk, never at a loss for words. Granny using animated gestures and Whisperer responding with his head nods and dazzling smiles. I take a quick glance at my watch and notice I have about fifteen minutes before first-class boarding starts. I gather my purse and rolling carry-on and make a quick stop to use the facilities. I'm hopeful I can stay calm and not have a panic attack because I'm flying alone.

———

MY EYES SHIFT across the bowler hat of the man in front of me. His straight posture and impeccable dress are reminiscent of a dying age when passengers wore their Sunday best, no matter the reason or destination, for their travel. He passes through, and I step up next, my boarding pass in hand. The agent scans the barcode and gives me a smile before I continue down the jet bridge. If all goes well, I'll be sliding into my 1500-thread count sheets, my front to the warmth of Joe's back, in about four hours.

I walk onto the plane and take the few steps toward seat 2B. Except someone, or shall I say something, occupies my seat. A familiar, tattered purse catches my eye as I sidle up to my space.

Oh, hell no.

Mentally gathering ammunition for my argument for a new seat on a plane I already know to be booked solid, I turn toward the nearest flight attendant catching a glimpse of Whisperer quickly organizing the area around my seat. He looks up and gives me a shy smile before rising to his feet.

"Yeah, sorry." He hurries to situate his belongings—like a college student right before parent's weekend—as Satan's spawn stares at me from *my* seat. "I thought I'd be settled before my seatmate arrived. Here, let me move this."

Reaching down, he grabs the purse/carrier and gently stows it under his seat. A hiss rises from the floor as he bites his bottom lip. "Cat sitting for a friend. Hope you don't mind."

I raise an eyebrow staring him in the eye as I cling to my annoyance. The man with sparkling green eyes, who has already piqued my curiosity, is my seatmate for the next three hours, give or take. Before I can bend down and grab my carry-on, he steps into the aisle, grasps the handle, and hoists it into the overhead compartment shutting it with a loud click.

"Thank you." My lips tip in a half-grin as I brush invisible dirt from my seat before sitting down and immediately buckling my seatbelt.

"Mitchell Anderson." His large hand darts across the armrest.

A forced smile slides across my mouth. "Hope." I drop my hand and rest my head against the back of the seat attempting to tame the anxiety that's wormed inside my body. Mitchell sits down and settles in, folding his long legs into the small space.

My heart rate picks up while I struggle to breathe in through my mouth and exhale through my nose. With the precision and regularity of a Swiss timepiece, my panic sets in. For some, it's a visit to the dentist, a speech in front of the class, or going to a party full of strangers. My torture is flying. Panic for impending motion sickness coupled with irrational fear turns my stomach.

Mitchell's hand falls on my forearm. "Hey, are you okay?"

I shift my eyes and meet concerned green. My shoulders lift as I close my lids. "Not a fan of flying, especially alone."

His breath flirts with my face leaving evidence of his visual scrutiny. Embarrassment heats my cheeks. His weight shifts against my shoulder as he leans toward me. "I once exposed my nipple to an auditorium of five hundred colleagues."

My eyes pop open, and I turn my head as a rouge giggle tickles my lips. "Excuse me?"

A mischievous grin lights his face. "You heard me. I suffered a UNE—unfortunate nipple exposure. Unintentional, of course." His head dips as his eyes tilt upward reminding me of a small puppy trying to convince his owner he wasn't the one who ripped apart the garbage.

I debate the merits of closing my eyes and ignoring him or engaging in this ludicrous conversation. My brain brews several crazy scenarios, and I can't let this thread go. "Seriously? Do I even want to know?"

"Before I immerse you in my tale, I feel compelled to share

a little backstory. It was my first year of med school, and my wild undergrad ways still clung to me like a bad rash." He raises his hand and rubs his jaw while averting his eyes like he can't believe he's sharing this story with a stranger. "Friday night partying with my best friend, Brad, bled into Saturday morning. I woke up face-first on my living room carpet, the aroma of wet dog, stale food, and smelly socks wafting to my nose."

I giggle as his words feed my vivid imagination.

"I rolled to my back, my chest sore from who knows what. My shirt was sliced down the front like I'd come in contact with a machete-wielding fashion ninja and my jeans were unzipped and rested half-way down my thighs. The creme de la creme was Brad's size thirteen foot stuck to the side of my head."

My hand slides across his forearm. "Did you say 'stuck'? How? With what?"

His eyes bounce to mine. "I have my suspicions, but to this day, I refuse to talk about it." His exaggerated shiver and wide eyes pique my curiosity.

"That was rude of me to interrupt. Please continue."

"I remember looking at my watch and having a strange sense I was missing something. I didn't think anything of it until I remembered my Saturday morning class AND the presentation I would be making a mere thirty-four minutes in the future."

My blond locks slide across my shoulders as I shake my head while trying to hold in a laugh. My mind is already racing toward the finish line of his story. "What did you do?"

He lifts a shoulder and lets it fall. "What do you think? I grabbed some clothes and hightailed it to class."

I lean into his personal space. "You didn't make it did you?"

He nods his head, disgust pouring from his features. "Now,

you're just being mean. You tricked me into thinking you wanted to hear my story." His emerald eyes sparkle with mirth as he lifts an eyebrow. "Cruel, just heinous."

My foot thumps the floor, "I do!"

A reprimand in the form of a hiss filters up from the floor, and I startle forgetting Fluffy's cozy quarters below the seat. It's like she's scolding me for coming between her and the rest of the story.

"If you'd been paying attention, you'd remember the UNE which hasn't even entered the story yet."

I don't need to see my face to know it's red. The heat coming from it is strong enough to roast marshmallows. "You're right. I got ahead of myself. It won't happen again." I dip my head and offer him a half-smile extending my hand as a peace offering for him to continue.

He shakes his head, "Where was I? Yes. Sprang up, threw on clothes, tried to remove stickiness from my head, grabbed my backpack, raced out the door, and arrived at class." Mitchell taps a finger on his armrest like he's checking each action off of a list. "I darted through the door and dropped into a seat with two minutes left to spare. I slid my backpack off my shoulder and set it on the floor as the professor welcomed everyone and signaled the start of the presentations. I absentmindedly rubbed my chest wondering why it was so sore and deciding it probably had to do with some asinine, liquor-fueled bet with Brad the night before. My eyes were trained on the presenters, but my brain was stuck on the throbbing across my chest which seemed to be getting worse."

I watch as Mitchell rubs his forearm, his eyes distant like his body's being transported back to his college classroom. His discomfort sweeps over me, and I debate if I should stop him. My heart rate rises as I scan his face which has turned a deep red.

"By the time my turn was called, sweat covered my forehead and collected under my armpits. I smelled like stale rum, and my skin burned like I'd taken a swim in a lava pit. I gathered my notes, moved to the front of the room, and stood behind the podium. Everyone. Every single person in the five hundred seat auditorium was staring at me. I should clarify. Everyone was staring at my *chest*. Mouths fully open, jaws dropped, human fly traps."

I lean closer as his voice lowers to a whisper. I swear Fluffy is holding her grumpy cat breath.

"You know, I'm really parched. I could use a drink about now."

I latch onto his forearm and squeeze. "Don't even think about it. If you value your body and your traveling buddy stowed under your seat, you will continue your story. Now."

A warm, velvet chuckle vibrates from his chest as his gaze travels down to my hand firmly wrapped around the sleeve of his white shirt. He tips his head from side to side as he plans his next words. "Where did you say you were from?"

I sit up straight and pull my arm into my lap. "I didn't. Why?" Confusion laced with suspicion wrinkles my forehead.

"When I offer the rest of my story, you're going to look at me differently. Judgments will be made. Like a runaway train, I'll have no way to stop your thoughts. No way to erase the feelings my words will elicit."

I slowly shake my head while maintaining eye contact. He raises his palm between us heading off my arguments before I give them a voice.

"I promise I'll tell you. I just want to bask in your non-judgmental aura for a few more minutes. I know you think you won't form opinions. But the truth is everyone passes judgment on others. We're human, and that's how we're wired. I'm not blaming you. I just want to prolong the inevitable. Seeing as how I've shared so much about me, maybe now would be a good time to learn about you. Quid pro quo if you will."

His face remains neutral as he looks to me for capitulation. I swallow words of frustration as I study the sharp angle of his cheekbones, peppered with scruff that's not quite a beard but too thick to be a five o'clock shadow. My attention moves to his mouth as his tongue darts out and wets his full lower lip. His emerald-green eyes roam over my face as he waits.

Butterflies flit through my stomach as Mitchell's attention zeroes in. It's been a lifetime since someone asked about *me*. "Um, well." My tongue stumbles over words like I've been given a shot of Novocain. "I live in Boulder."

Mitchell nods and remains silent compelling me to share more.

"I'm an EMT." I fold my hands in my lap and look to him while praying I've said enough.

Silence stretches between us. Minutes that feel like hours pass before he cocks his head and narrows his eyes. "Hope, a poised, beautiful woman such as yourself can surely share more than two sentences about herself."

Wetness dots my palms as I mull over his question. *What else can I say?* I work and go home. I'm pretty sure he doesn't care about the cleaning I do around the house and my meticulous attention to lawn care. I drop my chin as tears gather on my eyelashes. I cannot think of a single interesting detail to share.

The flight attendant pulls back the drape and steps through the doorway dividing coach and first-class before quickly closing the curtain. The tinny sound surprises me, and I jolt in my seat.

Mitchell's fingertips enter my vision as they slide over my clasped hands. The warmth of his skin seeps into my own. "I didn't mean to be intrusive. My questions were not meant to upset you. They were a way to include you in our conversation. My apologies." He pulls his hand from mine to cover his mouth as he coughs. "I believe I owe you the UNE conclusion." His lips lift in a lopsided smirk that lights his face and makes his eyes sparkle.

I meet his eyes and give an affirmative nod. "The suspense has left me breathless."

He leans back in his seat and fixes his stare straight ahead. "Where was I?"

"Entire class, jaws unhinged. Creepy, laser eyes."

"It's about the same time I notice their focus isn't necessarily on me, but more on a piece of my anatomy. I follow the direction of their eyes and see red smears across my hand. The same hand that had been rubbing my chest earlier."

"Oh my gosh. No. Please don't tell me it's what I think it is." Shock and surprise crawl across my face.

Mitchell glances at me and throws his head back releasing a loud laugh as he points at my face. "That look right there. Identical to my classmates."

I school my features as he continues.

"If you think it was blood. You'd be right."

A grimace contorts my face, no doubt turning it into a caricature painted by Este Lauder.

"I'm not 'gonna lie. I may have been a med student, but it was *my* blood. I admit I freaked out." He takes a breath while running both hands through his wavy, light-brown hair. "Adrenaline raged through my body, and the Hulk popped out." He pushes his hands forward in a jazz hands motion. "Totally forgetting where I was, I ripped my shirt open exposing my nipple *and* the pain culprit."

My eyes are the size of quarters as my entire body crowds the armrest. My heart rate stutters worried by the story, yet mesmerized by the smooth, low timbre of Mitchell's voice.

"It seems my drunken, wild night included a stop my brain had conveniently wiped from my memory. Apparently, I'd visited a piercing parlor at some point between Friday's five o'clock sobriety and Saturday morning's skunk-drunk phase.

I'd been drunk plenty of times before but never to the point of body mutilation. My drunk brain had assumed sliding a shiny ring through one of the most sensitive places on my body was a good idea. My sober brain vehemently disagreed. The best I could guess, my new nipple ring had gotten caught on my backpack straps when I'd pulled them from my shoulders in my haste to sit down. Needless to say, I garnered a nickname from my med school buddies that still haunts me to this day." He turns his body toward me and gives me a smile full of straight, white teeth. "And that, Hope, is my UNE story."

When he stops talking and remains silent, I circle my hand indicating he should continue. He raises his eyebrows silently asking the universal question *"What?"*

He doesn't elaborate, so I bump him with my shoulder. "And your nickname was?"

A rumble escapes from his chest as he shakes his head. "Nope. Not today. I already met my embarrassment quota for the day."

An unladylike sound of disgust bursts from my lips, and my face heats. "Totally not fair, Mr. Anderson."

A high-pitch nasal voice startles me, and I cringe as it fills the cabin. "Good evening, ladies and gentlemen. We are making our final approach into Denver International Airport. We ask that all tray tables and seat backs be placed in their upright positions as we prepare for landing. We know that you have a choice when flying, and we thank you for choosing United to get you to your destination. Have a great evening."

A three-hour flight is nearly over, and I haven't thought once about being in the air.

Mitchell gives me a grin while sharing a look that says, *"My work here is done."*

I feel the bump of the plane and the roar of the engines as it touches down and taxies down the runway toward the gate.

My heart speeds to a gallop as I get closer to disembarking and losing the connection I've made with Mitchell Anderson.

I'm unsure if it's the situation or Mitchell's willingness to distract me with an embarrassing story, but my mood makes me feel bold with my words.

I lean toward his ear, my breath raising goosebumps along his neck. "That's some story. I'm not sure I trust it's validity without some form of evidence." I pull away, shifting my gaze between his chest and his face, raising an eyebrow for emphasis.

He places his hand over mine where it's draped over the armrest. "Hope, I'd love to appease your curiosity, but trust in a person is all you need to believe their words." He winks and gives my arm a squeeze as pinpricks of electricity surge through my body.

I watch as he pulls Fluffy from under his seat setting her purse/carrier in his vacated spot before retrieving both of our suitcases from the overhead compartment.

"Thank you, Hope, for the pleasure of your company. It's been the best flight I've had in years."

By the time I focus my thoughts, Mitchell has deplaned and left me watching the backs of each passenger as they file out on his heels.

After the last person has left, I stand up and grasp the handle of my rolling carry-on pulling it behind me as I step from the plane, a feeling of heaviness surrounding me. Deep in my gut, I feel like my whole world is about the change.

16

HOPE

Two hours later, I hit the button and open the garage door. Two empty stalls greet me as my eyes move to the clock on the dash. It's after nine p.m., and Joe isn't home. I'm not surprised, but I am disappointed. I hadn't expected him to meet me at the airport considering he'd left our car for me to use, but I did anticipate he'd be home and waiting to hear about the four days he'd missed.

I've missed him, and my brain is trying its best to build his absence into an argument. I park and pull my bag from the car. I walk through the mudroom and drop my suitcase in the kitchen as I look at the house I've made into a home over the past three years. Not one item is out of place. It's so immaculate in its appearance that I can't tell if Joe has even been home since he arrived back.

Taking my bag into our bedroom, I unpack before pulling a camisole and pair of sleep shorts from my drawer. I walk to the bathroom, and turn on the shower. I want nothing more than to wash the stench of travel from my skin and erase the negative thoughts running through my head since seeing my empty garage. I step under the spray and allow the stress of the day to leave my body as the water circles the drain.

Fatigue hangs on my shoulders as I step from the shower. Rushing through my nighttime routine, I allow sleep to pull me into bed. I should call the hospital and leave a message for Joe. Let him know I'm home and anxious to see him. I have memories to share and goals to discuss, but sleep pushes me under and steals my plans before I can give them a voice.

———

MY HEART FEELS like someone is trying to pull it from my chest. I gasp, my hand grasping at my skin as I open my eyes. The pale light of sunrise filters through my room, and I sit up. Disoriented and confused, my breath comes in short bursts until my nerves calm. I have no idea what startled me, but I'm wide awake and alone in my bed. I swipe my phone from the nightstand and look at the time. It's a little past five a.m.

I strain my ears listening for disturbances outside of the normal house noise. I hear a fan and see the subtle flutter of the curtains indicating the air conditioner is running. The red light blinking next to the bedroom door indicates the house alarm is on and engaged.

I scoot off the edge of the bed and walk to the bathroom. My heart rate is finally returning to normal though I'm at a loss as to what woke me and why my heart is racing. I run lukewarm water over my wrists and stare at my reflection in the mirror. Something niggles at the back of my brain out of reach of my mind's consciousness. I pad back to bed and slide between the sheets staring at the ceiling until sleep pulls me under once again.

———

THE SUN IS FULLY SEATED in the sky when my alarm chimes four hours later. Trained to be a morning person during medical school, I'm amazed I've slept so late. Stale, cool sheets meet my arm where it drifts across Joe's side of the bed. He hasn't been home. Without the ability to call me, he has no idea if I ever made it home. My anger from last night simmers as I contemplate what I want to do.

I roll out of bed, heading for my closet. The hospital is a twenty-minute drive from the house. If I hurry, I can catch him during the nursing staff's mid-morning break. Usually, he has a lull in activity during that time. I put on a bra and shimmy into a pair of lace underwear before pulling Joe's favorite sundress over my body. Its flowing skirt is short but tasteful provided I don't bend over to retrieve anything from the floor. Joe told me he gets hard just looking at me in it because it makes my petite legs look a mile long. I'm hoping for the same reaction when I walk into the hospital. I haven't decided if I'll accidentally drop my keys on the floor when I see him.

I hope Dr. Roberts is up for a little teasing. It's a *look but don't touch* kind of day, and I'm annoyed enough to follow through with my plan. He needs to understand that his wife isn't going to stay quiet any longer, and his nights of staying at the hospital past his scheduled hours need to change immediately.

I circle the parking lot looking for my husband's Tahoe. It doesn't take long to find the big, black vehicle parked in the back row of the lot. It gleams, the sparkling chrome of the exterior throwing sunbursts across my eyes as I pass. I find a spot not far away and make my way through the lobby and up to his office on the fourth floor.

The elevator is empty. The car jars and makes my stomach do a little flip as it comes to a stop, and the doors open. Nurses walk through the halls on the way to patient's rooms. I spot one of Joe's colleagues leaning against a counter speaking to the unit clerk and walk in his direction. I nod at nurses as I pass, their strange looks registering but not making sense as I approach Dr. Glen McDonald. The unit clerk's startled expression reaches my eyes as Glen turns his head. I smile and witness the color drain from his face.

I see the indecision on his face as debates if he should embrace me or turn away.

"Hope. What are you doing on this floor?"

His voice is breathy and unsure. His question, paired with his strange reaction, wipes the smile from my face. Unsure what's happening, I lean in and give him a botched hug full of extended arms and no grasp.

"I'm here to see Joe. I got back last night and thought I'd surprise him."

The look he shares with the unit clerk is brief, but I catch it, and I'm instantly suspicious.

"He's here, I presume? I saw his car in the lot."

Glen's eyes dart around the hall landing anywhere but on my face.

"Glen, what is it?"

I step closer, my shoes stopping at the tips of his. My voice rises as I press him to answer. The urgency to know what's going on increases with each second he avoids my stare.

"Hope, let's take a walk." He grabs my elbow and starts walking down the hall toward the bank of elevators from which I came.

My mind is racing. Scenarios swirl through my already annoyed and confused mind. My feet stop moving, and the motion pulls my elbow from his grasp.

"Glen. I'm not going anywhere until you tell me what's going on."

Panic registers across his features. His eyes are pained, and his face pulls tight in a half grimace. "How is it you don't know? Didn't you get a call?"

"Know what? A call? I don't understand."

Knowing I won't leave this floor without some answers, Glen steers me into a private office. He ushers me in and steps behind me, closing the door and stealing the oxygen from my lungs. Suddenly, I don't want to know what he thinks I should already know.

My heartbeat picks up speed, and I remember waking up hours ago in a panic with no reason. There was a reason. The universe just took its time in revealing the catastrophe it had already set in motion.

"Hope, have a seat."

He indicates a couch, that looks older than me, pushed up against the far wall. I walk to it on feet as heavy as bowling balls and take a seat perching on the edge of the couch.

He sits down and takes my hand in his. My mind focuses on the softness of his skin. Men don't have hands this soft or gentle. It's a crazy thought, but my brain is diverting my mind from the chaos it knows is coming.

"Hope, Joe is here."

His words rattle through my brain. Of course, I know Joe's here. He works here, and I saw his car. My confusion must be evident because his eyes turn dark as discomfort rises to the surface.

"Joe is downstairs. There was an incident. He was brought in yesterday morning."

Incident? Denise and the phone call that changed my world three years ago flits through my mind. *There's been an accident.* No. No. NO. No one should ever have to hear those words in their lifetime, and I already have. I've reached my quota. This can't be happening again.

"NO."

The denial bursts from my lips as I slide from the couch hoping the ground will swallow me and save me from this anguish. I gasp, trying to gather air into my lungs, but they're throbbing to the point of suffocation. The unforgiving carpet pricks the backs of my legs like hundreds of mosquitoes feasting at the same time. I'm drowning on land, and Joe isn't here to save me.

Glen's hands come around my shoulders as he pulls me to his chest. "He's in bad shape, but he's still with us."

A pinprick of light pierces the darkness that descended only moments ago. I hear his statement, but confusion laces the thread of my chaotic thoughts. Glen's words are like fireflies, sparking joy then disappearing before I can catch one and hold it tight.

Joe hasn't left me. He's here, and he needs me. I lift my hands to my tear-streaked face, wiping the wetness with the back of my hands leaving dull, black streaks across my cheeks.

"I don't understand." My lungs barely squeeze enough air to voice my thoughts.

Glen turns on his doctor voice, the one that delivers information minus emotional inflection. "It happened around two a.m. yesterday. He was leaving the hospital. Two guys, hyped up on who knows what, jumped him as he walked to his car. He was stabbed multiple times in the chest. It was over in less than a minute. The security guard saw a scuffle and immediately called the police. By the time they got here, the guys were gone. I'm so sorry, Hope. I thought the hospital called you. I thought you knew and were already here." The emotion he's tried to hide leaks from his voice as his eyes hold mine. "He's in critical condition, but he's alive."

Why am I wasting time huddled on the floor while my husband's life is being measured in heartbeats? I rise to my full height, pulling strength from the fact that Joe is still alive.

"Take me to him, please."

17

HOPE

I STARE AT THE GLASS DOORS OF JOE'S ICU ROOM. GLEN stands beside me. He's giving me a review of Joe's injuries and trying to prepare me for the torture I'll endure as soon as I walk through those sliding doors.

The curtain, drawn mostly across the door, flutters in the wake of a nurse as she exits. Her head is down, yet I see her profile, and her jaw is set in a hard line. I try to decipher her emotions, and my stomach knots as I realize she's lost hope for her patient. Something she's seen tells her not to count on this patient's recovery.

My nausea is replaced with anger. Anger at the situation and annoyance with her acceptance of the circumstances. Joe is alive. He's still with us. He shouldn't be written off while his heart is still beating.

I can't be prepared for what I'll see, but I know to the marrow of my bones I need to be with my husband. I need to touch him and assure myself he's fighting to stay here with me.

Glen's mouth is still moving, but my ears have stopped listening as I walk forward hoping he doesn't follow me into the room. His retreating footsteps tell me he's sensed my need to be alone, and he's giving me the space my body asked for when my mouth couldn't form the request.

I've completed three years of medical school and made countless rounds and observations, but no amount of preparation could have saved me from the assault to my eyes when I move around the curtain. Machines line both sides of the bed. The erratic beeping and buzzing overpower my ears as I stare at the broken body of the man who's spent the last three years as my husband.

His eyes are shut, the right one is puffy and blue, and his mouth is propped open to allow for the stiff vent tube that's taped to the side of his cheek. My eyes trace from his mouth to the ventilator that makes a rhythmic, vacuum sound and reminds me of a city bus when it stops and opens its door. I track his face, noting the dark stubble covering his cheeks. He would hate knowing he missed his morning shave.

A chair is pulled up to the side of the bed, and I walk toward it to take a seat. My sandal slips on the polished floor, and I stumble into the side of the bed. My eyes dart to Joe's face looking for any indication I've disturbed him, but his face is a mask of stone, and his limbs lie motionless under the covers of the bed. I lower myself into the chair and continue my visual inventory.

The neck of his hospital gown has been pulled down to allow for the PICC line draped across his shoulder. His chest is wrapped in layers of gauze; the bright red color indicates it's time to redress his wounds.

His hand sits on top of the covers. I lace my fingers through his squeezing once, noting the strength in his fingers though he doesn't return the action. Cuts pepper the back of his hand, and I note a small bandage across his palm.

I've seen wounds like these before. I once observed the care of a man who was an MMA fighter. His hands had similar wounds, though his injuries were confined to bruises and not the number of lacerations Joe has. Tears stream down my cheeks as I realize Joe fought his attackers. He didn't stand and take the abuse. His hands are an example of his will to live.

"Baby, keep that drive. This is the most important fight you'll ever have."

I bend and kiss his knuckles wondering when the attending physician will be in to discuss his current plan of care. I could step out to the nursing station, but now that I'm here, I have no intention of leaving my husband's side.

A nurse breezes through the door, disturbing the curtain and bringing my attention to the wide smile she has on her face. Her expression is warm and, best of all, positive. I drop my eyes to her name badge. Amelia has hope. With her attitude, she's become my new best friend. My presence startles her.

"Oh, I'm sorry ma'am I didn't know anyone was in here."

I give her a small smile. "I slipped in a few minutes ago." I try to force a friendly smile to my lips, but I fear it resembles more of a grimace. "I'm Hope. Joe's wife."

Her expression turns thoughtful and pained.

"I'm sorry. I can't imagine how horrible this must be for you." She checks the leads to Joe's monitors. "Have you been updated on his status?"

"No." My voice comes out in a scratchy whisper, and I feel a pink flush rise across my cheeks as I admit how little I know of my husband's condition and medical plan.

Her eyebrows disappear under her straight bangs as her eyes widen. She belatedly realizes her face broadcast her surprise, and she schools her features. "Well, I can give you the basics, but I'll page Dr. Noe, the attending, and let him know you've arrived. He may want Dr. Hartzog here when he meets with you."

She sees the question on my lips before I ask. "Dr. Hartzog is our heart surgeon. I've heard his hands are magic when it comes to surgeries." She stops, biting her lip and looking away. "That was rude of me to gossip. Please disregard my flapping tongue."

Her admission makes me smile. Amelia is exactly the type of medical professional I want taking care of Joe. Her compassion and bluntness are refreshing in this abyss of uncertainty.

"Thank you, Amelia. I look forward to speaking with them soon."

I turn my attention back to Joe and squeeze his hand. I see a spike on his heart monitor, and hope rises in my chest.

MY NOSE PICKS up the scent of disinfectant at the same time my cheek registers the scratchy texture of an over-washed blanket. My eyelids flutter before they are fully open, and it's in that split second, I hear my heartbeat as it thrums through my ears. I glance at the wall clock and realize I've missed the past couple of hours. I must have dozed off after Amelia left. The stress had stolen my energy and forced my body into slumber.

I push myself from my slumped position, noting the black mark my cheek has transferred to Joe's white sheet. I straighten and stretch, working the kinks from my neck. My ears pick up low male voices, and I strain to hear their conversation.

"...I'm not sure if his body can take it."

"If she doesn't agree, the prognosis is poor."

They are talking about Joe. One's voice is hesitant like he doesn't fully agree with the other. Two sets of shoes, expensive Italian loafers just like Joe prefers, arrive on the other side of the drawn curtain and their conversation ceases just before a hand pulls back the curtain.

Two men. One older with salt and pepper hair and kind eyes. The second, younger, more rugged looking with auburn hair and a solemn face. The older one steps forward.

"Mrs. Roberts, I presume? I'm Dr. Hartzog, and this is Dr. Noe. We're both familiar with your husband's work in our hospital, and we're doing everything we can to make sure he receives exemplary care."

While he doesn't smile, I glimpse compassion hidden within the lines etched across his face.

The younger doctor walks forward and offers his hand. "I'm Dr. Noe, your husband's attending doctor." His expression is closed and more guarded than Dr. Hartzog's. He cuts his eyes to Dr. Hartzog, and they exchange silent words.

Dr. Hartzog clears his throat and steps forward as Dr. Noe begins examining Joe. His attention is on us, though his eyes and hands are moving over Joe.

"Joe sustained multiple stab wounds to his chest. While we were able to stem the bleeding and make temporary fixes, the MRI shows a small tear in the outer wall of his heart just to the right of the aortic valve. We've continued to monitor his vitals, but the instability of his blood pressure indicates we cannot wait to see if the tear heals on its own. I feel the best course of action is to repair it as soon as possible to avoid ruptures or further stress on his heart."

I look to Dr. Noe, who has finished his bedside exam. He comes to stand next to Dr. Hartzog and the older doctor continues. "With your consent, I'd like to perform surgery this afternoon."

A dozen questions run through my mind, but I allow only one to leave my mouth. "Do you feel he's stable enough to withstand such a delicate surgery?"

He pulls in a breath and releases it before answering. "Without this surgery, he runs the risk of heart attack, stroke, blood clot, or further tear which could be fatal. While it's risky, I believe it's the best plan considering the possible alternatives."

I stare at him knowing my permission will be the most important choice I'll ever make. "I need to think about this.

My heart is telling me to do everything medically necessary, but my brain is urging me to stop and consider all possible alternatives."

His eyes and face reflect compassion as he nods his head. "Please think about it, and have his nurse page me as soon as you decide."

"Thank you." I give them a quick nod, turning my back to them as I pace to the furthest corner of the room away from their expectant gazes. I don't know what to do. I feel like my medical training failed me in the ways of patient and family emotions. I've never been on this side of the bed, and it's isolating and terrifying.

My eyes never leave Joe's face as I pace. My brain knows I need to give my permission, but I can't convince myself to let him out of my sight. I won't be able to hold his hand, see his face, or beg him to hold on. I close my eyes and recall his embrace; his whispered words tickling my sensitive flesh, *"My heart beats for you. Only you."*

I know what must be done. I pray his heart remembers its promise.

HOPE

LIKE IT CAN SENSE MY FEAR, THE PEN STUTTERS ACROSS THE final sheet of paperwork giving my consent to Joe's surgery. The nurse gives me a warm smile as she stuffs the papers, which could decide Joe's fate, inside a large binder before scurrying way.

My medical background tells me this is necessary, but my heart isn't so sure. It's a delicate procedure, and one that isn't done often, which has my stomach in knots.

Dr. Hartzog explains the procedure, estimating the length of surgery, and the expected recovery time. He shakes my hand, giving it a squeeze, before turning and heading toward the operating room.

I walk to the desk clerk and request a pager so I'll be free to roam the hospital if the waiting room environment becomes too much for me to handle. I take an empty chair near the window and do my best to melt into the stiff cushions. I look around at the semi-busy waiting room. An older woman, in her Sunday best, sits by herself, knitting in a corner. Her face is serene and calm as she concentrates on what looks to be a blanket.

A woman, who looks a little older than me, sits with a boy I'd guess to be about seven years old. They're playing a card game, and the boy is smiling every time he plays a card. While the woman's lips are tilted up in a smile, her red eyes reflect the evidence her life isn't as pleasant as her smile indicates. I study them further. The wrinkles in their clothing, the big bag with a pillow sticking out of the top, and the blanket lying beside them tell me they've been here way longer, and possibly more often, than me.

I pull a magazine from the side table and stare at the cover, not registering who the celebrities are or the significance of the gossip splashed across the cover. I page through the articles, but my brain fails to comprehend the words.

A week ago I was celebrating my belated honeymoon, two days ago I made plans to fix my marriage, and today I'm praying for God to spare Joe's life.

———

I GIVE up trying to read my magazine and allow my gaze to fall upon the boy and his mother again. He pulls a card from his overstuffed hand and slams it on the small end table next to their chairs. Joy for the game radiates from his features, and he's completely oblivious to the turmoil I glimpse in his mother's eyes. I'm thankful I do not have to shield a child from today's realities.

My hospital-issued pager beeps, and I jolt awake not realizing I'd nodded off in the stiff, unforgiving waiting room chair. The last thing I remember is watching the doctor come out to talk to the woman as she clutched her young son in her arms. From her reaction, the surgery had been a success. My own eyes had misted watching her joy fill the entire waiting room. I'd smiled and mentally cheered for the future she and her young family would have.

I make my way on quick feet to inquire about Joe. It's been four hours, and even though I try, I can't seem to remember if this length of time is favorable or not. The nurse takes my pager, and I study her face as I watch her eyes scan her computer screen.

Her kind smile wipes away some of my nerves. "Dr. Hartzog will be out in a few moments to speak with you."

She leads me to a small patient conference room and closes the door. A chair and a two-seater couch are the only furniture that fit inside the tiny room. I take a seat but soon realize the room's size is suffocating, and I jump up and start pacing trying to rid my thoughts of the fear worming its way into every part of my mind. What seems like an hour passes before Dr. Hartzog slips through the door.

"Please have a seat."

He gestures to the couch, and I search his neutral expression, but he gives me no clue as to his next words though my heart takes off at a gallop. The goosebumps rising across my skin and the prickles teasing the back of my neck whisper his words before they leave his mouth. "Hope, there is never an easy way to—"

His words feel like millions of icicles pelting my body and instantly numbing my soul.

"NO!" I rise to my feet and turn to him, tears already creating rivers down my cheeks. "Don't say it. You said you'd take care of him." My words burst from my lungs, burning as they pass my lips. "You said it was necessary. I trusted you!"

His face remains stoic, lips pressed into a firm line while his eyes stare at me, as I rage at him.

"I'm sorry, Hope. The damage was more severe than the MRI had indicated. The attack made his body weak. When we took him off the bypass machine, his heart started beating, but then it stopped, and we couldn't get it started again. Please know we did everything medically possible. I'm sorry for your loss."

He takes my hand and squeezes it, and I have the irrational desire to return his gesture with an iron fist in hopes of breaking his hand. I take a breath and lift my eyes to stare at the man whose pain of failure sits prominently on his face. My heart stutters, and rational thought returns. He didn't kill Joe; he simply couldn't save him.

"I'm sorry. I didn't mean to accuse you. What happens from here? I d-d-didn't even get to say goodbye." My voice cracks as my breathing attempts to return to normal. "Can I see him?"

"It's not going to be easy. Is there anyone I can have the nurse call for you?" His eyes are warm, but concern rings through his question.

I shake my head. Joe's father is the only person who could help shoulder the burden, and I've already left two messages over the past eight hours asking him to call me at the hospital. I have yet to receive a response. I take a breath trying to calm my inner chaos.

"No. I don't have anyone to call. I know it won't be easy, but I need to say goodbye." Goodbye. How I've come to hate the single, innocuous word. *How do I say goodbye?*

Dr. Hartzog stands and nods. "Okay. I'll speak with the nurse and have her come get you once he's ready."

A current like a lightning bolt burns my skin. I'll never hear his voice again, see his smile, feel his embrace. Joe's heart is silent, and mine feels like it will never find the rhythm of life again.

19

HOPE

THE SUN IS BRIGHT, AND THE WARMTH OF ITS RAYS HEATS MY back through my black dress. Thankful for the need to wear sunglasses, I stare through the pastor as he gives Joe's eulogy.

I know his message would be uplifting and reverent if I could concentrate on the words, but I cannot get my ears to listen any better than I can get my eyes to stop leaking. Joe is... was my life, and I can't ignore the hole that's been burned through my heart.

I fidget with the crumpled tissue in my hand, unable to lift my head and face the empathy painted on the faces of Joe's colleagues and former patients standing behind me. Joe's father hadn't been able to make it to the funeral due to his own failing health, so I'm alone and seated in the lone chair in front of the casket.

He's been gone five days, and I still can't bring myself to step foot in his walk-in closet. McNair had to pick out the suit he's being buried in because I couldn't stomach the sight of his clothing hanging untouched, never to be worn again. The first time I'd crossed the threshold of our bedroom, I'd fallen to my knees and sobbed for hours as the bed we shared loomed across the room.

Our bathroom held the most difficult memories considering his smell assaulted my nose. I'd stumbled across the floor and walked directly into the shower where I sat as the water poured over my head until it ran cold making my skin as numb as I wished my heart to be.

Sleep has evaded me, and my stomach has forsaken any and all sustenance. I made the arrangements, contacted the pastor, met with the funeral director, and picked out the casket.

I know I'll probably have regrets in the future, but I opened the book and pointed to the first dark wood casket with pale blue satin interior my gaze landed on. Dark for the shadow that had descended, and blue to match my eyes. Joe often said he could lose himself in the color of my eyes, so I figured the blue would be a comfort to him in his final resting place.

It's all bullshit. The casket, the satin, the elegance is for nothing. It won't bring him back, help him find peace, or ease my broken heart.

A hand lightly rests on my shoulder, and I jump, not expecting the foreign touch. I turn and find Shawn McNair nodding and angling his chin to indicate the pastor standing at the head of the casket.

The pastor's expectant eyes rest on me as he gestures to the spray of flowers lying across the casket. Flowers I have no recollection of choosing. McNair steps to my side and helps me from my chair before I walk forward on trembling legs. Prickles raise up my spine as I feel the heat of the mourner's stares boring into my back.

Breathe in.

Breathe out.

My heart speeds forward anticipating my final goodbye.

I place my hand on the smooth surface of the box my

husband's body will forever be trapped within. Without the sun. Without life. Without me.

Until next time.

One beat.

Two beats.

My fingertips melt into the wood as my mind screams at him to wake up. Don't leave me here alone.

Silence greets my shattered heart as I turn and walk away.

Away from my friend.

Away from my lover.

Away from the life I thought we'd share.

———

THE RIDE HOME IS TORTURE, but I breathe a silent word of thanks to Chief Matthews for insisting McNair pick me up and drive me home. McNair cuts the engine, and I'm surprised to see the front of my house considering I don't remember any part of the drive.

Silence blankets the interior of the car as I search for my voice. I've been unable to utter a single word today. I shook hands with dozens of people, but I could not push one syllable beyond my lips as I forced a smile and moved on to greet the next person.

"If you'd rather not be alone, I can stay."

He moves his hand and lays it atop mine. The warmth of his fingers seeps into my skin. It's been over a week since Joe and I held hands. McNair's feels foreign and strange, and I pull back not wanting another man's touch to taint or erase my mind's memory of Joe.

I look at him. Straight teeth poke out from his warm smile as he waits for me to answer. My mind searches for words. I don't want to be alone, but I also don't want to curb my emotions out of fear of being seen by assessing eyes.

"You." My voice breaks as I gulp air. "You head home. I'll be fine."

He searches my face looking for the lie I've hidden behind my wide smile. He knows me well enough to gather that I'm lying, but he also knows when I've reached my breaking point and not to push an inch farther.

"I'll walk you to your door, then get out of your hair."

He jumps out and rounds the car before I piece together the steps to exit the vehicle. My brain can't focus, and I'm grateful for his support. As he opens my door and takes my arm to help me out, I'm reminded of my first date with Joe. I'd thought he was the last of a dying breed of gentlemen, but apparently, I'd been wrong. It appears McNair was trained in the same art of manners. I small smile curves my lips, and I wonder if Joe hears my thoughts and remembers the happiness and the fun we had that night.

"Do you have your keys?"

I jingle my ring and hold it up in front of his face. He grabs my keys and has the door unlocked and pushed open before I can blink. He holds it open for me and allows me to pass as he remains on the stoop.

He hands me a box, and my breath catches. It's a phone. Consumed by grief, I'd forgotten I didn't have one, but McNair had known and taken it upon himself to keep me connected.

"You have the same number, but you'll have to transfer your contacts. I've programmed my number. If you need anything, use it."

I nod as he steps forward and pulls the door shut tapping once from the outside as a reminder for me to lock it and set my alarm. I walk through the house, sliding between the rays of the afternoon sun as they filter through the living room windows.

Joe loved this house. *"Do you hear it, Hope? The footsteps and laughter? The carols at Christmas, the jack-o-lanterns illuminating that window for Halloween, the squeals of the egg hunt on Easter morning. It's perfect."*

His eyes had been huge, and his smile had nearly overtaken his face as he'd wrapped his arms around me and swept me off the floor, much to the surprise of our realtor who gaped like a fish at his display of excitement. It hadn't been my taste, but I'd immediately agreed with him instead of watching disappointment shadow his face with denial.

Maybe it was a reflection of my simpler upbringing, but I'd never felt comfortable in this house. It was too big, too grand, too ostentatious to suit my tastes, but I'd done my best to add touches to make it feel like our home.

My eyes fall on the purple pillow sitting askew on my dark leather couch. I purchased it last year because the color and feel of the fabric reminded me of the dress my mom had made for my eighth-grade graduation. When I'd seen the pillow, I'd bought it immediately, and every time I glance at it a smile crosses my face.

A tear slips down my cheek at the memory. The only people I've ever truly loved have left me without warning or a goodbye.

My eyes fall on the bed as I cross the threshold into my bedroom. A niggling at the back of my mind pushes forward as my memory returns to the boat ride in New York. *Keep moving, and never give up.* I can sit down and let emptiness engulf me, or I can rise above my grief and move forward just as I intended to do when I returned from New York.

I slide into bed wrapping the sheets around my trembling body. Enveloped by Joe's scent, I feel his presence, and a calm falls across my heart. I may have been dealt a shit hand, but I refuse to give up.

20

HOPE

MY EYELIDS FLUTTER IN RESPONSE TO THE SUN'S RAYS FALLING across my face as a faint buzzing filters through my consciousness. I extend my arm, blindly reaching for my phone as it dances across my bedside table.

Wiping at my eyes, I answer. "Hello." My voice has a deep rasp as it brushes off the remnants of sleep.

"Hope?"

I sit up and pull the covers to my chest. The familiar voice on the end of the line is loud and demanding. I drop my head back to stare at the ceiling to keep the wetness flooding my eyes from falling down my cheeks. Shit. In the fucked-up chaos of the past few weeks, I'd forgotten to call the one person who would have dropped everything and raced to my side.

"What's with Joe? His cell number says it's no longer in service."

My eyes drift closed as I prepare my words. EJ's brusque manner always rubbed me the wrong way, but I'd tolerated it because of our common thread—Joe.

EJ had never liked me for Joe and had no qualms about sharing that opinion. For that reason, I'd chosen to gracefully decline as many *meet and greet* opportunities as possible when EJ was in town. I had no problem with Joe meeting up with EJ, but I'd be damned if I was going to waste my time sitting with someone who didn't like me and made no attempt to hide it.

I mentioned it to Joe a couple of times, but he'd shrugged it off saying EJ's impression didn't matter, and I shouldn't take it personally since EJ had never been fond of any of his other friends. It was one of the petty reasons I was glad Joe and I hadn't had a wedding or reception. It kept me from being subjected to a toast which I was sure EJ would have turned into a "Hope roast" if given the opportunity.

I inhale and steady my breathing in hopes I can make it through this call without losing my shit.

It had taken me a week after the funeral before I could get up in the morning without having a full-blown panic attack. It was like my brain had short-circuited and clung to the irrational hope that Joe's death was reversible, and I'd wake up one day snuggled into his warm body. We'd laugh that it had all been a strange nightmare before picking up where we left off in New York.

Returning to work two weeks ago—four weeks after Joe's funeral—had been gut-wrenching since every emergency call reminded me of Joe in some way, no matter how obscure. Some calls still shake me up, but I'm moving forward, sometimes with the smallest of baby steps. I'm beyond grateful to have the colleagues that I do who've helped me settle back into my daily life with as much ease as can be expected.

My brain has made a superb effort in evading this conversation, but I can't avoid the inevitable any longer. My thoughts are jumbled, and I have to force my words through my lips. They feel like lead as they tumble off my tongue.

"Joe. There was…Joe…he…Joe..is..de." My voice cracks before I can stutter through my painfully botched answer. "EJ, Joe. He…died. About a month ago."

A loud bang on the other end startles me.

"EJ?"

An eerie silence filters through the line. I pull the phone forward and look at the screen seeing the call is still active. I return it to my ear, listening for EJ's voice. If it wasn't for a rhythmic click on the other end—a fan, maybe?—I'd think our connection is compromised and end the call.

"EJ?"

I'm almost yelling at this point, not sure what is happening on the other end. There's a loud crunching sound before I hear a scratchy, tortured "Shit. Dropped my phone," filter across the line.

It reminds me of the times Joe used to call me on his way home from the hospital. As soon as he hit Baxter Bend, the final leg of his commute, the connection would flake and his voice would sound scratchy and far away like he was talking with a bag pulled over his head.

I drop my lids searching my memories for his voice. I smile as it wraps around me, like a warm blanket, though my recollection is fleeting like my brain has its own connection problems.

"You're lying." EJ's voice is harsh, and it crushes my composure.

"I'm so sorry I didn't call you." I inhale before uttering my next sentence. "I forgot."

Tears leak from my eyes as guilt settles like a noose around my neck. Outside of me, EJ was Joe's best friend, though they'd drifted apart since Joe and I had married. I hate to think it was because of me, but maybe it was. Joe had spent what little free time he had taking care of me and trying to lift me out of my depression after my mom died. I'd failed to consider what he'd lost or given up in helping me. Shame covers me, and my mind starts to shut down.

"Damn it. I am his BEST friend. Hell. I've been around a lot longer than you. YOU robbed me of my goodbye."

My face heats, and my head feels fuzzy as I absorb EJ's angry words. I deserve every venom-laced word EJ spews at me. I had been blinded by my own grief, and I'd failed to recognize EJ's need to grieve alongside me.

"FUCK!!! Why couldn't it have been YOU!"

EJ ends the call, and I gasp for breath as tears stream down my face and pool in the crease of my cleavage. EJ's words are talons ripping at my freshly scabbed wounds. I'd made a mistake—an honest, but painful mistake—and hurt someone who Joe loved like family.

21

HOPE

"Approaching Baxter Bend. Five minutes out."

The drone of the siren nearly suffocates my adrenaline-fueled voice as McNair takes a left onto Baxter and the rig begins ascending the side of the mountain.

Considering my brain is still wrapped around yesterday's phone call with EJ, and I clocked two hours of sleep as a result, I'm glad Shawn's driving. I've driven Baxter millions of times since it's the only road leading from my neighborhood to the base of the mountain, but the chaos screaming through my mind makes it feel like I'm seeing this asphalt for the first time. It's no wonder the curves and blind corners of this stretch make it one of the most dangerous in Boulder, and the keeper of multiple lives each year.

McNair's knuckles turn white as he grips the steering wheel. "Seven years. Countless runs, and I still cringe every time I'm dispatched to this stretch. Don't know about you, but as soon as I turned onto this road, my heart took off like a gunshot."

"Way to talk me through, McNair. Are you sure you didn't

slip a dose of adrenaline in my cup this morning? I think a strong breath could push my heart right out of my chest."

I quirk an eyebrow which is totally unnecessary considering McNair will kill us both if he glances my way. I take my last sip of coffee and place it in the cupholder before pulling a pair of gloves from my kit between the front seats.

Years of medical school did nothing to prepare me for the carnage first responders see daily. Hospitals and doctors stand removed from the visual nightmare that is an accident scene.

The twisted metal.

The blood.

The metallic stench.

The victims.

The thin thread of hope flickering in eyes that often won't survive long enough to see the ceiling of the ambulance.

I shake my head, clearing my mind before my musings derail my focus. The victims, a driver and a small child according to the dispatcher's notes, deserve my full attention and my expertise. This road is deserted for the most part, unless it's between seven and eight in the morning or five and six in the evening when people who live on this side of the mountain leave for or return from work. Luckily, a passerby, who was running late to work, had seen the car and called it in.

McNair steers around a sharp corner, and the smoking scene rises from the hot pavement like a grotesque mirage. If I didn't know I was looking at a car, my brain wouldn't have comprehended what it was seeing. The guard rail looks like a corkscrew of silver and dark red. The color is identical to the blood smeared across the veins of the spiderweb that was a solid windshield not more than thirty minutes ago.

"Shit." The word leaves McNair's lips on a resigned sigh.

His reaction convinces me this call will be branded on my heart, leaving a scar that will fade but never disappear.

His words, barely more than a whisper, are laced with steel.

"Our experience may be the difference between life and death. Draw from what you know. Suffocate your emotions and lock them down tight. They will not help these people live."

I nod as he slows and throws the vehicle in park, and we both jump out. Each second is a grain of sand in the hourglass of a victim's life.

We rush to the vehicle. I scan the back seat as McNair scans the front. Quick and efficient in our routine.

McNair's voice is strong and clear as he paces around the car, looking for the safest access points for vehicle entry. "Adult. Female dress. Frontal lobe damage. Blood oozing from the nose. Eyes not visible. No restraint across the chest. Steering wheel protruding from the abdomen."

My voice is strong as my eyes check through the car and land on the back of the driver's head and my gut clenches. "Child. Toddler. Child seat. Still restrained. Visual indicates eyes open, crying. No open wounds visible."

The distant siren of the responding fire truck sits atop the stagnant air. McNair and I are this woman and child's key to survival, and I'll be damned if my emotions extinguish a molecule of the hope they so desperately need.

"I've surveyed the vehicle. The right front tire is gone, and the axle punched right through the guardrail. Touching the vehicle is too great of a risk. Our guys are on their way. I'll grab whatever else we need from the rig. You stay here. See if you can talk to the little one in the back."

I nod, and McNair turns to rush back to the ambulance.

I approach the window nearest to the screaming child and bend close. A shaky smile, identical to the obnoxious red, wax lips I used to love as a kid, stretches across my mouth.

"Hello, princess. I'm here. I'm going to help you, okay?"

Her matted curls bounce as she turns her eyes my way. Her gaze is intense as her chest stutters and heaves while she fights to get her crying under control. As she quiets, she studies me with soulful eyes, silently asking me why this is happening.

Infusing my voice with strength, I concentrate on keeping her calm and work to develop a bond of trust I'll need between us once the guys get here and start working on the vehicle.

"My name is Hope."

My smile is instant and genuine when she lifts her little palm toward the window in a wordless hello. My hand touches the cool glass, and she returns a gap-toothed smile that grabs my heart. I wasn't there for my mom when she skidded off the road, but I will be there for this little girl who sits smirking at me and holding out her arms in a universal request to get her out and pick her up.

"I can't get you out yet, pretty girl. What's your name?"

I know she hears my question because she cocks her head, eyes sparkling in the rays of the sun as she contemplates my request.

"Thadie." Her voice is like the flutter of a baby bird's wings, faint and gentle, as it filters through the window.

"Thadie?" I repeat wondering if that is, in fact, her name.

Her curls swish across her cheeks as she shakes her head, a look of disappointment covering her face as she stares at me.

My mind races as pieces of my child development knowledge filter through my head, specifically speech sounds. My mental reach is failing me, and I struggle to keep my face neutral, not wishing to alarm her with my own frustration. Like a puzzle piece clicking into place, an idea settles in my brain.

"How about a game, little one?"

She blinks, and a slow smile stretches across her apple cheeks, her annoyance with my inability to understand her name momentarily forgotten in favor of my suggestion of fun. I shoot a quick glance to the front seat and hope life still lingers within the woman's damaged body.

I look above my head and point to the sun before returning my gaze back to my little friend.

"Do you know what that is in the sky?"

Her nose crinkles as she nods, obviously confused with the point of my game.

"What's it called?" I nod in encouragement as she stares at me.

"Tun."

I clap my hands. "Yes! That's the sun."

Excitement flies from my tongue, and she waves her arms pleased with my response. My eyes land on the ground, and I bend to pick up a handful of sand and silt. This is going to be a long shot.

"I love sand! What about you? Do you like this stuff?"

She nods again, "Yes! I love tand, too!"

I think my game has paid off. I lean in close to the glass and hold up my hand like I'm getting ready to tell her a secret. She tries to lift her head like she's leaning in even though the straps of her car seat keep her restrained. If the situation weren't so dire, I would laugh at her efforts.

"Is your name Sadie?"

A giggle bursts from her mouth as she drops her head to the back of her seat. "Yay! You dot it."

Her infectious laughter nearly wipes the reason I'm standing next to this car from my mind. I look over what's left of the mangled vehicle and spy Shawn approaching with the large duffle that only gets brought on the scene when the possibility of airlift is imminent. He's been doing this for years and knows when to make that call.

"Sadie, honey? How old are you? This many?" I hold two fingers up to the glass so she can see them as I wait for her response.

"You tart, Hope." She punctuates her approval with a thumbs-up sign and a wide grin.

"Does your tummy hurt?" I run through a checklist making mental notes as I scan her small body while waiting for her response.

"No. I done fint so." The errors in her speech make her difficult to understand, yet the earnestness of her expression relays her message loud and crystal clear.

"Good, baby."

Sadie lifts her head a few inches as she lowers her brows and squints at me. "I no baby, Hope."

I hold up my hands, palms facing her, and nod my head, "You're right. You're a big girl."

The fire truck stops abruptly just down the road. The flashing red lights throw shadows across the ground reflecting off the car's fluids as they trickle across the road.

Chief Matthews jumps from the truck. His voice booms directives as it echoes across the canyon directly below us. "Briefed by dispatch. Road's closed. Chopper is ten minutes out. Safest and closest place to land is two miles down the mountain. Anderson and Gill, secure the vehicle. Mathison and Whitcomb, douse the perimeter. The goal, open it up within five minutes. McNair and Roberts, you'll transport for airlift."

The scene blazes to life on a rush of adrenaline. Sadie looks at me with wide eyes hearing the voices but too young to know the reason for the urgency. Fear blankets her features that two minutes ago had flared with smiles.

I've known this child five minutes, and I yearn to punch through her window and pull her to the safety of my arms and consoling whispers of refuge. Her lips quiver and I flatten my palm against the window hoping she can somehow seek solace in the nearness of my hand as it rests against the glass.

Anderson yells a confirmation that the vehicle is secure, as Gill approaches with the hydraulic tools for extrication. It's going to be loud, and I need to explain to Sadie what's coming so she isn't frightened by the sound of grinding metal.

"Sadie? There are some men who are going to help get you out. It's going to be loud. I'll be right here the whole time. You'll need to cover your ears until I say stop. We can have silly face contests with our ears covered, ok?"

She nods her sweaty head.

Gill catches my eyes over the roof and gives me a thumbs up.

"Honey, cover your ears just like me?" I lift my hands and cover my own ears so she can understand what I want her to do. I keep my ears covered and flash her a big smile as she lifts her tiny hands to her ears.

The squeal of the Jaws of Life cuts through the air as the machine slices the doorpost. Sadie's lips start to tremble, and I stick my tongue out and rapidly pull it back in like a frog catching a fly. She smiles then puckers her lips like she's giving a kiss. I cross my eyes and roll my head being careful not to do anything that will scare versus entertain her. We trade expressions while Gill and Anderson work in tandem to free the woman in the front seat, presumably Sadie's mom.

In mere minutes, the door is lifted away. McNair loses no time in securing a neck brace as he gathers vitals while Anderson and Gill begin work to remove the steering wheel. McNair catches my eyes and flashes a grimace before returning his focus back to the woman's head injuries.

A final thud echoes through the car signifying Anderson and Gill's success. They clear the space allowing Whitcomb to step forward and take what would normally be my place working in tandem with McNair. On the outskirts of Boulder, every first responder is adept at stepping into multiple roles.

Taking just enough time to step around the vehicle, Anderson and Gill pop the back window from its casing. The shrill drone of the machine now gone, I remove my hands from my ears and give Sadie a thumbs up. She follows my lead, but is startled by Gill as he reaches in and unbuckles her seat belt.

"Hope!" Sadie's scream tears from her lungs as she wiggles around searching for my face.

"Sadie, I'm here. He's helping me get you out." The fight immediately leaves her body as my voice connects with her ears.

Her feet, encased in Minnie Mouse sneakers, clear the back window, and I walk alongside Gill as he brings her around and sets her on the back of the fire truck, away from the view of the men trying to save the woman's life.

I start Sadie's medical evaluation as I hear the distinctive sound of the gurney as it snaps into place. I speak directly to Sadie, voice low and calm, as I check her pupils, neck, abdomen, and limbs.

McNair closes the first door of the ambulance, and Sadie's head snaps in that direction in response to the shrill squeak of the hinges. I try to shield her vision, but I know the second her eyes land on the end of the gurney.

She reaches her hands out as I physically restrain her from jumping off the truck.

"Mommy? Mommy! Don weave me."

The scream tears from her mouth, and the agonizing sound is forever tattooed on my brain.

Gasping, I jolt awake. My heart slams against my ribs as my fingers grip sweat-soaked sheets. A rivulet of wetness slides down my drenched chest as I focus on the bare, blue walls of my bedroom.

A hint of morning light filters through a crack in the window shade. I lift my head reaching out a hand to tap my phone charging next to my bed. I note the five a.m. alarm, set to go off in twelve minutes and drop back to my pillow, allowing my thoughts the rare opportunity to return to the events of that day.

The blood.

The turmoil.

Sadie's innocent trust.

My failure to find out what happened to her or if her mother survived.

Three years have passed, but the vivid memories have burrowed so deep within my subconscious I know I'll never eradicate the nightmare.

PART 2

Hope is the thing with feathers that perches in the soul - and sings the tunes without the words - and never stops at all.
Emily Dickinson

22

HOPE

1 YEAR LATER...

The scratch of the pen sounds loud to my ears as it glides across the paper. Mel, my realtor, smiles as I push the signed documents across the massive table.

"Great! I'll finish up the rest and let you know when the closing is. I've already talked to the title company, and they assured me you don't need to physically be in the office to sign the final paperwork."

I nod, blindly searching for my keys inside my purse while standing from the ergonomic desk chair my butt has conformed to over the past forty-five minutes. Signing the paperwork to officially accept the offer on the Boulder house had been the final hurdle before I could jump in my packed car and head back to Illinois.

Leave it to my luck. My small hurdle turned out to be a giant six-hour mountain and a major drain on my tight schedule. A missing document had been the culprit, shooting my original driving plan to shit. Leaving now, I'll be smack dab in the middle of Denver's Friday night rush hour traffic.

Lucky me and my best-laid plans.

Mel hurries to an apartment-sized refrigerator tucked into the corner of the large conference room. She returns with a couple of bottles of Fiji water and pushes them into my hands. "Here's some water for the road. I'm slipping you two because you never know when dire thirst is going to strike."

She gives me a quick wink and a wide smile as she holds the glass door open for me. Wow. Two bottles of water? She is set to earn five percent commission on the $1.8 million sale of my house, and here she is playing up the advantages that I scored not one, but *two*, bottles of water. Yep, I'm one lucky lady.

Don't get me wrong, I like Mel. She's witty, ambitious, and one heck of a saleswoman. It's what made me choose her when I decided to sell the house Joe and I had bought nearly seven years ago. But, her enthusiasm is a little over the top at times and doesn't always jive with my personality.

She walks me to the door, and my hands finally close around my elusive keys which happen to be hiding under Colleen Hoover's *Verity*, the book I finished during my unexpected delay. Anyone who can pull a story like that from her brain is a genius word wizard, though I wonder if her husband has read the book and sleeps with one eye open.

Mel extends her hand, and I shake it before turning and walking to my SUV which is loaded with so much junk the driver seat is the only free space in the entire vehicle. I open the door and slide in hitting the ignition button and welcoming the lukewarm air that keeps the moisture gathered at the corner of my eyes from dripping down my cheeks.

Today is supposed to be a happy day, though the hole in my chest is doing a convincing job of telling me otherwise. It's taken me four years, but I'm ready to take on the world. Well, the Chicago suburbs, at least.

I am finally in the home stretch of becoming a pediatric orthopedic surgeon. My path hasn't been easy. Some days my mind has been filled with darkness, and I've wanted to quit and accept defeat. But then I remember the significance of Dr. Johansen's words, *"Defeat lies in the failure of doing nothing and never moving forward,"* and I plod ahead knowing every step is a choice I'm making in moving forward.

My work family has been a blessing since Joe passed. When I'd told them I planned to finish my medical degree, the guys had been avid supporters often stopping by to cut the grass or drop off groceries knowing I didn't have time between my school and work schedule for such tasks.

I've always wanted to be a doctor, but it wasn't until I considered going back to school that I rationalized why. After Joe's death, aided by a Dr. Johansen, I chose to rip away my roots of self-doubt and found the flowers of hope I'd let wither for years.

Hope. I wanted to be a doctor who encouraged others to see hope in situations where it was often hidden. I wanted to show them its power and the miraculous changes that occurred when they held it tightly within their hearts.

With that goal in mind, I'd applied to finish medical school. Though it took me nearly three years rather than the one I'd expected, I never doubted my choice because it had been born from my experiences, both good and bad.

An uncomfortable lump tickles my throat, and I crack open one of my *two* bottles of water. The cool liquid passes my lips, and it immediately washes away the melancholy I'd unknowingly let creep in as I'd driven past the mountains that had witnessed some of the highest and lowest points in my life.

I scrub the sadness from my face, drop my sunglasses over damp eyes, and hit the gas. I'm filled with hopefulness and ready to open the next chapter of my life.

———

Two DAYS and roughly a thousand miles of Midwest cornfields later, I follow the directions on my phone and exit off of I-90 toward Geneva. I'd scoured the Internet and found a little two-bedroom house in a quiet neighborhood close enough to the hospital so I can walk to work on days when the weather is pleasant.

Though pictures of the completely remodeled marble and stainless-steel kitchen were drool-worthy, I'd been leery of signing a lease on a place I'd never seen in person. After ninety minutes on the phone with the landlord, I was sold. Twenty-four hours later, I'd signed and emailed the contract, wired the money, and started a mental inventory of which small appliances I'd be bringing with me to add to the kitchen.

Cameron, the owner and landlord, is a nurse at the hospital and a riot to speak with on the phone. I don't think I've laughed that hard since I was in high school and Mrs. Stotz flashed my entire English class when Beowulf was accidentally replaced by a home movie of her getting frisky with her husband. I hadn't been sure a person's face could turn that color of purple, but Mrs. Stotz made me a believer. Needless to say, her blunder resulted in her losing her job, which was unfortunate because she was one of my favorite teachers prior to the porn show.

My smile had been huge while I'd listened to a description of the house and the surrounding neighborhood, until Cameron said I would be responsible for all of my own yard maintenance. The grin fell right off my lips, and I nearly hung up the phone and dialed the second place on my list. That is until Cameron went on to describe the kitchen and I heard the home had a Viking six-burner gas stove. I'd given a hoot of joy which led me to explain my love of baking. Cameron had asked what I liked to bake then listened intently, throwing in an "mmm" or "oh yeah" as I explained.

When I was done, Cameron proposed a verbal baking

trade agreement which stipulated I could opt out of yard maintenance responsibilities provided I supplied him with two dozen cookies, brownies, tarts, or muffins each week. He'd also given me the option of baking a cake in lieu of two dozen cookies one week a month as long as the cake was not a pineapple upside-down cake which, according to Cameron, should not qualify as a cake. I'd laughed and readily agreed considering the lawn mowing had been my only stumbling block for the rental.

I'd hung up and sent a mental thank you to Dr. Johansen for encouraging me to find a hobby where I'd meet new people and explore the benefits of participating in an activity of my own choosing. Baking had been an easy choice since it had always fascinated me, and I already excelled at it. My confidence fell a few pegs when the first intermediate class kicked my butt, and I'd had to call and request a transfer into the basic baking class. I'd been humbled by the experience, but it also lit a fire under my skin which had me compelled me to go back every week.

I drive down Main Street, and excitement flows through my body as my eyes scan the quaint shops of the small downtown. Tall, black street lamps flicker to life and give the street a warm glow.

I'm hit with a memory of my mother. We'd taken a day trip to a small town called Woodstock, and we'd proceeded to spend the day sampling homemade treats from the bakery while we strolled past the shop windows before heading home for the day. My lips tip up as goosebumps rise across my skin. I swear my mom's telling me this move is going to change my life.

I spy a coffee shop that appears to be open, so I signal and pull into a spot in front of the cafe. If I'm going to survive unpacking tonight, I'm going to need a caffeine boost.

No sooner has the bell over the door rung when I'm nearly

knocked down by a mini-tornado with long dark pigtails followed by a mountain of muscle who breezes by me, with a gruff "sorry" sans eye contact, as he continues down the street on swift feet, presumably to catch the little storm who fled in front of him.

A moment of annoyance warms my skin before I brush it away. I have no idea what it means to walk in that man's shoes, and I'd be a hypocrite if I claimed to know. One very important lesson I'd learned with Dr. Johansen: *Never assume the stranger next to you isn't dealing with a burden heavier than your own.*

Sometimes it's the people you least expect who are falling apart inside. It's human nature to hide one's baggage from the world in favor of creating a public perception that hides the ugliness of your reality. People need kindness, not judgment, which is why I try to keep my thoughts pointed away from ignorant assessments of strangers. Though I'm not without my moments of judgment, especially when I'm tired.

I step to the counter and order a black iced coffee. I hope it will give me the jolt I'll need for the next four or five hours. The girl behind the counter gives me a warm smile before turning to make my drink.

I look around the quaint shop as my eyes take in the small two-top tables and cozy armchairs scattered throughout. It reminds me a little bit of Rise and Grind, and my mind immediately floats to the first day I saw Joe. With his tweed jacket over casual jeans, I'd been smitten from the second he'd walked through the door. Little did I know at the time, I would talk to him, marry him, and lay him to rest less than four years later.

My adopted mantra whispers through my head. *The events of life can never be controlled, but the choices for how we live are the greatest gift we've been given.*

I hear the shake of ice and turn to accept my drink with a quiet "thank you." The smooth taste of coffee coats my tongue as I take a long pull from my straw and meander through the tables before heading out to my car. I'd told Cameron to expect me around six p.m., and a quick peek at my phone tells me I'm already a few minutes late. I hit the button to unlock my vehicle and jump into the driver's seat. Caffeinated and excited, I'm ready to see where my most recent choices have taken me.

23

MITCHELL

"WHAT DO YOU MEAN SHE'S NOT A GOOD CANDIDATE? I LOOKED at the bloodwork, examined the MRI, and did the physical myself. She is a perfect candidate."

My eyes scan Common Grounds, the little coffee shop that sits exactly between my house and the hospital and is just a few blocks from my daughter's dance class.

My little ballerina is doing figure eights and weaving through the tables while sipping from the strawberry banana smoothie she suckered me into getting for her since I forgot her water bottle at home. She swore she was going to die of thirst if she had to suffer through an *entire* car ride home before she could get a drink.

I'm half watching her as I listen to my friend and the best cardiothoracic surgeon I've ever met. He lays down a valid argument for why my current patient is not a candidate for a valve replacement. Though I'm not happy with his recommendations, I admit I'd missed a very small, but critical, part of the medical history that pointed to a high rate of failure for this type of procedure.

I fist my hands in an attempt to fight the disappointment

filtering through my system. I'd missed something vital. That's not to say I would have missed it on the second or third review since I never speak to a patient about a procedure until I've triple checked the medical history.

"You're a fine surgeon, Mitchell, but if you think you'll be able to save every patient who walks through your door, you're setting yourself up for disappointment."

I squeeze my eyes shut before opening them, not wanting to take my eyes off of my active daughter for more than a second. I know he's right, but I don't want to think about the reality.

"Thanks, Dan. I appreciate you taking a look."

"My pleasure. Tell me, how have you been?"

I run my hand through my wavy locks and exhale. It seems I'm due for another haircut though I have no idea when I'll have the opportunity to fit one in within the next month or maybe even the next year. Dan's words don't voice the question he actually asking. He's one of the only people who know the shitstorm of a story that's become my life, and he's also one of the only people I'm willing to give an honest answer.

"It hasn't been the easiest. I still don't know what I'm doing half the time, and the only reason I haven't accidentally killed or maimed my daughter is because someone is always around. I don't know what I'd do without Maggie or my parents. Though my mom has been reminding me she and my dad leaving for their winter home in Florida soon. To be honest, I keep ignoring her subtle hints because I think I may truly go insane without her."

I can practically hear Dan's words lining up in the silence. "There's nothing wrong with permanent placement. It may be better in the long run for all those involved. When was the last time you took a moment for yourself?"

My eyes flit back and forth as my mind reels, failing to

produce one example of the last time I sat by the lake or even saw the lake for that matter.

"Does taking a shower with the door half-cracked count?" Deflecting with humor is my primary defense strategy.

His grunt hits my ears, and I know he isn't amused by my response. "It's okay to admit you can't do it all. Just remember that."

I nod though he cannot see my reaction, and I try to keep the resignation from my answer. "I'll try to remember that."

"Good. I'm too invested in helping you stay at the top of your game. I'm not getting any younger, and Sharon's nagging about my retirement has gotten worse lately. My patients need someone like you."

A golf ball-sized lump appears in my throat, and I swallow to push it down.

A streak of black trails through my vision, and I turn in time to see a wooden chair go toppling over in the wake of my daughter. Whoever thinks giving a six-year-old a smoothie is a good idea should be given a swift kick in the ass—even if that butt is my own.

I reach the overturned chair in three strides and give an apologetic smile to an older woman who's giving me the evil eye from the corner. Unfortunately, my movement is too slow to catch my daughter's hand before she suggests we go to the pet store and sprints to the door.

I forget Dan is on the other end of the line until I hear a low chuckle. He's met her and knows the atomic energy level I'm dealing with, yet he still laughs in my ear. "Sounds like she hasn't changed or slowed down."

The door swings open, and a woman walks in. Something tells me I should have given her a second look, but my moment for scrutiny is lost when Sedona barrels between the woman and the door frame, nearly slamming the customer into the hinge before hanging a left and taking off down the street.

"Nope, still as active as ever. And some idiot just threw gasoline, in the form of sugar, on her fire. I've got to run. Thanks for the advice."

Phone to my ear and fire in my steps, I issue a half-assed "sorry" to the woman before passing through the door, ending my call, and making my way to the pet store three doors down.

My second shoe hasn't cleared the threshold of the store and my daughter already has her face plastered to the glass cage of a little yippie dog that is alternating barking and bouncing back and forth around the cage. This mutt is moving so fast he makes my daughter's energy level look like that of a one-legged turtle.

"Daddy, I can tell this one wants to go home with us! See how he's looking at me."

I'm not sure if Canine Crazy Eyes can stand still let alone have the attention span to glance at my daughter.

"Sorry, pumpkin, he'll have to stay here. I believe Maggie is allergic to all pets."

I make a mental note to bring Maggie up to speed on her *supposed* allergies, apologize for throwing her under the bus, and give her a bonus on her next paycheck.

I don't know what I'd do without Maggie. She's been Sedona's full-time nanny and my lifeline for nearly three years. A retired school teacher who'd tragically lost her husband to a massive stroke a year before she started working with us, Maggie is strict, yet isn't stingy with her praise or her encouragement. Sedona adores her, and while I'm not always ready for them, I appreciate the no-nonsense comments she reserves for critiquing my life. I often joke I'll likely buy her a house if she ever threatens to leave us.

While my parents are around and have helped immensely, they've also had no qualms telling me they've raised their children and their reward is spending time with each other. My dad suffered a heart attack a few years ago, and they vowed to not waste a single minute of their days together. I can't fault them for wanting to make the most of their time. What happened with my dad reminded me how drastically life can change in a heartbeat.

Sedona walks past every cage, whispering compliments into each as she drags her feet up and down the aisles. The smile on her face does little to hide the sadness brimming in her eyes. There is very little I won't do for my little girl, but unfortunately, getting a pet—another added responsibility to a pile that is precariously in danger of toppling—is one of the things I just can't bring myself to do.

I glance at my watch and track Sedona to the back of the store where a little bunny sits nibbling a carrot in the corner of its cage.

"Pumpkin, Maggie's waiting on us for dinner."

My little princess leans close to the screen and says, "Don't worry, someone will love you as much as I do someday."

I look to the ceiling, embarrassed that my eyes mist when I hear the promise my daughter's given to this little rabbit. *Why is life so difficult sometimes?*

24

HOPE

I TAKE A FINAL LOOK IN THE MIRROR PROPPED AGAINST THE floor behind my bedroom door. Ponytail secure. Check. Scrubs clean and pressed. Check. Running shoes, worn but clean. Check.

Nerves are making me a neurotic mess this morning. *When I see patients, will they believe I'm actually the doctor? Can I handle the responsibility and the stress associated with keeping the hope of so many people alive?*

I do a full-body shake and let my doubts and insecurities roll right off my neck. I am Dr. Roberts, and I have every intention of making the name as well renowned in pediatrics as it once was in oncology. Joe left me with huge shoes to fill, so to speak, but he also left me with the means to succeed in every step of the journey without him.

I walk to the kitchen and swipe the Tupperware of banana nut muffins I baked last night and my car keys off the counter and head to my first day at Geneva General.

"Well, aren't you a sight this early in the morning." The low cadence of Cameron's voice trickles across our shared driveway as I make my way to my car.

I glance across the space and see my tall, blond-haired, neighbor who looks like a California surfer transplant, standing in dark blue scrubs with little green blobs all over them. I squint. Wait. *Are those little Yodas covering his chest?* If I'd harbored any doubts about us getting along, they've all just fallen away. Fellow Star Wars fans shoot straight to the top of my "automatic friends" list.

"A sight, I am."

He approaches my car and stops to look over the roof from the passenger side and his smile grows as I do a poor imitation of the coolest Jedi master of the galaxy.

His chuckle is like warm frosting on homemade cinnamon rolls, dripping with warmth and sweetness. "Sorry about this weekend."

He'd texted me with a lengthy apology on Friday saying he'd gotten roped into hanging with a couple of friends from out of town which was why my keys were waiting for me on my porch when I arrived, but my landlord was not.

"A couple of college buddies didn't give me any notice they were coming into town. They showed up at my door, and before I knew it, I was being dragged on a bar crawl through Chicago and crashing at their hotel for the remainder of the weekend." He rubs the back of his neck. "I feel like the world's worst landlord for not being here when you arrived."

I school my features before turning my head and staring at him long enough that my lack of response blankets the air with an uncomfortable tension.

His smile slips from his lips as his eyes drift away from my stare. He'd left a note and keys to the house as well as a map of the surrounding neighborhood, two menus for local takeout, and a four-pack of bottled water that may or may not have been cold when he first left them on the doorstep.

I hadn't been bothered in the slightest that he didn't greet me when I arrived. I'm messing with him because I'm interested to see if he's truly sorry or just a jerk who says he'll be there for you and then bails. His tenant care package, which went above and beyond my non-existent expectations, has me thinking he's not a jerk, but I'm testing him just to be sure. Since I beat the moving truck by a full day, I'd had very little to unload, though it took a massive number of trips to transfer everything from the car to the living room floor.

"Uh, maybe I could order a couple of pizzas, and we could have dinner tonight? You know to make up for me being such a prick for abandoning you and everything."

Bingo. My assumption is correct. He's not a jerk.

He waggles his eyebrows which I assume is his attempt to lighten the mood.

The early morning sunlight reflects off his wavy, short-cropped hair, and the back of my neck tingles. Cameron is really good looking. My face heats, and I look away hoping he doesn't see the simmer of interest in my eyes.

I bite my cheek to hold back the grin that's fighting to burst onto my lips. "I guess it's the least you could do for leaving me hanging after you said you'd be here. Make one of the pizzas ham and pineapple, and you've got yourself a deal."

His eyes go wide. "You like ham and pineapple AND know who Yoda is." He leans to the side and stage whispers behind his hand. "Though her impression sounds more Kermit the Frog than the great Jedi master, she may have just bought herself a lifetime lease on her place. If she keeps up these surprises, I don't think I'll be able to let her move." He winks and taps the roof of my car before turning back toward his garage. "Oh, one other thing." He turns, his face grave as walks backward. "Don't, for any reason, go into the basement alone."

I blink and give him my deer-in-the-headlights expression. Shit. *What's wrong with the basement?*

He throws his head back and gives me a throaty laugh that annoys me and calms my nerves at the same time.

"Just kidding. Though if I would have taken a picture of your reaction, I'm one hundred percent positive I could have made that meme go viral."

He turns on his heels and holds his hand above his head giving me a dismissal waive.

I roll my eyes and smile as I open my door and climb in. No doubt in my mind, Cameron may be just what the doctor ordered for my new life.

———

I CHECK my phone and make a final circle through the designated doctor's lot. So much for doctors getting extra perks, like a parking lot, if I can't find a spot. *How many doctors work at this hospital anyway?* By the looks of the packed asphalt, I expect a two to one doctor/patient ratio.

I inch down an aisle, making sure to not only scan the one I'm in but also the rows on either side. I'm nearly ready to throw in the towel when I spy a perfect spot at the end of the next aisle. Thank heavens. I've nearly blown the thirty-minute cushion I'd given myself, and my heart rate is starting to climb.

I signal and begin making a turn before a sleek, black SUV zips in and parks. I tap my horn and lift my hands in a *What the hell? That space was mine* gesture feeling cheated when I can't even see the driver's face because of the blacked-out, tinted windows. Yeah, I'd have tinted windows too if I made a habit of stealing parking spots and driving like a madman.

I wait for a few seconds, ready to roll my window down and give this ass a piece of my mind. However, Mr. Andretti hasn't exited the vehicle, and another glance at my clock says I don't have time to wait.

I give the offending car a final, lingering look before making my way to the other parking lot which looks like a postage stamp because it's so far away. Welcome to your first day, Dr. Roberts.

25

HOPE

"Then she turned her nose up like the Miss Priss she is and told me she wouldn't have agreed to a date if she knew I drove the hunk of junk I arrived in."

Cameron lifts his chin and throws his hand out in an exaggerated pantomime of throwing hair over his shoulder. It's so out of character for his six-foot, muscled frame that I snort the water out of my nose and onto my plate of spaghetti.

"She actually turned her nose up? What a brat!" I reach for a napkin and dab water from my upper lip.

Cameron rips a chunk of garlic bread from the loaf and pushes it through the pool of red sauce on his plate. "Turns out, that night ranks in my top ten best dates." His eyes twinkle as he shrugs his shoulders and stares at his fork.

I reach across my table and lay my hand across his. My face is a mask of fake sympathy. "Uh, we may need to review Dating 101 if that ranks as one of your best."

He lifts his shoulders in a shrug and shoots me a mischievous grin. "Not with her. She left straight away. I ended up going into the restaurant and leaving with Amanda and Madison, two best friends who enjoyed sharing everything!" He waggles his eyebrows as he takes a sip from his bottle of beer.

I toss my dirty napkin at his face. "Gross!"

He bats away my napkin like it's a gnat and stands up. "Don't knock it 'till you've tried it, I always say."

He carries his plate to the counter and starts filling the sink to wash the dishes. I watch the muscles of his back as he tips his plate over the garbage before turning back to clear the rest of the table. With his sun-bleached, wavy hair and his fit body, it's no wonder he's the talk of more than one break room at the hospital. I can see the appeal, yet for all his hotness, I don't think of him as more than a great friend and the guy next door.

Though Joe has been gone four years, I still can't imagine myself with another guy. He'd been gone at least a year before my attraction to the opposite sex resurfaced. Though the attraction is where it stops for me. Dating feels unnatural, like I'm cheating on my husband. Needless to say, my hang-ups with dating tend to kill any inkling of interest within the first five minutes of meeting someone. Dr. Johansen had me warned the idea of physical intimacy may take a while to surface, but when it does, I should trust my heart and explore where it could go. I'm not in a hurry. I have work, a few friends, and my awesome patients. I am comfortable and content, and for me, that's enough.

Who would have thought the hospital hottie—as so many of the female staff refer to him—would turn out to be such a good friend? We have a comfortable rhythm. He gives me the friendship I need, and I give him insider tips on which hospital women to pursue and which ones to sprint away from.

He places the last glass on the drying rack and turns, the dishtowel thrown over his broad shoulder. "I see the grass is getting a little long. What confection do you have in store for me this week?" He raises an eyebrow and grins, making his dimples pop as he leans against my counter.

I return his look with a smirk of my own. "Uh, you just mowed my lawn two days ago. It's been hot as hell, and we haven't had any rain. If you cut it again, there won't be enough blades left to make a footprint. Plus, I gave you two dozen carrot cake bars on Thursday night. Tell me you haven't eaten all of them already?"

He folds his arms across his chest and bites his lip. "Damn. I was hoping for another dozen since I shared my sweets with a certain confection of the nursing variety on the fourth floor on Friday."

I roll my eyes and lock down the grin fighting to take over my face. Cameron is a Grade A, certified flirt, and he has no shame. "Please tell me you didn't start your flirtation with a lie and take credit for making them."

His hand slams to his chest above his heart, and he gives me a look of mock horror. "Who do you take me to be? I told her my grandma made them and told me to share them with someone special." He gives me a wink before grabbing another beer from my fridge, popping the cap, and flicking it toward me where I stand against the counter opposite him.

"You are horrible."

"But you'd still date me if you weren't married to your job, right?" He gives me a toothy grin.

He'd cornered me and asked me on a date the week after I'd arrived. I'd been flattered, and a teeny bit turned on, but I'd firmly told him I had absolutely no interest in a relationship other than friendship. He'd shrugged it off then asked, "Does that put friends with benefits on the table then?" When I'd hit him in the stomach with the bag of groceries I'd been holding, he laughed and proceeded to ask me if he could hide his porn collection at my house when his grandma comes for a visit. Since that's what friends do for friends, apparently.

Already knowing I'll be making him a treat so I can contribute to his shameless flirting, I give him a serious stare. "Yes, Cameron. As soon as I lose all interest in medicine and divorce my job, you'll have the green light for us to get together."

He tilts his head from side to side, giving me a smile that nearly blinds me with pearly whiteness. "What I hear you saying is the odds are in my favor?"

I walk up and hip check him, pushing him out of the way as I open the refrigerator door. "So, this sweet girl on the fourth floor?" My head snaps in his direction. "Wait. It is a girl, right?"

"Would there be a problem if it was a guy?" His expression is neutral and unreadable as he waits for my answer.

"Absolutely not. Though my choice of confection may vary a little if it's a guy."

He reaches out and bops me on the end of my nose. "Your first assumption is correct, though I'm touched that you wouldn't treat me any differently if I were into dudes."

I pull out a couple sticks of butter, two eggs, buttermilk, and a pint of strawberries. "I'm thinking a little strawberry for your shortcake." I stretch my thumb and index finger apart so an inch of space lies between them. "See what I did there? *Short* cake."

He grunts and walks into the living room, which is open to the kitchen, and drops onto my couch before throwing his heels up on the coffee table.

"You do know you have your own home literally twenty steps away?" I cock my head in the direction of his house as I flit around the kitchen pulling out tins of sugar, flour, salt, and baking powder.

I'm teasing him about leaving. I'm willing to admit I've grown fond of spending time with someone considering I've spent the past four years on my own and primarily alone. If he wants to stay for a couple of hours, that's fine with me, but I'm not going to pass up a chance to razz him about it.

What started as the prize for a bet we made during an evening jog, Spaghetti Sunday has kind of become our thing. I make the spaghetti and garlic bread, and he brings the beer, though he's the only one who ever drinks it.

We typically end up hanging out at other times, though I like knowing my week always starts with a friend. His flirting can be a bit over the top, but he's truly been a lifesaver to my sanity considering the number of hours I've been clocking and the stress I've been under as a new surgical resident at the hospital.

"If you're going to stay, at least be useful and come pull out my mixer. I pushed it to the back of the cabinet, and it's stuck under a cabinet drawer."

He huffs like moving is a hardship, yet he gets up and walks into the kitchen knowing the mixer is his friend in scoring points with Miss Fourth Floor. He bends down and wrestles with the appliance for a minute before pulling it out and placing it on the counter.

"How much does that thing weigh? And why the hell do you put it in a cabinet when you know you're just going to pull it out again the next day?"

I run my hand over its shiny red exterior, covering the sides protectively like it has ears. "Hush. Ruby is sensitive. She's bulky, not heavy. I don't want you giving her a complex."

He rolls his eyes and returns to the couch where he flips on the TV and cues up an *Arrow* episode on Netflix.

I plug Ruby in and arrange the ingredients across the countertop. I love my mixer. It may have cost a mint, but it's the first item I packed for the move. This little machine has brought me hours of contentment and saved me from spending the day in tears on more than one occasion.

Three hours later, a dozen shortcakes sit stacked inside a

zippered bag next to a bowl of homemade whipped cream and a container of sweetened, sliced strawberries. To the right of those is a Tupperware container of my favorite chocolate and caramel brownies. I figured I'd make a batch and leave them in the break room for the surgical staff. I can always use the *brownie* points.

Cameron is slumped over and passed out on the couch, and the TV is blaring unwatched across the room. I tiptoe over to his sleeping form and blow in his ear before taking a huge step backward. Five seconds later, Cameron jumps up and runs to the bathroom holding his crotch with two hands.

"Shit." A shout somewhere between a growl and a groan filters to my ears while I await his return.

The snicker that slides out of my mouth turns into a full-blown laugh when Cameron walks back to the living room with a large wet stain on the front of his white basketball shorts. A spot he's trying, unsuccessfully, to hide behind the hands he's casually crossed in front his junk.

Cameron has one ticklish spot on his body which I found completely by accident after I leaned over and whispered something in his ear during a horror movie marathon a couple weeks ago. Needless to say, his reaction is strange and horribly embarrassing…for *him*. However, that doesn't stop me from capitalizing on his little *problem* whenever the opportunity presents itself.

My eyes drift below the waistband of his shorts, and my controlled laughter threatens to bubble over.

He shakes his head before his eyes capture mine. "You're an evil, vile woman."

"I'm sorry. I couldn't resist." The sincerity of my apology is ruined when my lips tip up in a grin.

"Yeah. Just remember. Payback is a sneaky bitch."

I walk to the kitchen and put all of his shortcake fixings

into a plastic bag and hold it out in front of me like a peace offering. "Shortcake for your troubles?"

He rips the bag from my hand and walks to my back door, his flip flops flapping in response to his exaggerated stomping. He holds his hand above his head in a guy salute before slamming his free hand into the screen door and crossing the threshold without looking back.

I call to him before he's swallowed into the darkness of my backyard. "Tell me how it goes tomorrow."

His right-hand rises and I think I see the shadow of a middle finger before his gruff voice slides back to me through the screen "Payback. It's coming, Sweet Cheeks."

I grin at his use of the nickname he'd adopted the week after I gave him his first batch of cookies. He swears up and down it's because I like to bake sweet confections and I have pinchable cheeks, but considering his flirtatious ways, I'm not so sure it's the cheeks on my face that he's talking about.

26

HOPE

Thinking of my patient causes a sharp pain to lance through my ribs as I exit the operating room and pull the surgical cap from my head. A mother of three had come in last night reporting severe stomach pains and vomiting. Tests had shown she was suffering from acute appendicitis, and she had been cleared for an appendectomy this morning.

I'd just spent four hours standing next to Dr. Harris, my first surgical mentor, in an "oh shit" surgery. Harris had gone in to remove her appendix and found a black mass snaking around her appendix, liver, and lower intestine. No one in the operating room needed a degree in medicine to know this woman was in a bad way and had been for some time. Harris had immediately paged the oncologist on-call and proceeded to remove what he could without damaging her strangled organs. I'd said a prayer for her recovery, though my medical training tells me prayers are probably her only answer at this stage of her illness. Harris had claimed exhaustion and said he'd talk with the family before leaving me instructions to close. I'd been meticulous in my work, hoping she'd appreciate my efforts to make her scar the smallest possible when she wakes.

I scrub out and head to the break room/locker room where I keep my purse and phone. I'd left my chocolate caramel brownies in the middle of the table six hours ago, and I hope I'll be able to snag one, or at least a few large crumbs because I need a sugar high no matter how small.

I walk into the deserted break room and open my locker taking out my phone and shooting a text to Cameron to see if he's busy for dinner even though it'll be late considering I still need to check on a few patients before I leave. I buy a sparkling water from the vending machine and scan the surface of the round table before sitting down.

My eyes flare before I turn and survey the rest of the small room. My perusal comes up empty, and I start to panic. Forget snagging a brownie. My Tupperware is gone. The one with the white bottom and orange top. That container had belonged to my mom and held not only sentimental memories but had also housed some of my greatest baking masterpieces, including my chocolate caramel brownies just this morning.

I stand and rummage through the room, opening random cupboards and drawers not expecting to find it, but looking anyway. More tragic than going without a single morsel of brownie, someone had *stolen* my Tupperware container?

Maybe it's my frayed nerves, but my heart rate picks up, and my body grows hot. I'm pissed, and my mind is poised to attack.

My phone buzzes, and I pace to the table where I left it. I unlock the screen, and Cameron's unwelcome words hit me in the face.

Cameron: Can't. Taking the extra whipped cream to Shortcake's house tonight.

Damn my hospitable ways in making more whipped cream than his greedy little mouth needed.

Me: Okay. Raincheck?

Cameron: Raincoat? Yeah. Never leave home without one (or five).

His response paired with the winky face emoji he adds to the end of the message makes me smile through my anger. He's shameless, but at least he can make me laugh when I need it.

I make one last check for my Tupperware with no luck. I finish my drink in two long pulls and throw the can in the recycling bin then make my rounds checking on today's surgical patients before heading home to my empty house minus my favorite Tupperware.

I'VE FINISHED A RUN, eaten a plate of subpar Chinese leftovers, and cleaned my bathroom. My surgery today really messed with my psyche. It's a reminder of how fast life changes and how powerless one is in stopping the sands of time.

I scroll through the cable channels, failing to give my brain the time to focus on the screen before blindly flipping to the next station. While my body is physically exhausted, my mind can't seem to settle, and I'm anxious and jumpy as a result. I rise from the couch and walk to the kitchen for a glass of water hoping the little amount of movement paired with the distraction will calm my thoughts.

As I'm putting my cup in the sink after gulping down two full glasses of water, I get a taste for crispy rice bars. Walking to the pantry, I scan the contents and give myself a mental high five for having the foresight to buy the ingredients the last time I was at the store. I pull out the box of cereal, a stick of butter, and a bag of mini-marshmallows along with a big glass mixing bowl and a baking tin. Normally, I would spice them up by throwing in some chocolate pieces, a few candied nuts, or a handful of butterscotch chips. Tonight, I need the simplicity of the traditional recipe to occupy my hands.

Ten minutes later, I'm sitting on my couch with a baking tin full of sticky goodness perched on my lap as I debate how long I should let them harden before diving in and satisfying my craving. I divide the pan into four rows, then make a precise cut down the middle of the first row, pulling out a square and shoving half of it in my mouth before it falls apart. There's nothing like warm, gooey crispy rice and marshmallow bars straight from the pan.

My phone buzzes on the coffee table. I look over and see a text notification presumably from Cameron though it seems a little early for a report from him. I carefully pinch my phone between two fingers, using a knuckle on my opposite hand to unlock it and open the message.

Cameron: Tonight was a dud. I should have taken you up on your dinner offer.

I don't know if I'm pleased or offended that I rank a step above dud and somewhere way below whipped cream.

Me: Oh, poor baby. Don't forget to bring my bowl home. I've already sacrificed one container today.

Cameron: Shit. I guess I can go back.

Me: Tell her it's your grandma's bowl.

Cameron: Maybe I could just buy you a new one?

Me: That bad???

It must be. Cameron's so cheap he makes two calls to the local pizza joint when he orders so he can use two coupons instead of one.

Cameron: Worse.

I laugh and toss my phone back on the coffee table. I don't know what it says about me as a friend that I'm happy I wasn't the only one who had a crappy day.

I SLEPT HORRIBLY which means my butt is dragging when my alarm goes off at five the next morning. I'm thankful today's schedule is light, and I'm only booked into the operating room for a little over an hour.

I pull my hair into a messy bun and jump in the shower, pulling the curtain closed with one hand as I turn the water on with the other. Icy droplets hit my skin, and I release a low hiss while silently scolding myself for turning the knob in the wrong direction. The temperature has barely reached lukewarm before I'm done and grabbing for a towel.

It takes me ten minutes to finish getting ready before I walk into the kitchen and pick up my freshly brewed coffee and a small container of the leftover crispy rice bars from last night.

Before I'd gone to bed, I'd polished off three more squares and cemented my decision to take the leftovers to the hospital today in an effort to escape eating the rest of the pan when I get off work tonight.

My eyes catch on the sticky notes on the corner of my counter, and my mouth smiles as a plan takes shape. I grab a marker, scribble a short message, and tape it to the top of the Tupperware container.

I pull my lunch out of the fridge, snatch my keys off the hook near the door, and pick up my container of treats. A smile sits on my lips as I walk to my car.

I'm going to catch a thief today.

27

MITCHELL

I SLAP MY PALM AGAINST THE CLOSED DOOR OF THE BREAK room reserved for the surgical staff. I bend and root through the tiny refrigerator. It's stocked with plastic and glass containers of delicious looking meals, though I know none belong to me since I haven't stocked it with my own snacks for quite some time.

I rise and slam the door empty-handed. I may be known as a prickly, hard-ass around here, but I'm not about to be labeled a food thief. I've seen the way the staff members ridicule and humiliate a food burglar, and I want no part. Volunteering to be publicly flogged or caned would be more enjoyable.

I meander three short steps to the vending machine to check out the selection, though I can't contain my lip curl when I spy two rows of packaged pork rinds—*Is that a layer of dust on the front package?*—and the single serving of sunflower seeds hanging in the otherwise empty machine. That's a hard pass.

I fill a disposable cup with water from the bubbler in the corner and slump into a seat at the round table in the middle of the room. A glance at my watch tells me why the small room looks like a ghost town. It's just after nine a.m. which most likely means every OR is bustling with activity for at least the next hour or two.

I scrub my hands down my face and inhale, trying to soothe the ache in my chest. Today has been one hell of a downer. I would have been one of the doctors in the OR had Mrs. Mandiver's labs not come back with three, neon-red flags. I'd double-checked the stats, contacting the lab directly, to make sure her samples hadn't been compromised considering the bleak results.

I'd had to stand in front of the expectant faces of Mrs. Mandiver and her husband while telling them her surgery had not only been canceled, but there was no chance of rescheduling it today or in the future because she was no longer a candidate for the surgery. I'd hoped it would have given her the additional years she so desperately wanted to gain. Twin grandsons in high school, she'd told me. They'd just started their freshman year, and she was determined to see a high school diploma placed in each of their hands before she left this life. She'd faced me, her hands clasped tightly within her husband's, not blinking as I relayed the devastating news for the last avenue we'd had to offer her.

Tears had threatened the back of my eyes as I stood immobile and impotent to feed the hope she'd placed upon my shoulders. Life sucked some days, and today was one of those dismal, dark times.

When I'd finished relaying my news, Mrs. Mandiver had taken one look at me and said, "While I'm still breathing, hope is not lost."

Her courage and strength are commendable though I fear her bad days will soon eclipse her good before erasing them altogether.

I glance across the room staring at nothing and thinking about everything. I should have known today wasn't going to go smoothly considering Sedona's scream in the dead of night had jarred me awake and jump-started my heart like I'd been woken up by a set of defibrillator paddles.

I'd arrived in her room, boxer briefs the only clothing covering my otherwise naked body, in one and a half seconds flat. She'd been asleep, covered in sweat, and caught in the middle of a nightmare. Her thrashing had pulled the sheets from the corners of her bed wrapping her legs like a mummy and keeping her lower half from moving. She'd screamed, "Mommy, mommy, no!"

My racing heart had stopped like someone pulled a plug from the wall. She hadn't had a night terror this bad since preschool two years ago. I'd thought her subconscious had made peace with that day, but I should have known the brain is unpredictable and life likes to twist the knife when you least expect it.

I'd fallen to my knees beside her, running my hands through her hair and pulling her towards me as I helped her surface from her terror until she was fully awake and breathing normally. Her face was wet from her tears and mottled with dark red splotches. My heart had cracked as I'd wiped her tears while hiding the fear I felt for my little girl.

She'd spent a good portion of the last two years in weekly therapy sessions talking about her fears and memories of the incident, as much as a toddler could voice those types of things, until her psychologist felt she'd worked past her fears and flashbacks. I'd assumed, like an idiot, her nightmares were behind her only to be slapped in the face and reminded last night that while her memories would fade, her mind would never let her forget.

I am powerless against my own screwup. If I'd made an effort to listen, I might have been able to save her from experiencing the heartache of that day.

One day. One blink, and the life I'd had disappeared leaving broken bits of guilt, anger, and failure in its wake.

I shake my head to clear last night's turmoil as a nurse, who I've seen around on the floor but have never spoken to, hurries across the room. She gives me a glance and a half-smile as she fiddles with a locker before pulling a phone from the top shelf, slamming the metal door, and bustling back out into the hallway. While I feel guilty for not giving her more than a smile, I'm glad she didn't sit down next to me and expect a conversation. The chaos swirling through my brain makes it hard enough to concentrate let alone keep dialogue moving with someone I don't even know.

I push back my chair, thinking I'll step outside and take a quick walk around the campus to clear my gray thoughts. Before I stand, my eyes catch on a plastic container in the middle of the table, similar though not identical to one that was here yesterday.

I'd walked in after my scheduled bypass, tired and in need of something to appease my appetite before my next surgery when I'd overheard two nurses and a surgical assistant practically in the throes of orgasm where they'd stood over an open container stuffing their faces with what appeared to be baked chocolate bars.

Their moans and giggles had bordered on obscene, and I'd approached them to ask if I needed to shut the door to give them privacy. They'd all glanced at me with a cross between fear and embarrassment before sharing a look and hustling out the door with napkins pressed below their mouths to catch any dark pieces of chocolate that threatened to fall from their lips.

My Prickly Pete reputation had struck again. I'd vowed to make an effort to lose some of the prickliness I'd become known for as I'd strode to the table in search of what chocolatey goodness was hidden in the container.

A few crumbs, the size of a pencil eraser, were scattered

across the bottom of the plastic, and I cursed my timing in missing out on fulfilling the craving I'd had before I'd walked in.

A neat freak, by necessity, I'd taken a napkin from the nearby counter and wiped the table stirring up the air and lifting the velvety smell of chocolate to my nose. The aroma was heavenly, and I'd nearly allowed my own groan to escape as I sniffed the container like an olfactory freak. The arrival of another doctor had me lowering the container and tossing it in the garbage before I'd headed outside to take the walk I'd so desperately needed.

I let yesterday's musings lift from eyes as I pull the new container toward me. My fingers reach out to remove the lid, and I see bold black writing filling a yellow sticky note taped to the top.

Sweet tooth? Enjoy a snack.
Tupperware thief? No treat for you.
Trade the container you stole
and score monthly confections for a year.
Fact: My chocolate brownies are just one of my baked specialties.
Text Dr. Roberts, 555-920-1509, when you're ready to fess up.

I drop the lid like it's a hot potato and shoot a look over my shoulder to see if there are witnesses to my bizarre reaction. *Tupperware thief? What the hell is Tupperware? Is this person looking for me?*

My thoughts review yesterday's actions, and my eyes slide shut when I latch onto the memory of throwing the plastic container in the garbage. I had been courteous by cleaning the area. *How was I supposed to know the plastic wasn't meant for the trash?*

I fill my lungs with air before exhaling the tension and the shittiness of this day. I pull the note from the container, consider my options, and begin formulating a plan. My brain throws out ideas, and I run through them like I'm a quarter-back making the last big play of the day.

After ten minutes of strategizing, I know a couple of things: 1. The treats were baked by Dr. Roberts, a fellow colleague, and therefore, someone who I probably don't have the option of intimidating into accepting an apology.; 2. Dr. Roberts bakes orgasmic treats (if the reactions of the staff are anything to go by as well as my own reaction to the simple act of smelling the container.); 3. The trash in the locker room is changed daily. (I'd made a quick check to see if the offending item had been lying on the bottom. It isn't.); 4. I'm obviously the "Tupperware thief" considering my hands chucked the orange and white plastic into the trash.; 5. What the hell is Tupperware, and how do I find a replacement?

I take a final look at the note and stuff it into my pocket. I'm afraid to ask my mom what Tupperware is for fear it's some rare, priceless treasure and she'll rip me a new one for not knowing its worth.

There is one person who can help me with my problem. While she's scarier than my mom, I have the protection of an employment contract and the knowledge she loves Sedona just a fraction of an inch less than I do.

I walk out of the room, needing to check the status of my patients, before cruising home and begging Maggie to help me out of this mess.

———

I WALK INTO MY HOUSE, and the aroma of garlic hits my nose eliciting a wide smile as I kick off my shoes and drop my keys in the dish by the door. Maggie, whose parents immigrated from Italy when she was three years old, is a master of Italian cuisine, though she doesn't treat us to it as often as my stomach would like. She claims it takes all day and she'd rather spend those hours with Sedona.

I can't fault her logic, though some days my cravings for her homemade spaghetti and meatballs get so intense I come perilously close to giving her permission to plop Sedona in front the TV for the afternoon just so she can cater to the whims of my taste buds.

My home's open concept allows Maggie to see me from the kitchen as soon as I walk through the door, but I announce my presence letting Sedona know I'm home. There's not a single event I look forward to more than being greeted by my daughter's smile when I walk through the door.

"You're home!" I hear her small shout of joy and a flurry of footsteps as she races from the other room.

I bend and sweep her into my arms as her long, dark braid bounces against my shoulder. I give her a tight squeeze while placing a kiss on her slightly damp head.

She leans back, raising her hands to my cheeks before planting her wet lips on top of mine. "Guess what I've been doing? Wanna come see?"

Her pink cheeks and sweaty body tell me she's been playing the crazy dance game on the gaming console she begged me to buy for her last Christmas. I'm not a parent who advocates letting a child sit in front of a video game, but after having to take a ten-minute break to wait for my breathing to return to normal after playing just one round, I figured the console did what it promised in getting kids moving.

I give a little shake of my head before setting her back down. "How do you expect me to catch a beat in these pants?" I hold my hands out at my sides and spin around putting my dress pants and button-down on display like I'm a runway model.

She scrunches her nose and bites her lip. "Catch a beat? What's that mean?"

And just like that, I feel like the fifty-year-old dude at the gym who drops movie lines from the eighties as the young twenty-somethings roll their eyes and walk away. I purse my lips and move them side to side. "I meant, I can't dance in these pants."

"Why didn't you just say that, silly?" Her eyes twinkle as her hips sway to the music still playing in her head.

I bop her on the end of her button nose. "Why don't you go practice, and I'll be in after I get a report from Maggie and change my clothes?"

Her gaze shoots to Maggie's before bouncing back to mine. The guilty look she tries to disguise tells me the console may not be on for much longer tonight. My suspicions are confirmed when she gives me a rushed thumbs up and bolts back to the game room, her braid trailing behind her like a dark flag.

I strain my ears listening for the music of her favorite game before walking into the kitchen where Maggie stands brushing butter across fat pieces of bread. A huge salad sits to her right on the corner of the counter, and I snag a piece of hard-boiled egg and toss it into my mouth in the shadow of Maggie's laser stare.

She pushes a puff through her nose and shakes her head. "Between you and that daughter of yours, I'm inching toward a slow, painful death."

I shrug my shoulders and beam at her before grabbing a beer from the fridge, popping the top on the corner of the counter—a party trick leftover from my college days—while suffering through a glare from Maggie. I take a pull from my bottle as I lean back against the island.

"Don't you dare let your daughter see you do that! Knowing her, she'll try it on everything with a top, and who do you think will be the one to pick up the resulting mess on the floor. Not to mention, she could seriously hurt herself."

I know she's right, and her words make me feel like a stupid teenager instead of a cardiac surgeon and a father who knows better. "Sorry. I forget my habits aren't always the most child-friendly."

She nods as she arranges the buttered bread on a pan before sliding it into the oven. She sets a timer, then turns and pins me with a hard look. "What's going on? You never drink beer when Sedona is around."

I tip my bottle and take a sip letting the crisp coolness slide down my throat before I jump into my questions and beg for her help. I've known Maggie for a long time, and a little voice at the back of my brain tells me she's going to have a heyday with this conversation.

I start by telling her about Sedona's nightmare last night. Even though she lives in my house, her living quarters are totally separate from ours so she can maintain her privacy and feel like she has her own space. It's been that way since she started and it works well for us, especially if an emergency occurs and I'm called back to the hospital in the middle of the night.

Maggie listens while she busies her hands with tidying the counters, stirring the spaghetti sauce, and setting the table. She's like me, always needing to be in motion so she can process and think. It's what makes us masters at multi-tasking. When I'm done telling her about Sedona, Maggie looks at and me and asks what I think could have set her off. I honestly can't say and, though she considers it, neither can she.

"That may explain the tantrum she threw when I picked her up from camp today. She wanted to stop for an ice cream cone. When I told her no, she screamed that her mom would let her get one before she burst into tears. I had to pull the car over to the side of the road and wait for her to calm down. I hadn't been back on the road more than ten minutes before I looked back and she was sound asleep in her booster seat." I take another drink as she continues. "It makes sense. Her mom was skirting around her subconscious last night and floated to the surface today."

Maggie walks around the edge of the island and stops in front of me waiting until I meet her warm, golden gaze. "I know you avoid talking about it, but maybe it's time to consider making some changes. Sedona's getting older, and she's mature enough to see this arrangement isn't right. Not to mention, the suffocating tension that blankets this house when *she's* here."

I fix my stare to the floor and shake my head, not willing to voice the doubts I keep packed in the recesses of my soul. Letting go. Giving up. Closing the door. Those are all fears keeping me rooted in one place, not ready to move on, but not willing to return to the past. My thoughts are not in a place to think about this today, but I know my avoidance cannot be stretched much longer.

I look up, meeting Maggie's expectant stare, "I promise to consider your words. Today hasn't been my best day, and I can't think about or entertain those decisions right now."

She wipes her hands on the front of her apron and turns to check the bread in the oven before shutting the door and resetting the timer. She's voiced her concerns, leaving them at my feet, until I'm ready to pick them up. It's a trait I admire and appreciate, and one I wish my mom was capable of emulating.

"There is something else I wanted to run by you, if you don't mind?"

She walks across the kitchen and takes a seat at the table set with dishes and flatware for tonight's feast.

She taps the plate at the head of the table, "Why don't you have a seat and share what else is on your mind?"

I cross the floor and sink into the indicated chair before filling my mouth with oxygen and blowing it through my lips. The goofy sound is loud as it fills the silent kitchen. "I believe I made a terrible mistake at work, and I'm not sure how to fix it."

Her horrified eyes cut to mine, and I realize she's incorrectly assumed I've made a medical oversight. My words rush to calm her fears, "It has nothing to do with a medical decision or patient."

Her eyes narrow in confusion before she opens her mouth. "If it doesn't have anything to do with that, then what is it?"

"Let me start by saying, I didn't hurt anyone. Maybe just made someone a little mad." I think about the folded sticky note in my pocket. "Ok, I think the person might be a lot upset. In my defense, I never imagined my need for cleanliness and order would get me into trouble."

Maggie is silent, though confusion still wrinkles the lines on her face.

"Have you ever heard of something called Tuppermail?"

"Tuppermail? No. Then again, I can't keep up with all the new technology of the younger generations. What is it?"

"I think it's a basic plastic box with a lid."

Her eyes widen, and she laughs. Not a simple laugh and done. She roars to the point of tears. "That's Tupperware, not tuppermail."

"Yeah, Tupperware." I nod my head, though I fail to see the humor. "What is it?"

"Oh, honey, it's God's gift to all kitchen enthusiasts. It wears like iron, can be washed in the dishwasher, has a lifetime warranty, and is expensive as hell. But, what does Tupperware have to do with your mistake?"

I lift my palm and rub the back of my neck. Understanding for Dr. Robert's ire sinks in, and I exhale on an embarrassed sigh. "I found one in the locker room yesterday. When I saw it was empty, with just a few crumbs stuck to the bottom, I threw the container away."

Maggie brings her hand to her chest, the color drains from

her face, and the look of horror painted across her features has me contemplating if I should reach out and check her pulse. "Mitchell, tell me you didn't."

I pull in a breath and let it out slowly. "I did. It seems I've been branded a Tupperware thief by Dr. Roberts, who I've never heard of before by the way."

I pull the note from my pocket and hand it over.

She reads it and snorts. "Sounds like you've got some explaining to do. I'd start by offering to replace the container."

"Maybe I should make a run to the store before I call this doctor's number."

Maggie lays her hand over mine and gives a squeeze. "Oh, Mitchell, this isn't something you're going to find at a big box store. I'd suggest you start with the Internet, maybe a re-sale or auction site. And be prepared to pay quite a bit of your hard-earned money if the one you threw away was a retired style or color."

Little did I know how much money would end up leaving my wallet before I had a replacement in my hand. I think I could have fed a small village in Africa for less.

28

HOPE

I READ THE LETTER AGAIN, HOPING MY TIRED EYES ARE SEEING things, but knowing I saw it correctly the first time.

Damn. I hadn't realized my first rotation was nearly done. I've enjoyed Dr. Harris's way of mentoring. He is neither condescending nor egotistical. He values my opinion and is quick with his praise, though he doesn't pull any punches with his criticisms. Overall, I couldn't have asked for a better first rotation. Like all good things, my time is almost over, and I am set to start my next rotation.

Nothing like jumping from a bubbling brook into the fiery pits of Hell. I've heard the whispers and seen the cringes on the faces of my fellow residents whenever his name is mentioned. Dr. Anderson is an excellent cardiothoracic surgeon—who is also quite young—but he is known around the hospital as Prickly Pete because of his difficult personality.

To be honest, I've made a conscious effort to avoid gossip, preferring to draw my own conclusions once I meet him. I throw the letter next to my plate and pick up my fork. There isn't anything I can do about my assignment except show up on time and be the best kick-ass resident I can be.

I finish my dinner, placing my dish in the sink before returning to the table to finish my glass of wine. I don't have one often simply because I don't enjoy drinking alone. Joe and I had often shared a glass or two on the rare nights he'd get home before I'd been in bed. I've found the previous satisfaction I'd taken in drinking had been tied more to connecting with Joe than enjoying the wine itself.

I stare at the window facing my backyard. With the darkness, my reflection is the only thing I can see clearly in the glass. It's been two weeks since my Tupperware disappeared, and I'm starting to think it's gone for good. I'd berated myself more than once for using a container that held so much nostalgia.

My mom and I didn't have a lot of money, but she had been obsessed with Tupperware. Even though she couldn't afford it straight from a consultant, she'd spent hours scouring garage sales looking for the elusive plastic. I can still hear her "hoot" of triumph and her elation when she'd find a complete set—container and lid—for a fraction of what it would have cost new. The white bottom with orange lid had been the last one she'd bought just a year before she'd died. It's a hard piece of plastic to most, yet to me, it had represented my mom and her triumphant smile.

My phone buzzes, making little jumps across the table where it sits next to my dinner plate. Granted the late hour makes it more a late-night snack versus dinner, but missing lunch while standing in one place for over ten hours today had made me ravenous.

My gut clenches as my mind jumps to Mr. Lenox. He'd come through the surgery and had already been out of recovery by the time I left the hospital. He'd seemed to be doing well, but his recovery still hung in a precarious balance. My eyes close briefly before I pick up my phone.

The notification shows an unfamiliar, but local, number.

Considering so few people have my number, I figure it's a tele-marketer, but I check just in case it's from the hospital. I open my app and read the attached text.

Unknown: I have something you lost. I believe you offered a trade?

What? Definitely not from the hospital. I read it a second time, and I'm a little creeped out.

Me: I think you have the wrong number.

Three minutes pass before a response pings. The text field is empty, but the attached picture makes my eyes mist. Staring at me from its perch on the side of a white countertop is my orange and white Tupperware container.

Me: You have it? Is it okay?

I send my response, belatedly, realizing I'm talking about a plastic container.

Unknown: I do. Will you be at the hospital tomorrow?

I take a look at my watch and realize I need to clarify.

Me: Do you mean today (Friday)?

Unknown: Yeah, sorry. I guess it's later than I thought.

I debate my response. I don't know anything about this person other than he or she is a thief with a lazy conscience—considering it's been two weeks—and he or she probably works on the surgical floor at the hospital.

Me: No. I'll be at the hospital again on Sunday.

Unknown: Monday morning possibly?

Yeah, I was already dreading Monday morning and the beginning of my new rotation.

Me: Meet in the surgical break/locker room at 5:30 a.m.?

Unknown: Works for me. See you then.

I enter a reminder for my Monday morning meeting with the Tupperware Thief before taking the final swallow of my wine.

As I'm getting ready for bed, I realize the kleptomaniac who stole my container didn't even have the decency to apologize.

29

MITCHELL

I PULL INTO THE LOT AND SLAM ON MY BRAKES NOTICING AT the last second that a black SUV is parked in my favorite spot.

I'd been distracted thinking about the last two days and the stress caused by the conflict between the logic of my brain and the guilt on my heart. Even Sedona, who had looked forward to these weekends in the past, seemed especially eager to have Maggie return last night. After a couple of random, near accidents between Saturday and Sunday, I am embarrassed to admit I'm happy to have the two days behind us.

I'm also fortunate Tess, my Tesla X, has a faster response time than its driver or else I'd probably be buying the owner of the black SUV a new bumper. Though I could probably buy five new bumpers for the price I paid for the hunk of plastic sitting in my passenger seat.

I'd made the mistake of griping about the cost to Maggie, who laughed and pointed a finger at me asking when had I not complained about spending money. She isn't wrong, but she isn't entirely correct either. I have monthly expenses that would make most people's hearts stutter, not to mention the one expense draining nearly a third of my annual earnings.

Not that I'm complaining because that's what you do for family.

I circle the lot and find another spot two rows over from the SUV. I park, grab the container, and walk on quick feet, so I'm not late for my meeting. A reminder chirps on my phone, and I pull it from my pocket.

Shit.

I'd forgotten about the resident starting a rotation with me this morning. Having a resident is something I often manage to avoid, though I've gotten pulled in once or twice before. I slide my phone back into my pocket trying to think of random assignments I can give my resident to assess his ability levels before inviting him into my operating room.

I am a perfectionist and meticulous to a fault, and I don't tolerate mediocrity. Pushing the resident from my mind, for the time being, I enter the side entrance stopping at my office to drop off my coat and laptop before heading to the locker room.

As I walk down the hallway, I hear a low buzzing from multiple voices all laughing and talking at once. There was a time when my voice would have been the one giving a play-by-play of my weekend activities and shocking my colleagues with some of my more adventuresome dares.

Those days are a far cry from my current situation, and I'll admit, but only to myself, I miss the camaraderie and the feeling of belonging. My brain screams I can have those feelings again, while my heart points out the cost of allowing others to know what I try so valiantly to protect.

If I could figure out how to straddle the two, I'd do it. Or at least I'd consider it. Maybe Maggie and Dan are right. I need to make some tough decisions and move the fuck on.

I cross the threshold of the break room, and all conversation ceases. They stare at me, their mouths open and eyes wide like I'm the grim reaper here to claim their souls. I give them a tight nod as their eyes bounce, passing a silent discussion around the small circle. Without a word to their companions or me, each one stands and slinks out of the room before I take a seat at the table.

Seeing the room has emptied, I check my watch and see Dr. Roberts is one minute from being late, and my annoyance rises. I'm left to wait with nothing to occupy my time except for thoughts of the weekend.

This had been the first time I'd seen indecision and confusion mar my daughter's face. She is a people pleaser. She doesn't want to disappoint me, so she pushes her discomfort aside and willingly accepts my repeated efforts to a force a relationship that is never going to develop the way I've hoped. Sedona knows it, Maggie knows it, and deep down, I know it, though I let my guilt suffocate my ability to admit what needs to be done.

Disturbed and lost in my thoughts, I don't hear another person enter the room until her voice burrows into the dark crevices of my brain. Something tells me I've heard it before, though its smooth cadence fails to spark a specific memory.

"Two weeks. Your conscience is either really quiet or you have a weird fetish for vintage Tupperware. Neither scenario is attractive, I might add."

Since she's standing behind me, I don't know if she's smiling, though I swear I hear a smirk in her voice.

I shake my head thinking of the odyssey I've traveled to return such an innocuous-looking hunk of plastic. "I don't think you'd believe me if I told you the whole story."

I hear the whir of the coffee machine before she speaks. "To be honest, it's the sentimental value more than the box itself. It was my mom's." Her voice lowers like the memory has stolen the strength of her voice. "She used to collect them from yard sales and would be so damn excited she couldn't wait to get home and show me her find."

I pull my chin to my chest debating if I should tell her the Tupperware sitting in front of me never belonged to her mom. Her next words have me swallowing down my admission.

"That one there. It's the last one she bought before she died. When I use it, it's like I can feel her smile of satisfaction. It's stupid, but it's my favorite simply for that reason."

She moves around the table and takes a seat across from me. My jaw drops, and my eyes widen as I fail to keep the surprise from my face.

Her reaction mirrors mine as she brings her hand to her mouth.

"Hope? What are you doing here?" I look down in front of me and amend my question. "Other than claiming your mom's treasure."

No sound leaves her lips as she lowers her hand to her cup as her crystal blue gaze stays locked on mine. She shakes her head like I'm a memory she's trying to erase from her vision.

"Mitchell?" Her lips mouth "Anderson" though no sound rolls from her tongue. Her eyes slide shut, and I allow my own to search her face looking for clues of where she's been, why she's here, and what's happened in her life.

Damn. It's been four years since I heard her utter my name, and I can't contain the spark of excitement traveling down my spine. The last time I saw her a wedding ring kept my mind from spinning fantasies my dick was more than willing to indulge. My eyes drop to her bare fingers where they curl around her coffee cup. The huge diamond of four years ago is absent as well as any indication it's been recently removed from her finger. My brain feels like it's been wiped clean, which is why the inane question bursts from my lips without permissive thought. "Been on any airplanes lately?"

Her eyes sparkle as she takes a drink then chuckles. "Uh, no. Can't say I have." Her eyes drift over my shoulder, though I know her thoughts are no longer in this room. "I haven't been on a plane in four years."

She returns her eyes to mine, and I try to ignore the pleasure her presence gives me. She'd tried, unsuccessfully, to hide her anxiousness beneath an air of sophistication on the flight, but I'd glimpsed a sliver of it and provided a distraction in occupying both her mind and my own.

She had been an enigma. Beautiful on the outside, yet I'd sensed unrest simmering beneath her surface. I'd be lying if I said I didn't wish my life was as uncomplicated as it had been then. What had seemed difficult at the time had been a cakewalk compared to the position I sit in today.

My brain sifts through my memories, like I'm thumbing through my contacts, searching for her last name, yet I come up blank. *Did I ever know her last name?*

"I can't believe I'm sitting across from the guy who suffered a UNE."

Her smile is contagious, and I shake my head to hide the embarrassing warmth creeping across my cheeks. Though an entire lecture hall of colleagues had witnessed my unfortunate mishap, I'd never shared the story with anyone else.

"Please tell me you're not obsessed with social media sharing, and I won't one day read my story on some random website."

Her smile falls, her face turns serious, and my stomach rolls. She looks left then right as she leans forward. "You didn't tell me it was supposed to be a secret." Her eyes widen, and I scrub a hand down my face missing the sneaky grin that tips her lips. "Don't worry, I kept it one."

A low chuckle rumbles from my chest, and I shake my head. I catch her eyes and point across the table. "And I thank you for keeping it that way."

"Not my story to tell." She lifts her shoulders letting them fall before continuing. "I don't know about you, but I don't gain satisfaction by spreading gossip. Even when a story is as entertaining as yours."

She glances at the watch on her wrist before tilting her head to the Tupperware container still sitting in front of my chair. "Thank you for returning it."

I start to slide the box toward her but stop before it makes it halfway across the table. "If I remember correctly, you mentioned a trade?"

She lifts her thumb to her mouth like she's going to bite the nail before dropping her hand and biting her lip instead. "That was more than two weeks ago. The offer already expired."

I lift up and pull the yellow sticky note from the pocket of my scrubs. "Unless it's written in invisible ink, I don't see any expiration dates."

She drums her fingertips on the table before giving me a smile sweeter than cotton candy. "Well, I don't want to be accused of reneging."

"Excellent." My face splits into a wide grin.

"Do you have any allergies I should be aware of? Likes? Dislikes? I wouldn't want to provide a sub-par trade."

Something tells me she's not in the habit of delivering sub-par anything. I glance at my watch, noting my new resident will most likely be at my office door within the next ten minutes.

I rise and pick up the Tupperware walking slowly around to her chair. I feel her eyes track my movement, and my body responds by straightening my posture allowing me to tower over her by another half inch when I stop next to her chair.

She tips her head to look at me as I extend the box. She grasps it brushing my hand in the process. I'm not sure if she feels the current of energy as her skin slides over mine, but I sure as hell do.

I swallow my reaction, hiding it from her inquisitive eyes. My throat is dry lending my voice a husky quality as soon as I open my mouth. "Seeing you again has been one heck of a surprise, but it's been a pleasure, Hope. It's a pity I'll forever be branded a thief in your mind." I lick my lips and shoot her a grin as she stands. "Honestly, I think I prefer it to UNE sufferer though." I glance at my watch. "I've got a resident to meet, so I've got to run. Maybe we can catch up over coffee downstairs sometime? You can tell me the story of how you ended up here."

I know I don't imagine the look of sadness passing over her face before she smiles and nods. "How do you feel about a ten-minute chat each morning?"

My skin warms in response to her suggestion. This meeting is turning out to be more interesting than I'd originally expected, and a silent curse floats through my head for the resident who's pulling me away from standing here with her for another hour. We both walk into the hallway, though I search for a way to stall my departure.

"Sounds great, but I'm usually in surgery by six or seven." I slide my jaw to the side in an exaggerated cringe and wait for her to amend her offer.

She gives me a big smile and shoots me a wink that stabs me right in the gut. "I'll double-check my schedule for the next couple of months to make sure, but I'm pretty confident the timing will work perfectly."

This woman spells trouble for me. "Great, sounds like a plan. You have my number…if you didn't delete it."

"Nah, I didn't delete. It's saved as T Thief, though I may need to make a minor change considering the circumstances."

I give her a wide grin. "I appreciate graduating from Thief to Mitchell."

"Oh. I'm afraid anything less than Dr. Anderson may be disrespectful."

"Why is that?"

She looks at her watch and pushes air out of her lungs.

"Because as of one minute ago, I'm officially your new surgical resident for the next two months."

My smile disappears from my lips, and I barely manage to hold back my curse though my brain hears it loud and clear.

Shit.

She's a resident.

More accurately, *my* resident.

I'm technically her boss for the next eight weeks.

I run my hand through my hair and turn toward my office as my dick's vehement "NO!" pulses through my blood.

30

MITCHELL

I STIFLE A YAWN, THANKFUL MY MASK COVERS THE MAJORITY OF the lines of fatigue painted across my face.

"Water."

A straw is immediately pushed to the side of my mouth allowing me to drink without breaking my focus on the table in front of me. My eyes are tired, and my brain is screaming for a break, but there's nothing I can do outside of stepping aside and letting Dr. Roberts finish the procedure. I've pushed through worse fatigue, and I'm nearly done anyway.

Hope isn't used to be being an observer, and Dr. Harris spoiled her by permitting her to do far more than my comfort level has allowed. She does well to keep her frustrations and impatience from bubbling to the surface, but I've come to recognize the set of her jaw or the tightness in her smile telling me she is most likely screaming at me in her head.

I shift my eyes to where she's standing across the table. Her focus is so intense, I don't think a bomb would startle her. With her patience and ability to think quickly coupled with the compassionate way she handles patient's questions, she's proven to be one of the best residents in the surgical program.

I remove the clamp from the carotid artery and nod to the nurse letting her know I'm finished. Hope's eyes shift to mine, and I tilt my head toward the table. "Think you can finish from here, Dr. Roberts?"

I catch her surprise in the slight uptick of her eyebrows before spying the wrinkles at the sides of her eyes which tell me her mask is concealing a satisfied smile. I step back and watch as she moves forward directing the team before settling in.

Thirty minutes pass before I hear her request for roll call. While I'd felt like I was asleep on my feet before I'd relinquished control, her skill had arrested my attention, and I'd become mesmerized by the movement of her hands and the confidence of her words as she spoke with the team. She'd bantered back and forth inquiring about their families while creating the most precise stitches I'd ever seen. I hate to admit it, but I could learn a thing or two myself from Dr. Roberts.

She is an excellent doctor, not to mention a beautiful woman whose personality blurs the proverbial line I've drawn in the mentor/mentee sand. It's been five weeks since we started working together, and my ability to separate my romantic and professional interests becomes more difficult by the day.

I've read through the Human Resources manual twice making sure I'll have the green light to pursue her as soon as her rotation with me is completed. I feel like I'm a damn teenager waiting for the girl I like to break up with her boyfriend, so I have a chance to sweep her off her feet.

My eyes are continually searching her for clues. Ones that may give me insight into who she is on a personal level even though she holds her cards firmly against her chest. I'm like a man in the desert searching for water, and she's the oasis, elusive and right on the edge of my vision just out of reach. I know she's been married, or maybe still is, yet she never mentions her husband or her home life other than her sprin-kled comments for her love of baking.

Speaking of which, it's a new month which means I'm due my promised batch of baked goods. She wasn't exaggerating when she said she could bake.

Embarrassing as it is to admit, I'd devoured the chocolate coconut crunch cookies she'd made the week after I returned her Tupperware. I'd taken a bite of a cookie the size of my palm as I'd pulled out of the parking lot, and I'd put away six by the time I hit the button for my garage door. Needless to say, I'd spent an extra hour on the treadmill that evening deter-mined to work off at least half of the calories so I could partake in a couple more cookies the next day.

I'd been surprised when she'd delivered them in the same Tupperware container that started our exchange. When I'd raised an eyebrow at her, she'd shrugged and said she knew how to find me if I didn't bring it back. Little did she know, I treated the hunk of plastic the same as I did my Tesla consid-ering the exorbitant amount of money I'd shelled out to beat TUpp4Me in a vicious bidding war. I'd silently questioned if Maggie was TUpp4Me until I'd nonchalantly mentioned what happened, and she laughed until tears streamed down her face saying she was disappointed she hadn't thought to do it herself.

I push through the scrub room doors and pull my mask from my face. Dr. Roberts is hot on my heels as she steps to the sink to scrub out. She grabs two packages of soap, nudging one my way before beginning her routine. Every surgeon has one, and I've noticed hers differs only slightly from mine.

"Nice work, Dr. Roberts."

She tilts her head at me and continues scrubbing. Her lips tip in a half-smile. "Thanks, Dr. Anderson." She waits for a beat. "Can I ask you a question?"

I figure she's going to ask me why I let her close or why I

changed my technique midway through the surgery, so I'm surprised when the next words fall from her mouth.

"Do you like vanilla?"

I stop the motion of my hands. For a split second, my brain sprints to the edge of the cliff that rises above the sea of my dirty thoughts. It peaks over the side and spies my cock doing the backstroke in a sea of vanilla. I swallow and push my waist against the edge of the sink to hide the erection I feel creeping up the inside of my boxer briefs. "Uh." I stifle a cough, and my voice comes out in a strangled whisper. "Could you be more specific?"

Finished, she grabs a towel and stands up straight. I feel the path of her gaze as it travels over my face. "Do you like the taste of vanilla?"

My cock winks and shoots my brain a high five. I school my features knowing I cannot conceal the redness racing across my cheeks in reaction to the erotic path of my thoughts. "Like vanilla cake? Ice cream? That sort of thing?"

She glances at me for a second before a smile stretches across her mouth in slow motion. "Great." Though I wait expectantly, the single word is the only one that comes from her mouth.

When she doesn't offer more, I step away from the sink, crowding her space as I reach around her head and grab a towel. She lifts her lashes and meets my stare as I take my time wiping my hands before speaking. Her thoughts are elsewhere as she drops her eyes to focus on my lips.

"Is there a point to your question, Dr. Roberts?"

Her gaze shoots back to mine, and I catch a glimpse of her embarrassment before she clears her throat and speaks, though her voice is tinted with a thickness not normally present.

"I need to treat you to another set of goods." Her eyes widen a fraction before amending. "I need to bake you. Bake for you."

I witness the pink as it glides across her cheek like the dawn of a sunrise. Her nostrils flare, but she doesn't break eye contact as we share a wordless conversation.

I turn, throw my used towel in the receptacle, and walk to the door. With my hip against the door, I glance over my shoulder pinning her with the heat of my emerald scrutiny. "While I do like vanilla, given the option, the surprise of spice feeds my craving way better. Just in case it makes a difference." I give her a wink and push through the door.

The wink.

The innuendo.

The heated stare.

Her blush.

Her husky voice.

The line is drawn in the sand.

Something tells me we've just pole-vaulted beyond the hospital's definition of professional, and I couldn't be more pleased.

———

AFTER MR. LOPEZ's surgery and my conversation with Hope, I feel energized. I spend the rest of the day and part of my evening holed up in my office answering emails, reviewing consult requests, and clearing shit from my desk so I can actually see the surface.

I go nuts when things aren't in their proper place at home, but my office is one corner of heaven where my life still feels like my own. I electronically sign my final order for the day and log off my computer before standing and stretching the fatigue from my back.

I lock my office and walk to my car. A glance at my watch tells me I spent way more time in the rabbit hole of my office than I'd planned. I need to call Maggie as soon as I get in the car. Sedona will throw a fit if I'm not home by the time she goes to bed, and I hope the traffic is light because I'm cutting it close. I unlock my vehicle and slide in the driver seat, giving a command to call Maggie as I back out of the space.

"Long day, I take it?" True to Maggie's personality, she dives right in instead of answering with the customary "hello."

"Yeah. Sorry. Papers were threatening to swallow my desk. It took a bit longer than I expected. How's my girl?"

"Today's been a good day. We already had dinner. You'll have to be the one to explain why you weren't here for Pizza Night. I saved you a few slices, though your daughter ate five by herself tonight. I may need to make an extra pizza from now on."

I grin. Sedona's always been able to pack away food as long as she's not upset about something. Hearing she put down five pieces alleviates some of the worry sitting on my heart lately.

"Taking after me, I guess."

Maggie chuckles. "You can say that again. I'll read her a story, and you can slide in and give her a kiss when you get home. You remember your appointment tomorrow, right?"

I exhale. No. I didn't remember. My brain's form of self-preservation, maybe?

"Nine o'clock. You're still available to watch Sedona?"

"It's on my calendar. I figured you may need all day, so I'm taking her to the zoo."

"Thanks, Maggie. I'll be home in about thirty."

I hang up, and my mind drifts to the appointment I'll be sitting at in a little over twelve hours. I have no idea if I'm doing the right thing, but I rationalize I don't have to make any decisions tomorrow, though I don't know how much longer I can wait to move forward.

Sedona has had three nightmares in the past two weeks, and I'm both physically and mentally exhausted from the stress of worrying she's slowly gaining momentum for a relapse.

The year after the incident was hell. Having no choice, I moved her from the home and daycare she loved, which started a chain reaction of night terrors. Coupled with selective mutism, her loss of appetite, her twice-weekly therapy appointments, finding a care facility, and completing my fellowship, I nearly buckled under the pressure. My parents had tried to help, but I'd been bitter and riddled with guilt for the role I felt I'd played in throwing our lives into turmoil. Once I found Maggie, I was finally able to hold my head above water and get our lives on track. Whoever said God doesn't give you more than you can handle must have thought I had a clone to hold half of my burden.

I'd finally broken down and talked to Maggie last week just before she'd left. She always makes herself scarce on the third weekend of the month, and I can't really blame her. On those weekends, the house feels like a balloon filling with stress to the point of bursting. I can feel it, and if Sedona's recent nightmares are anything to go by, she is also feeling the burden.

Maggie hadn't pulled any punches, not that I thought she would. "You've buried your head in the sand far too long, Mitchell. You cannot continually expose your daughter to a virtual stranger and expect her to understand her role. You know what needs to be done. It will be better for Sedona and better for you. Your life is sitting in limbo. You don't have to cut ties, but you do need to make changes, set boundaries, let her know you aren't the person she thinks you are. It's not good for any of you."

I pull into the garage and lower the door before stepping from my vehicle. I'm bone-tired and scared to death of the decisions I can no longer avoid.

I kick off my shoes and drop my crap at the door before heading toward Sedona's room. I stop in the doorway, careful not to make a sound, while I take in the scene. Maggie is sitting in the rocking chair in the corner reading one of her favorite thriller novels while Sedona stares at the ceiling and hums softly to herself like she does when she desperately wants to stay awake.

I cross the threshold, my feet finding the squeak in the wooden floorboards. "Hi, princess."

Maggie stands from her seat and tiptoes from the room, while Sedona's head lolls toward the doorway. She lifts her arms straight in the air, the universal sign for a hug, as I approach her bed. My girl is so exhausted, she doesn't have the energy to lift her little body from her pillow. I bend down and wrap her in a hug, placing a kiss on the top of her head, before laying her back down in her bed. "I love you to the moon."

A lopsided grin appears on one side of her face, and her voice is breathy and laced with fatigue. "I love you to the moon and back, Daddy."

I lean forward and brush my lips across her forehead before turning out the bedside lamp and leaving her room.

Tomorrow's meeting, and what it means for our little family, hangs like a noose around my neck. I want to give my daughter the world, but to do so, I'll have to remove the part that at one time *was* her world.

31

MITCHELL

I WALK INTO MY KITCHEN AND GRAB A BEER FROM THE refrigerator before making my way to the container of two dozen vanilla cupcakes topped with clouds of chocolate frosting laced with some kind of spice. If I were a betting man, I'd say it's jalapeño, but who puts spicy pepper in chocolate? The mere thought of it sounds nasty.

I lift the lid and notice someone's swiped one since dinnertime. Maggie would be my guess because my princess doesn't like anything spicy. She would have broadcast her gag throughout the house if one dab of the frosting touched her tongue.

I grab a paper towel before pulling a sweet confection from its neatly arranged friends. Hope had snuck into my office at some point today leaving me the Tupperware full of baked heaven and a note written in her precise dark letters.

M -
Since we work together and
you like spice, and I like vanilla,
I thought I'd mix the two. I think

it's a winning combination.
-H
P.S. I know where to find you. Return the
Tupperware and no one gets hurt.

I'm not going to lie; I went full girl-mode and analyzed the shit out of her note. Stuck in my own head, I hadn't heard Maggie when she'd come into the kitchen after I'd gotten home from work and read the note while peering over my shoulder.

Worst mistake I've ever made. She's been hounding me since dinner asking who H is and why she's baking me cupcakes.

Luckily, she knows not to question me in front of Sedona, but I know she's not going to let it go until I give her the truth, or a truncated version of it. I figure I'll wait a few days and see if it slips her mind, though I know I'd have a better chance of Sedona eating an entire plate of peas than Maggie forgetting something to do with my personal life.

I lick a path through the chocolate frosting and relish the slight burn it leaves on my tongue as I swallow it down. Since I'm by myself, I let my thoughts wander as I continue eating. *When she says she likes vanilla, is she being coy or literal? Are the flavors a winning combination, or does she think we are a winning combination?* Damn. I sound like a teenage girl.

Fourteen more days.

She's my resident for two more weeks.

I'll finally be able to avoid the torture of standing across from her in surgery fantasizing about the color of her panties and what she looks like under those panties. I don't know how I've made it this long without accidentally saying something that could get me reprimanded for sexual harassment or at the very least make her uncomfortable. The day last week after Mr. Lopez's surgery was the closest we've come to a sexually-charged exchange, though that conversation could have been a fluke of innuendo.

My phone sits on the edge of my counter. I know I shouldn't engage, but I can't stop my fingers from sliding toward the screen and tapping out a quick text to thank her for the cupcakes.

Me: You're in my mouth right now. Thank you.

I hit send before proofreading the text, and my eyes practically bug out of my head when I read what I sent.

I type out a correction as fast as possible, but the "read" receipt pops up on my screen before I have a chance to send the revision. My fingers fly across the screen, and I jab my thumb on the send button.

Me: Damn. Autocorrect forgot a word.

Me: Your tits are in my mouth right now.

NO! Abort. Fuck you autocorrect. The read receipt shows, and I practically throw my phone against the wall. My face feels like it's on fire. My phone dings indicating an incoming message, and I slap my thigh in frustration.

Hope: What???

Me: TREATS!

Me: Your treats are in my mouth right now.

Me: They are delicious. Thank you.

I stare a hole in my screen waiting for any type of response.

At this point, I'm not sure if she's screenshotting the exchange as evidence for Human Resources or laughing because she knows autocorrect can be a little bitch.

The dots appear at the bottom of the message thread before disappearing and reappearing thirty seconds later.

Hope: I can barely type.

Hope: I'm laughing so hard, tears are dripping onto my phone screen.

Hope: First, the UNE story, now this. What's next? A story about streaking the quad at college?

Little does she know, she's just plucked another embarrassing tidbit from the overflowing bucket called *The Stupid Shit Mitchell Did in College*.

A chuckle falls out of my mouth, and my heart rate takes a spike north at her cheeky response. Dr. Anderson will be keeping his job and survive to perform another surgery. Thank you, Jesus.

I throw my paper towel and cupcake wrapper in the garbage and head to my cave. With dark grey walls and dark furniture, it's nearly pitch black when I drop to the couch after choosing to leave the switch off. The only light in the room is the glow of my screen. I stare at her messages for a good five minutes before I shoot her another text.

Me: I'm bored. Wanna play a game?

Hope: Depends. You may need to disable your autocorrect to preserve your dignity. LOL

Hope is saucy, and I like it. Dr. Roberts is cordial and polite but also serious and strictly professional.

Me: It's simple. I name a place, and you tell me two lies and one truth about the place. I have to guess the truth. Then we'll switch.

Hope: Sounds innocuous enough.

Who uses words like innocuous in everyday speech, let alone in a text? I smile. Hope is a mystery, and I'm about to go Inspector Gadget on her ass.

Me: The gym.

After about a minute, dots bounce across my screen as I wait for her truth.

Hope: 1. I peed my pants while lifting a ten-pound weight. 2. I've never been a member of a gym. 3. I witnessed a guy crush his 'man parts' when he did a chest press without a spotter.

My eyebrows raise to my hairline when I read her response. With the shape her body's in, she's definitely been a gym member. Seeing a guy crush his nut sack is just too painful to imagine. Leaving me with pee as the truth.

Me: 1. Truth 2. Lie 3. Lie

Hope: Nope.

Hope: My turn.

Me: Wait. Which one was the truth?

Hope: That wasn't part of your rules. Sorry :)

Damn. She's smart with a dash of spice just like her delicious cupcakes.

Hope: My turn. Grocery store.

I rack my brain to come up with three things that will be impossible to figure out.

Me: 1. I worked in a grocery store as a bagger when I was a teenager. 2. I saw a mom rip open a box of diapers and change her infant in a shopping cart. 3. I cut coupons and only go on Coupon Tuesdays.

Hope: 1. Truth. 2. Lie. 3. Lie

Me: Damn. How did you guess?

Hope: Moms always have a diaper with them whether it's in their pocket, their purse, or the diaper bag, and it's Coupon Monday, not Coupon Tuesday.

Me: You're good.

Hope: Thank you.

Me: Hospital

Hope: 1. I get butterflies before every surgery.

2. It took me more than four years to finish medical school. 3. I hate my mentor.

Me: This one's easy. 1. Truth 2. Lie. 3. Lie.

Hope: Nope, and you're horrible at this game.

Me: Did it take you more than four years to finish medical school?

Hope: Yes. I requested emergency leave after my third year. When I returned, I got stuck re-doing some of the coursework.

Me: That sucks. Why'd you have to do that?

Hope: Different school, different requirements.

Me: No. Why'd you have to leave and go back?

Five minutes pass and my phone rests silently on my thigh. My mind flips through the various reasons why she'd leave after three years of medical school, and none are positive. I've exposed a nerve I didn't mean to uncover, and now I feel like I've shot this conversation to shreds.

Me: Never mind. I don't need to know.

Hope: It's okay. It's just tied to times I'd rather not think about.

Ten minutes pass and I know I've killed the banter we had

going. I pray my mistake didn't peel a scab and leave an old wound open to the maggots of negative memories.

Me: See you at 5:30 a.m. to discuss tomorrow's surgeries. Maybe, I'll even let you do more than assist.

Hope: I'll be there, and yeah, right. I won't hold my breath.

Her response quiets my worries. Hope is a professional. I'm fairly certain she'll avoid discussing anything about tonight's messages. I need to convince my brain, both north and south, to be just as professional, and I'll have no problems making it through the final two weeks of her rotation.

32

HOPE

"Last day with Anderson the Prick tomorrow?"

Cameron busies himself with setting the table, swiping a cucumber from the bowl of salad I'm preparing for Spaghetti Sunday, though it's actually a Thursday. Cameron has to work on Sunday, so we've moved it to Thursday instead of canceling it.

"Be nice. He's not that bad you know."

"If you say so, my friend. And I chose the nicest nickname of the bunch, by the way."

He winks and swipes another cucumber before I manage to slap his hand away from my finished masterpiece.

"Word on the floor is you've been cheating on me by baking for someone else." He pins me with a serious stare. "Why is the guy always the last to know? I expected more from you."

I roll my eyes and grab the Italian dressing from the refrigerator and a bag of croutons from the pantry and place them in the middle of the table. The sauce has five more minutes to simmer, and I'm suddenly intent on watching it every second of the final minutes.

"Becky on the fourth floor said she saw you walking in a couple of weeks ago with a Tupperware container, but instead of putting it in the break room like you've done in the past, she saw you slip into Dr. Anderson's office and emerge *without* the plastic in question."

I turn from where I'm stirring the sauce at the stove as sarcasm gathers at the tip of my tongue. "Thank you, Colonel Mustard, are you sure I wasn't carrying a lead pipe on the way to the conservatory, too."

"Go ahead and deflect. But she confirmed what I already suspected. I didn't want to believe it, but garbage day evidence doesn't lie. The cream cheese wrappers, empty whipping cream containers, a large number of egg cartons, it's all there. I just didn't think this would happen to us, you know?" He wipes a fake tear from his eye.

"Oh my gosh, you're a freaking drama queen. He had something I wanted, so he accepted a trade." I recognize my mistake before the final word clears my mouth.

"He *had* something, did he? I *have* something too, all you had to do was ask. I wouldn't have required a trade in return. I'm a gentleman like that."

He flashes me a wicked grin, and a laugh pops from my lips. While I don't want to explain, I know the fastest way out of this is through an explanation.

"If you must know, he's the one who took my Tupperware. Before I knew it was him, I offered a reward for its return. My container for baked goods."

He inhales a sharp breath behind me as I turn off the stove and carry the pot of sauce to the table. He slams his hand to his chest. "Well, I never thought I'd see the day when I wasn't the only one who got your oven hot."

I raise an eyebrow at his Broadway-worthy performance. "Give it a rest, Nathan Lane."

He huffs, then gives me a huge smile like a cat who just

drank every last drop of cream. "So, what's he got that I don't have?"

It's on the tip of my tongue to whisper *he makes a thousand butterflies take flight in my stomach, and he's the first man, in four years, who makes me yearn to be touched,* but I lock the words firmly behind my lips unprepared to share the ache in my heart. Knowing we've already agreed our relationship is better left as friends, I humor him and spit out the first fact that crosses my mind. "He's a surgeon."

I dish his spaghetti and hand him the plate. His fork dives into the mass of noodles before continuing his inquisition.

"He's good with his hands. One point to Prick. What else?"

He takes a drink of his water, and I recognize the keen sparkle in his stare. He's the big brother I never had, and I have to admit, I'm loving the protective vibe he's throwing over me.

"He keeps to himself. Doesn't gossip."

Mitchell's silence regarding his personal life is extreme. I've been working with him for eight weeks and the only personal things I know are he likes spicy food, he has a sweet tooth, his car is named Tess (though I have no idea what he drives), and he worked as a bagger at a grocery store.

I've also been an obedient observer where he's concerned. I find him compassionate with patients, meticulous and confident in the operating room, and possessing a sense of humor that's had me in tears on more than one occasion.

"Read: boring and doesn't have any friends. No points." He rolls his wrist in the universal sign to continue.

"He's got a wicked sense of humor." I decline to admit it comes out to play in late night text messages.

I've purposely avoided bringing up the night he'd asked about medical school, though I'd felt bad for shutting him down. He hadn't been nosy, but I'd been too exhausted to handle the intrusiveness.

"I'm taking your word for it since the gossip says otherwise. Half a point."

"If you're done being scorekeeper, can we drop Dr. Anderson from our dinner conversation?"

He purses his lips then gives me a wide smile. "Did I tell you Rachel from the third floor had an accidental threesome with Bob in respiratory?"

While I have no desire to hear the BobRa story, anything is better than potentially exposing my growing feelings for Dr. Anderson.

I KNOCK on his open office door and wait for an invitation. He glances my way and gifts me with a wide smile before extending a hand toward the chair opposite his desk. My shoes sink into the plush carpet as I cross his office and take a seat, more nervous and conflicted than I ever remember being.

He pulls a file from the corner of his cluttered desk and scans its contents before returning his eyes to mine. "Let me start by saying I've completed the paperwork. You've passed this portion and will be moving on to your next assigned rotation on Monday. This interview is a formality, but one I'm hoping will provide insight on both sides of the table."

I nod. I'm relieved he's no longer my boss, and I'm no longer his student.

"Why don't you start by telling me three different things you've learned during your rotation with me." His posture is professional as he clasps his hands on top of his desk and waits for my response.

I've read the Human Resources manual more times than I care to count, so I know there are no restrictions on employees dating provided it is consensual and neither party is in a position of authority over the other. I may die of embarrassment, but I need to see if what I've been feeling is more than just one-sided. I lace my answer with honesty and a little humor praying I haven't misread the heated glances when he thought I wasn't paying attention.

"I'd say I've learned the proper way to do an incision near the carotid, the proper procedure for installing a pacemaker, and you have a sweet tooth for my baking as well as a penchant for stealing Tupperware containers."

His eyes widen as I finish before his face returns to an unreadable mask. If I didn't know my rotation was finished, my mouth might have murdered my chances of passing the past eight weeks.

I'm exhausted, and my body screams for release from the sexual tension that pools between us. I don't know if he desires a relationship free from the hospital's confines, but I've reached my capacity for denial.

Grab life by the wings and soar. Dr. Johansen's favorite quote is burned in the flesh of my soul. I've always had the wings, but the desire to fly has remained buried beneath the ash of the past.

My tongue darts out to wet my bottom lip, and his gaze is riveted to the movement before he snaps back into his professional pose and continues the interview, unperturbed.

"I want you to feel like this is a safe place to voice concerns you may have for me or the way I deliver instruction."

A small smile sits upon his lips, and my mind nearly forgets everything I've prepared to say. "I'll admit I was frustrated at the beginning when I felt like a surgical assistant instead of a doctor. I've studied your work and know you demand perfection in yourself and others so I had an inkling of what to expect, but I experienced a good amount of irritation at the onset. I appreciate you releasing control to me in the operating room. By the time you gave me the reins, I felt prepared and honored. Thank you."

A soft look flashes through his eyes before he moves on. "You're welcome, Dr. Roberts. You are one of the most talented doctors I've seen come through this hospital. I wish all of our medical students walked the same path and had your drive."

My heart twists, yet I keep my face from responding. There had been a time when I'd rejected my choices and followed in the footsteps of others instead of creating footprints of my own. That path had been paved with devastation and heartache, yet I would not relinquish one step of what I've conquered to be sitting here today.

He plucks his phone from his desk and types out a message just before my phone buzzes from its position where I've hidden it my under my thigh.

"I've written a list of items for you to focus on going forward. If my ears didn't deceive me, it's already waiting for you on your phone. Also, I'm still expecting the full year of baked goods. Finishing your rotation does not negate our trade. Thank you for your impeccable service, Dr. Roberts."

He holds out his hand, and I lean forward and place my palm against his, the friction sending warmth from my wrist to shoulder. He picks up his pen and looks down at the folder spread out in front of him, effectively releasing me from our interview.

Could this man be any more strait-laced and professional? Maybe I've been wrong, and he's silently rejoicing that I'm no longer his problem. I straighten, slide my phone in the pocket of my lab coat, and give him a brittle smile before exiting his office.

Water threatens at the base of my lower lids as I walk to the locker room determined to escape to my car before I lose the ability to stem the flow of my tears. With my interview completed, I am on the fast track to my house where I can wallow in disappointment.

I grab my wallet and keys from my locker and slide into the

driver's seat ten minutes later. I throw my car in reverse and do a quick shoulder check before backing out of the space.

I've nearly made it to the exit when I spy the shiny black SUV I've dubbed the "parking spot thief." Turning my head to give it a menacing stare as I cruise by, I note the T symbol and Model X emblazoned on the back. T for "thief," why am I not surprised.

———

GATHERING the numerous bags filled with a plethora of random crap I've purchased at the neighborhood grocer on the way home, I stumble out of my vehicle and hit the garage floor on both knees when my pant leg gets caught on the edge of the car door. Baking chocolate, colorful bags of sprinkles and two cartons of cream cheese fly across the cement as I howl in pain from my position on the floor.

I crawl through the old oil stains as I gather the scattered items while cursing my day. I'd been blindsided by my own stupidity in thinking my boss—ex-boss—wanted anything more than a professional relationship with baked goods benefits. I'd performed a cannonball off the high dive during my interview, and I'd hit the water in a belly flop of epic proportions.

After a good five minutes, I finally collect all of my junk and stagger into the house. Throwing the pile on the counter, I gingerly walk to my room wincing when my pants stick to my sore knees. It seems they may be a little more than bruised. I strip down to my underwear, my scrubs hitting the floor with a thud reminding me of my cell phone I'd stashed in my pocket before getting into my car after my meeting with Mitchell. He became Mitchell in my mind the exact moment "boss" no longer tethered my professional name to his.

I clean up my knees, grab a pair of yoga pants and t-shirt

from my drawer, and slip into them before scooping up my cell, noting it's deader than an ice rink in the summer. I plug it into the charger next to my bed and make my way to the kitchen planning to lose myself in a couple hours of stress-relieving baking.

Three hours and ten dozen cookies later, my body and my mind are on the same page, calm and drained of energy. Normally I'm one who is anal about washing the dishes and making sure the kitchen is spotless, but tonight I can't bring myself to care. I'm single, live alone, and have a rare day off tomorrow. Nothing will change before morning.

I perform the bare minimum of my bedtime routine, turn my charged phone back on, and crawl into bed, closing my eyes seconds after my head hits my pillow.

Two minutes in and my brain won't shut down because my stupid phone's notification alert keeps beeping in my ear like a freaking hearing test. I roll over to clear the incessant noise only to notice the text Mitchell sent while I sat in his office fighting to keep my emotions from spilling across my face.

My brain, which checked out minutes ago, lights up like a child on Christmas morning, as I open the notification and read his words.

Mitchell:
Items needing Hope's attention:
1. Nine additional months of sweet confection
deliveries. I enjoy cookies, cakes, bars,
pastries, cupcakes, eclairs, and muffins. (Pro-
vided the muffins are not bran because muffins
and bran in the same recipe are just *wrong*.
Always.)
2. Devote time to texting Mitchell (texting
about work DOES NOT COUNT and won't be
tolerated.)

**3. Commit to two coffee dates with Mitchell
(Not to be confused with that prick, Dr.
Anderson.)**
**4. Engage in something spicy with Mitchell
(including but not limited to: A visit to Taco
Truck Tuesday; a night of chocolate tasting at
Chocolates by Daniel; viewing the movie *Spice
World*)**
5. Agree to a date with Mitchell

A smile big enough to hurt my cheeks stretches across my mouth as I re-read his text. I didn't imagine our connection, and our chemistry isn't one-sided.

My skin tingles as I consider if I should answer him tonight or wait until the morning when my brain function isn't sketchy. I'd love to think I'm an independent woman who doesn't need a man to put a smile on her face. Yet, when the first man who's lit a fire within my soul since Joe's death sends me a text like this, I don't need to be a martyr for the feminism movement.

I fall to my back and consider my response, starting and stopping numerous times before I make it to the final bullet and hit send.

Hope:
Hope's attention is as follows:
**1. Treat deliveries will continue. Special deliv-
eries may be honored.**
2. How many constitute devotion?
**3. I drink coffee from anywhere but prefer
Common Grounds not far from the hospital.
I'll meet you there at five a.m. this Friday. Is
that too early? *Additional coffee dates made
upon request.**
4. I'm willing to try spicy, but I'm vetoing *Spice*

World. There's no way my eyes could unwatch that train wreck.
5. Name the time, name the place

I stare at my screen considering he may be sleeping or away from his phone when I see the read notification pop up and dots immediately dance across my screen.

Mitchell:
1. My mouth is filled with requests.
2. Devotion = one text per day, minimum. Feel free to text at any hour of the day.
3. I'll be there. 5 a.m. Friday, Common Grounds *Bring your calendar
4. No *Spice World*, noted. Did I mention I like sassy, too?
5. Angelos, two weeks from today. *Wear something that makes you feel gorgeous. I'll pick you up at 8:30.

My heartbeat sounds like a cannon in my ears as I read his response before firing off a final text.

Me: I like a man with a plan.

I re-read the texts, and my skin tickles like a mass of butterflies are skimming across the surface. He's witty and confident with a twist of sarcasm.

I feel the protective shell I've worn like armor for four years slipping away, and I'm equal parts terrified and excited to finally break free of my emotional slumber.

33

MITCHELL

I read her text and choke on the gulp of water I've just taken after finishing a thirty-minute climb on the treadmill. Fortunately, her words didn't arrive two minutes ago, or I'd probably be nursing a broken ankle from stumbling off the back of the machine.

Hope: Have you ever enhanced? Public service announcement. Do. Not. Do. It. Your manhood thanks you.

Her off-the-cuff humor mixed with a sassiness she keeps hidden when in a professional capacity is by far my favorite thing about her. Her tight, athletic body she keeps hidden under shapeless scrubs and white lab coats runs a close second on my list.

We've been texting back and forth for the past week, and it seems like we've been doing this for as long as I remember.

Me: So, you saw roid effects up close and personal?

Her response hits my phone less than a minute later.

Hope: Something I cannot unsee. My retinas are burning.

I wipe my sweat from the machine and walk to the locker room. I hate being at the gym by four a.m., but missing a day makes my skin itchy and my mood dark. I strip out of my wet clothes and head to the shower, suddenly wishing I hadn't read her texts before getting naked.

I turn the water on and step in hoping the two minutes it takes for the temperature to warm to something more palatable will cool the fire in my groin. It's been a long time since I've spoken intimately with a woman, and my body has remained in a constant state of semi-arousal since she walked into the surgical locker room nearly three months ago.

I've never been happier for being a neat freak as the day I accidentally threw away her brownie container. Best decision ever, and I'd do it again—provided I knew the container wasn't a treasured keepsake from her deceased mother this time.

I finish shampooing my hair, making a mental note to replace the bottle I've been nursing for the past week. I grab the soap and run it across my slick body allowing myself only two swipes past my straining cock.

I'm at the gym, and while I'm sure quite a few guys have rubbed one out in this shower bay, I can get loud no matter if I'm with a woman or sans female company. I don't get off— pun intended—on filling another dude's ears with a live audio feed of Mitchell's morning show.

I towel off, mentally running through today's schedule to avoid any thoughts of Hope which could prove embarrassing. Dr. Ortiz, a colleague from the hospital, is currently leaning his foot on the bench directly behind me to tie his shoe. I'd like to avoid being known as Man Muscle Mitch or any one of a hundred crotch-sponsored nicknames considering my UNE-inspired nickname still haunts me over a decade later.

Dressed and in my car ten minutes later, I use my short commute to see if Hope is available. I didn't realize what a high I'd been riding working side by side with her until she'd finished her rotation, and I'd crashed like an addict jonesing for his next Hope fix.

I know very little of her current schedule, only that she's in a sports medicine rotation and she's literally up to her eyeballs in a fuck-ton of athletically built dudes on a daily basis. None of which are me. If I were into labels, the correct one would be jealous, but I don't own a label maker so no sweat there.

My interest in her is much stronger than three months should allow, but as Maggie reminded me, the heart knows no timeline. It's been more than four years since I've even gone out on a date much less considered pursuing a woman, and my body is encouraging me to make up for lost time.

Though Maggie has been pro-Hope since I brought home the vanilla and spice chocolate cupcakes, they haven't met because I'm too chickenshit to introduce her and my daughter to another woman without assurances the woman in question is sticking around.

I can't be sure if Maggie's cheerleading is tied to her desire for me to find a life partner or her cravings for Hope's baked creations. I'd like to think she wants me to be happy, but I've sampled the deliciousness of Hope's baked goods so I can't be sure of Maggie's intentions when it comes to her push for a relationship.

I give Tess instructions to call Hope as I cruise down the freeway. She picks up on the third ring, her breathing heavy and her voice husky. "Hello, Dr. Anderson. What can I do for you?"

I'm turned on by the cadence of her voice, and I adjust in my seat searching for a position that will alleviate the growing tightness in my pants. I lower my tone. "That's a loaded question, Dr. Roberts. One I beg extra time to consider."

She pauses, and I wonder where her thoughts have run to before she answers. "Granted. Now is that all you needed?" She waits on the other end, and I hear her breathing begin to level out.

"We're still on for tomorrow night, yeah?" I'd wanted to play it cool, throwing the suggestion of Angelo's out two weeks into the future when we'd first texted. At this point, I'd only succeeded in making myself a stressed-out, hot mess obsessed with every detail of tomorrow's date.

At the time, I'd also forgotten Saturday was the final day my family unit would spend together before the treatment plan changes took effect. I should have canceled my date, but my desire to know Hope had grown to a raging inferno. I had no idea how to extinguish it without seeing her.

"Absolutely. I'll text you the address and be ready by eight-thirty." She pauses. "Is it too gauche to say I'm looking forward to it, but I'm nervous as hell."

Her admission has me grinning considering I'm in her boat and riding the same waves.

"Not at all. Full disclosure, I cannot remember the last time I went on a date. You're getting a virtual dating newbie."

"And you think I'm a serial dater? I haven't been on a date since my husb—"

Her sentence cuts off like she's hit it with a machete, abrupt and clean. I don't want her shutting me out, so I remind her of our first meeting.

"Husband. I know you've been married, Hope. I remember being blinded by your ring when we met on the flight to Denver and thinking he was a lucky guy." I stop, considering if I should share my next words before I continue. "This may make me sound like a bastard, but your ring was the first thing I looked for when we met the first day of your rotation."

I hear puffs of breath as she listens to my explanation, and I hope I'm not screwing my chances with her before we even sit down to our first date.

"He…died."

Divorce isn't shameful, a secret, or taboo in our society so my brain had just assumed she'd been married and it hadn't worked out. I never considered this beautiful, intelligent, young woman is a widow.

Questions, I have no right asking, bombard my mind like hundreds of paper airplanes thrown at once. Assuming there wasn't a huge age gap, he would have been young. Young guys don't die. But my brain immediately tosses pictures of patients, ones I couldn't save, through my head as if to say *you know better, Dr. Anderson. Was he sick? Was it an accident? Did he take his own life?*

My silence is doing nothing to validate Hope's admission, so I say the first words that surface. "I'm sorry, Hope."

"Thank you, Mitchell. I'll see you tomorrow night. Goodbye."

The line goes silent, and I'm left sweeping up the remains of our conversation long after she ends the call. She was courteous, but her dismissal strips me of the excitement I felt minutes ago. She's shut me out, and I'm left wondering how much she'll fortify her wall before I see her.

———

THE GLOW of my computer screen fills my office as I listen to the voicemail. My hand rests across my eyes trying to hide from the tirade filling my inbox with angry, pleading words. I don't know how the call was made, considering the rules in place, but her call couldn't have come at a worse time.

When I'd arrived at the hospital, still trying to sift through the ashes of my aborted conversation with Hope, I'd had thirty minutes to prep for two, back-to-back surgeries. I was physically and mentally exhausted and didn't have the patience to deal with the accusations that clouded my past. Anger flares through my blood before it's extinguished by the icy reality of guilt.

Four years. It's been four years, and I'm finally ready to plan for what I want, what I need, and what Sedona needs.

I make a mental note to speak with Mr. Carson when I see him on Saturday to make sure a phone call doesn't accidentally reach my house where Sedona could inadvertently pick it up.

I open a new tab on my laptop to confirm the schedule for my date tomorrow night. I'd called Angelo's last week and secured a table for nine p.m. Daniel, the proprietor of Chocolates by Daniel, had been a little less accommodating when I'd asked about an after-hours private tasting. It seems a certain number of green presidents are good enough to stall any arguments against keeping a shop open after hours. I'd also asked him if he had any specialties employing spicy flavors to which I received a thirty-minute education on the differences between using powder-based seasonings, like cayenne pepper, versus the whole fruit, such as jalapeños, to flavor the body of chocolate. I personally didn't care about the process only the reaction of Hope's palate.

My schedule would be tight tomorrow, but if I left the hospital by seven, I could read Sedona her bedtime story before taking a shower and leaving by eight to make it Hope's house by eight-thirty.

Maggie, who usually chose to be gone on the third weekend, had volunteered to give up her free Friday night so she'd be available to watch Sedona. She'd even offered to sleep in the guest bedroom just down the hall from Sedona's room in case I was *too tired* and chose to stay at Hope's house instead of driving home.

I know I haven't been in the dating pool for a good stretch of time, but I'm pretty sure sex isn't the norm at the end of a first date. Not that I won't be prepared or partake if the opportunity arises, I'm just not banking on it happening.

Plans finalized, I shut down my laptop, lock up, and walk to my car. If I'm lucky, I'll slide into Sedona's room in time to read her bedtime story.

34

MITCHELL

The minutes on my watch toy with me as I glance at my wrist for the fourth time in the past…twelve minutes. It's five p.m., and I'm stuck between two attending physicians and three medical students as we round through the cardiac care unit.

Since I've been at this hospital, I can count on one hand how many times I've not been able to excuse myself from rounds. Today is one of those days, and I'm feeling the saltiness as it swishes through my system. Between the monotony of inane questions mixed with the bewildered expressions of the medical students when asked simple questions, I want to slam my pen through an eye socket.

I was never this stupid in medical school. As if to say *liar liar pants on fire*, my brain starts flipping through a video reel of stupid shit I did in medical school reminding me I've blocked out the worst of it.

I see my frustration for what it is, a fear the Hope I see tonight will be different from the one I've come to know these past few months. I've failed to come up with a casual way to broach the subject of her marriage, and I'm hoping yesterday's phone call doesn't hang like a cloud over our heads all night.

We finish rounds, and I slip away before I'm pulled into a conversation about aortic valve repair. Any other day, I'd be right in there throwing my opinions and research findings around like little hand grenades, but today is not any other day, and my thoughts are firmly planted outside this hospital. I lock my office and head home, ready to know Hope on a much more personal level.

———

Sedona shuts the cover of *Harry Potter* and looks at me expectantly. Her eyes bore into mine, and I feel like I'm being silently interrogated by the FBI. My six—almost seven—year old is a master manipulator, and I feel myself caving under the pressure. She knows Maggie will be with her tonight, but I haven't shared why, and I'm dragging my feet. I've vacillated between telling her about my date with Hope and just keeping my mouth shut. Silence is currently winning, though I feel like I'm lying to my kid by omission which negates my bid for *Father of the Year*.

I switch gears and prepare her for tomorrow. While it will virtually be the same from her perspective, I want to prepare her for the possibility of increased tension and tantrums. "Tomorrow is the last day Emily will be visiting our house for a while. I've thought about it, and I think it's best if we take a break."

My daughter's eyes bore into mine. "Kind of like summer break at school?"

"Yeah, like a vacation."

"I like that idea, Daddy." My daughter's entire body relaxes and melts into my side where she's nestled under my armpit.

Until this very moment, I've been too blind to recognize

the stress I've placed on my princess. Her reaction wipes away a good portion of my guilt and gives me the validation I didn't know I needed.

She turns and places her hand on my cheek. "You don't smile when she's around. I'm glad she's going away." She leans over in a conspiratorial whisper which is louder than her normal speaking voice. "She makes really bad choices, and she doesn't listen. I've tried to help her, but she just gets mad and runs away. It's exhausting." She nods her head putting a punctuation point at the end of each statement.

My daughter is wise beyond her years. It makes me sad her life experiences have forced her to grow up far faster than other children her age. I've failed her by trying to force a relationship that isn't there and hasn't been for some time.

Tonight is the first step in fixing me, and tomorrow is the first step toward a new future.

I PULL Tess along the curb and park, taking a moment to steady my nerves before exiting my vehicle holding a bouquet of flowers.

The small, white house sits at the back of the lot and shares a driveway with an exact replica of Hope's house all the way down to the light blue shutters.

Though it's dark, I can see her sidewalk where it winds across the freshly cut yard ending at the mouth of a small covered porch edged in blooming window boxes. An instant feeling of nostalgia settles over me. Hope's house reminds me of my Grandma and Grandpa Anderson's place where summers were spent passing the football with my brother and drinking iced tea on the cement steps.

I knock on her door, smiling as I stare at the two white rockers sitting like sentries presiding over the quiet street. The nob jiggles back and forth, and I swear I hear a feminine curse before the door swings open sending a swoosh of air across my face and disappearing into the warm summer night.

Blinking the dryness from my contacts, I recover to find Hope standing with one ankle crossed behind the other, one hand on the door and one on her hip. My eyes travel from the hot pink of her exposed toenails to the cut of her dress. Like the blue of a peacock's feathers, it wraps across her front and is tied closed by the bow sitting enticingly over the curve of her right hip. Her glossy blond hair falls in loose waves around her shoulders. I've never seen her dressed in anything outside of her work clothes. She is stunning, and I'm rendered speechless by her beauty.

"Hi." Her smile is shy and a bit unsure, a total one hundred and eighty-degree change from the confident surgeon I've seen in the operating room. Her eyes flick to my hand, and she raises an eyebrow. "Are those for me?"

"Huh?" My mouth struggles to combine sounds into intelligible words. "Oh, yeah. These are for you."

I pass her the bouquet of daisies Maggie pushed into my hands while muttering about "kids these days" as she shoved me out the door tonight.

She leans in and closes her eyes, inhaling the subtle fragrance. I'm mesmerized by the flutter of her thick lashes where they meet the curve of her cheek. "You look beyond beautiful, Hope. The flowers pale in comparison to you."

She pulls the door wide, inviting me into her space before closing the door and turning to walk toward the back of the house.

The older home has been completely renovated from the white and stainless kitchen to the hardwood floors. The open concept of the rooms allows me to appreciate the slight sway of Hope's hips as she walks barefoot into the kitchen and takes down a glass jar she'll presumably use as a vase.

I follow her into the kitchen, taking note of the bright-colored bowls artistically displayed around the room. She chuckles and fills a jar with water before moving to stand in front of the granite-topped island.

"Thank you. I love flowers, though I don't buy them for myself. Hence the mason jar vase."

I look around the kitchen noting the bright yellow wall clock, the shiny red appliance pushed to the corner of the counter, and the black towels hanging on the handle of the oven.

"Something tells me you'll make it work."

Her teeth sparkle beneath the smile stretching across her full lips. I tap my fingertips on the counter.

"So, this is where the magic happens?"

Her eyes rise to mine before dropping to arrange the rest of the flowers. "Sounds a little weird, but I guess you could say that."

She carries the arrangement to the small round table in the corner and pushes the jar to the center before standing back and taking a look like a photographer does before he catches the perfect photo. A broad smile lights up her face as she examines the view. "I like it. Looks like I'll be buying flowers for my table from now on."

I step toward her, my shoes coming within an inch of her painted toes. "If you smile like that every time I bring flowers, I'll take care of keeping you supplied."

Her sky-blue gaze darts to mine before she unleashes another radiant smile.

I swallow, trying to rid my mouth of the thirst I have to pull her into my chest and kiss her. Her eyes drop to my lips, and I'm unable to resist touching her. I lean down meeting her mouth with a brush of my lips. Her intake of breath stalls my movements leaving me frozen as the beat of a drumline echoes behind my ribs.

She shifts her weight aligning our bodies from knees to chest lifting her fingers to feather across the back of my neck before pulling my lips into the lush softness of her own.

I melt into the warmth of her skin, the aroma of oranges intoxicating my senses, and driving me crazy with thirst. I tease her lips with the tip of my tongue, tracing the delicate seam hidden in her perfect bow. Her mouth opens and her minty breath mingles with the heat of my lungs.

My hands cup her cheeks, my thumb pulling at the dent in her lower lip before my tongue dips into the wet warmth of her mouth. Her arms wrap around my waist, and I'm lost to the drag and pull as my tongue explores her mouth with steady, slow strokes. She feeds me her moan, and I collect it with a swipe of my tongue, savoring its richness as it inflates my lungs.

I break the kiss, unwilling to let her go, but knowing we need to leave so we aren't late. "We should go."

Her lips are plump and rose red, my new favorite color. "Yeah, let me slip into my shoes. I'll meet you outside."

"I'll wait for you on the porch." I turn and walk toward the door thankful to be wearing a dark suit to hide the raging erection straining the confines of my dress pants.

She pulls the front door shut and bends forward to lock it before turning and extending her hand. I reach forward and place it in the crook of my arm to help her down the stairs and across the cracked sidewalk.

I hit a button, and my vehicle wakes from the darkness as the lights come on illuminating our final steps. I step forward to open her door when she stops so abruptly her hand falls from my arm. She walks to the back of Tess. Her face is a mask of concentration as she surveys the rear end. Looking for what, I don't know.

"Hope, are you okay?"

"Tell me this isn't your car." Her demand is clipped and my brows lower in confusion.

"This is my car. Her name is Tess."

She bites her lip. "T for Tess. Like the one on the back of the vehicle?"

"Yes." I stretch out the word, turning it into a question.

She drops her chin to her chest and takes a couple of deep breaths. "Good thing he's an amazing kisser." Her mutter is barely audible, and I strain my ears to catch all of her words. "You are a thief with a capital T, Dr. Anderson."

"I'm sorry." Shit. I'm apologizing, and I not sure why.

She starts to pace as she relays the story of her first day as a surgical resident. "On my very first day, I'd circled the doctor's parking lot no less than eight times. My heart was racing, afraid I was going to be late, even though I'd allowed for a thirty-minute emergency cushion. I finally spied an open spot, turned on my blinker, and someone—who I've just discovered was you—swooped in and *stole* my spot. The windows were so dark, I couldn't see the driver, but I made sure to memorize the car. THIS car!"

She throws up both hands and stares at me, daggers of blue flames hitting me in the chest. Her reaction is so contrary to her normal mood, I can't tell if she's on the verge of tears or laughter. I scan the quiet street waiting for neighborhood lights to flick on in response to the commotion.

I close my eyes, trying to remember the day, but my memory comes up empty. I run my palm across the back of my neck. "I'm sorry. I usually return calls during my commute. I was probably distracted and didn't even see you before I pulled in. Please forgive me."

I walk to her, bending my knees and trying to catch the attention of her downturned eyes. "If I promise to never steal a parking spot again, am I forgiven?"

She flicks her eyes to my face meeting my raised eyebrows and questioning smile. "My first day was supposed to be awesome, and you gave it a crappy start."

I take her head in my hands and rest my forehead to hers. "Brand me a thief. Ask me to park in the staff parking lot. I'm at your mercy."

Her body leans forward in an almost imperceptible movement, but I feel her forgiveness in her stance before I feel it on my lips. "You're lucky you have magical kisses. Let's go to dinner."

I open the door and help her into her seat. "Your chariot awaits, Madam."

35

HOPE

WE FOLLOW THE HOST THROUGH THE DIM RESTAURANT, PAST two large parties of jovial patrons laughing and talking animatedly with their loud voices and busy hands, to a cozy table in a back corner away from the din of the busy dining room.

Mitchell pulls out my chair, making sure I'm situated before taking his seat across from me. We both smile and thank the busboy who fills our water glasses before being pulled to the other tables needing water service.

"I know we started off a bit rough, but I'm hoping the rest of the night will be smooth sailing."

His eyes sparkle, yet his face remains neutral as his eyes caress the contours of my brows, moving to my cheeks, and ending at the bow of my lips.

"Your car caught me off guard. It's received the brunt of my annoyance, and I've lashed it with multiple insults as I've walked or driven by it. It's childish, I know. Dr. Johansen, my psychiatrist, would chew me a new one if she knew I was harboring unhealthy thoughts toward an inanimate object."

His face morphs into a look of horror, becoming more

pronounced with each word. "Do I need to file an order of protective custody for Tess?"

"Not unless you steal a parking spot again." My words get caught in the middle of my chuckle before I continue. "I propose a truce. How about you promise to stop 'borrowing,' my belongings, and I'll stop calling you a thief."

He nods as a wide smile pulls his cheeks up causing wrinkles at the corners of his eyes. When he smiles, his whole face is part of the action. He busies himself with his napkin, pulling it from beneath his silverware and placing it on his lap.

"Let's start out on more neutral ground. How did you know you wanted to be a cardiothoracic surgeon?"

"Being a surgeon has always been my goal, but it wasn't until about five years ago I figured out what specialty." He looks to the side like he's grasping for information hidden on the other side of the room. "My dad had a heart attack that resulted in an emergency triple bypass several years ago, two months before I was set to declare my surgical specialty. Ironically, I'd attended a cardiothoracic seminar in Boston a month before my dad's attack. I'd really only signed up so I could get continuing education hours and visit my buddy who worked in Boston at the time. I ended up enthralled by the information. I'd sat in the front row and didn't move a muscle for eight hours in fear of missing one word of the cardiothoracic surgeon's presentation. When my dad had his attack so soon after I attended the seminar, I took it as a sign that cardiothoracic was the calling I'd been looking for. Over the next couple of months, I secured recommendation letters, and I applied for every cardiothoracic fellowship I could find. As luck would have it, I received an offer from Geneva General." Mitchell's eyes are lit with excitement turning them dark.

"I wish my story was as inspiring as yours." I succeed in keeping my voice even, hoping he won't ask me the same question.

"What's your number one goal in the next five years?" His question is innocuous, but it carries a weight that attaches to my shoulders pulling them forward as I stall to answer. Four years ago, my answer would have included babies and preschool applications. Today's answer is vastly different, but no less significant. I take a sip of water, swishing it around and loosening my words.

"I hope to be a pediatric orthopedic surgeon since I love the challenge of surgery, and I love kids. I'd hoped to have one or two of my own by now, but my path took a left turn some years back, and I was forced to pave a new route." Unshed tears blur my vision, and I tilt my eyes toward the ceiling to stem their flow.

Mitchell's hand covers mine, and he smiles. "Life can throw some nasty curveballs, but you're here. Whatever the circumstances. You are an excellent surgeon. Kids and parents are going to love you."

Our server, Martin, approaches the table and recites the specials before offering Mitchell a wine list. He tips the list at me and raises his eyebrows.

"No wine for me, just water. Thank you."

Martin crosses his hands in front of his waist. "Might I suggest the manicotti special for your dinner? It is excellent."

I smile and take a sip of water. "Sounds great to me."

"And for you, Sir?"

Mitchell hands Martin the wine menu and orders a ginger ale and the dinner special. Martin excuses himself and takes off in the direction of a door I assume is the kitchen.

Mitchell leans forward and clears his throat as his eyes bounce around the table.

"Hope, I need to mention something to you. I've not brought it up before tonight because the timing hasn't been right." He folds his hands. "What happened at your house, before the Tess debacle? I want more. Maybe not tonight or

tomorrow, but I'm looking for more than one date with you."
His tongue wets his bottom lip. "Are we something you'd be
interested in pursuing?" He flicks his hand between us.

I swallow and take the leap I've wanted to take. "Yes. I've
wanted to do this since I found out you were the one I'd
dubbed the Tupperware Thief."

His smile stretches across his face, but it doesn't reach his
eyes. He takes a sip of water, then clears his throat.

"I'm happy to hear you say it. But, before we take any
more steps forward, there's something you need to know." He
takes a breath and releases his words on an exhale. "I have a
daughter. She's a beautiful six-year-old who's smart, insightful,
and full of energy."

I pull my hand from his, taking a moment to process.
Emotions swirl through my chest, but I can't pinpoint a single
feeling. It's not anger or jealousy or shock. It's tinged with
sadness. It's disappointment wrapped in longing.

I've wanted a child since I was one myself. When Joe died
my plans for a baby with *him* perished, but my dream never fell
away. I buried it under medical school, residency, and my
future fellowship, but I still feel the heat of desire where it
burns the back of my heart. A single tear escapes, running
down my cheek, and landing on the goosebumps raised across
my arm. "Your face lit up when you mentioned her. What's her
name?"

His lips, which he'd pulled into a straight line while he'd
awaited my reaction, morph into a smile of relief and release
his secret of how much he cares about the future of our
budding relationship.

While this is our first official date, my heart recognized the
song of his months ago. Playing softly in the background,
weaving its melody throughout my blood, and working its way
into my consciousness as it waited for my mind to catch up.
This man, with his sensitive heart and prickly professional exte-

rior, isn't a stumbling block. He's a rock placed in my path, not to stumble over, but to act as a step so I can rise above and see the landscape of my future.

"Her name is Sedona, and someday in the future, I'd like for you to meet her."

My heart soars as a feeling of contentment falls over me like a warm blanket. In wanting to introduce us, he's giving me his trust. A priceless bond more expensive than the rarest diamond.

"I would love to meet her when you feel the timing is right."

Martin arrives with our plates, arranging them in front of us and checking if we need anything before disappearing as quickly as he arrived.

Mitchell cuts a piece of pasta and spears it with his fork. "I feel stupid saying this, but very few colleagues know about my daughter."

He puts a forkful of pasta into his mouth, and I'm hypnotized by the play of his jaw as he chews and swallows. He takes another bite, shutting his eyes in reverence while savoring the richness of the dish. Never have I ever been jealous of a fork until it entered his mouth. Tingles play along my spine as I drop my eyes and concentrate on lifting my own food to my mouth.

His voice, low and melodic, startles me from my sensual thoughts. "I go to great lengths to separate my hospital life from my personal life. It's not easy juggling family responsibilities with the kind of work we do, but I'm lucky to have Maggie, Sedona's nanny. She lives with us. Truth be told, if adults could have nanny's I'd claim her as mine as well. She maintains my house and keeps me sane. She's worth her weight in gold, which is close to her actual salary now that I think about it."

His quip makes his eyes sparkle, and I cannot keep my own smile from my lips.

"She sounds like Wonder Woman. Does she wear a cape around your house?" My tease plays at my lips.

He stares to the side for a moment, his fork paused midway to his lips, "You know I haven't seen it, but I wouldn't be surprised if it was hidden under her clothes. Not much surprises me with her anymore."

Curiosity pushes my next question from my tongue before I can pull it back. "What do you mean?"

"She's not afraid to speak her mind and call bullshit when she sees it. She's one of the reasons I asked you out. I work and spend time with Sedona. Other than my daily trips to the gym, I don't carve out time for my own interests. She's been pushing me to make friends and find an outlet. She says hermits aren't young and handsome, just unhappy, old men."

His self-deprecation is endearing, but also a surprise. Outside of the hospital, he's not the confident, controlling surgeon who's made me bite my tongue and want to scream until my lungs bled. Sitting in front of me having dinner, he's a sensitive, quiet father who works to give his daughter the best of life and the best version of himself.

Blinders fall from my eyes as I stare at him. Mitchell is not like Joe. When Joe and I were married, physically I had everything, but emotionally I was always struggling to rise a step above his job on his scale of importance. Mitchell is a man who's made his daughter his capstone at the expense of keeping nothing for himself.

The faint memory of sitting on a bench, my clothes stuck to me like a second skin from the humidity as I stare at the crowd in the busy theme park, floats through my vision. A heart neckless suspended in a teenage boy's grasp. *Hope is the music of life.* I'd nearly forgotten the words that were wise beyond the years of the boy who'd spoken them. I'd swallowed those words and tethered them to my soul, allowing the neckless to act as their guard where it lay over my heart.

When the clasp had broken my freshman year of high school, I'd mistakenly assumed I no longer needed the reminder and tucked the neckless into a jewelry box of forgotten keepsakes. As the years passed, the stranger's words faded like an old tattoo, visible but no longer holding the detail of remembrance.

Joe's music was drumbeats and steel guitars, commanding and full of energy. I'd ignored my melody and embraced *his* music and borrowed *his* happiness, even though I'd never liked the reverberation of drums or the harshness of the steel guitar.

Looking into Mitchell's eyes, seeing his smile, and feeling the softness of his hand where it covers mine, realization hits me. I'd mistaken Joe's song for my own. When his song had been silenced, I'd finally recognized the melody of my forgotten anthem.

A weight of sadness lifts and my chest expands like I've been swimming toward the light and finally broken the surface of the water.

"Mitchell, a wise young man once told me 'Hope is the music of life,' and this, you, us is the music I long to hear."

His eyes narrow, and he cuts his vision to the side before returning back to me. His eyes are clouded by confusion like he's trying to remember something that hangs just beyond his grasp.

The clouds clear and his green eyes sparkle at me from across the table.

"Since we're in agreement. I propose a toast. To a soundtrack of happiness." He winks, clinking his glass to mine before taking a drink.

36

MITCHELL

She sucks her fingertip then uses a cocktail napkin to dab the final evidence of chocolate from her lips. "Devine. That's the only word I can pull out of my brain right now."

My cock, which has been halfway to a full erection since we left her house, twitches in my slacks as I watch her mouth envelop her finger before her cheeks hollow. The movement is an unintentional erotic tease as she licks the sugary remnants from her digit.

"Which was your favorite?"

She bites her bottom lip before her face lights with mischief. "The jalapeño dark chocolate truffle. Sweet and smooth, with just the right amount of kick at the end." She purses her lips and taps her mouth. "I think my baking rotation just gained another player."

"Won't hear any complaints from me, and I agree. Jalapeño was my favorite. Then again, I've always liked spicy."

She lifts a blond eyebrow, and I bite my cheek, containing the urge to outline it with my tongue.

"Tonight's been quite the flavor adventure."

Her comment sends my thoughts straight to the cherry of

her gloss I'd removed with my kisses. I scrawl my signature across the bill that sits at my elbow. Glancing at my watch, I lean toward her, "I should probably get you home."

Her smile dims as she nods her head. "Probably best. Are you working tomorrow?"

"No."

Her schedule at the hospital probably hasn't been consistent enough for her to notice I'm never there on the third Saturday.

She wants more, which involves throwing open all of my doors no matter the darkness of the rooms beyond. Refusing to ruin the magic of our date, an explanation lies suspended on my tongue. I have every intention of telling her, but tonight doesn't afford the time necessary to work through all of the questions bound to arise.

I tuck her hand in the crook of my elbow and pull her toward me as we exit through the front door of the chocolate cafe. Her head rests on my shoulder, and the smell of citrus fills my nose. I unlock my car, helping her in, making sure to push her purse into her lap to avoid shutting it in the door. Rounding Tess, I slide in and start the noiseless vehicle.

Her fingers dance across the back of my hand where it rests on my thigh. "In case I forget to mention it later, I had a fabulous time tonight. Thank you." Her words are followed by a soft smile.

The light from the dashboard gives her an aqua blue glow. Placing my opposite hand on her cheek and angling my body, I pull her in for a soft kiss. Her lips part and my tongue meets hers in a slow dance of desire. I retreat, and she advances raising her hand to massage the back of my neck. My hands move to her sides, my fingers splaying to mold to the ridges of her ribs.

"Watching your hands as they repaired the lives of your patients, I burned for your touch. Fantasized how I'd open for you, pull you within me as you memorized my body." Her sensual words punctuate her breaths setting my lips on fire.

I withdraw from her mouth. Keeping a hand locked on her waist, I capture her chin with the other. "Damn. I need to get you home while I can still claim the title of gentleman. Make no mistake, this isn't a rejection. Hell will freeze over before I deny your fantasies."

I throw Tess in drive and take off for her house hoping I can drive safely considering the steel rod threatening to break through the zipper on my pants. Heavy breaths fill the cabin as I accelerate through yellow lights and test speed limits. I keep my eyes glued to the windshield, though my peripheral vision captures the rapid rise and fall of her full, round breasts.

"Park in the drive. My neighbor is gone, and it'll get your car out of the street."

I come to a stop next to her house, and she's out of the vehicle and sliding her key into the lock on the side door before I'm able to catch her. I lean into her, her ass cradling the warmth of my erection. I feel her moan as the vibration transfers through her body to mine. She pushes through the door, our combined weight throwing her off balance and making her stumble. I pull her against me while slamming the door with my foot.

She turns her head, throwing her hair over her slim shoulder. Her profile reveals the curve of a small smile. "Multi-tasking. That's hot."

I nip at her ear lobe, my mouth hovering above the sweet expanse of her neck.

"You haven't *seen* my multi-tasking skills."

I bite her neck, holding her in place when her knees buckle.

Her stuttered breath ends in a moan as she lifts her hand to the back of my neck pulling me forward and urging my mouth to lay a trail of wet kisses down her neck.

"You taste like temptation. A sweet morsel waiting to be devoured." My words whisper across her skin.

She releases my neck, running her hand to her hip to tangle with mine. She steps forward pulling me through the kitchen and down a darkened hallway toward what I assume to be her bedroom. We cross the threshold, and a nightlight throws muted shadows across the walls making her bed look like a fluffy gray cloud.

She moves to walk toward it, and I bend and scoop her into my arms and carry her the rest of the way to the mattress. I release her feet, and she slides down my front. Her breasts press against my chest. The warmth of her core skims the sensitive head of my hard cock where it strains against my pants separating it from the promised land between her legs.

I advance a step, and the backs of her knees hit the side of the bed as I tower over her. She tips her head back, teasing my heated gaze with the silky-smooth skin of her neck. I cradle her head, skimming my eyes across her body, ending at her electric blue stare.

"You're beautiful. But you, like this, are exquisitely breathtaking."

Starting with the shallow divot at the base of her throat, I alternate light nips and soothing licks as I make a path to her waiting lips. Her hands are in motion, gripping my waist, trailing streaks of heat across my back as she untucks my shirt exposing a sliver of my skin to the coolness of the air and the bite of her nails.

I take her mouth in a fevered kiss. My tongue circles hers, tasting the sweet remnants of the chocolate we'd consumed earlier. I explore her, swallowing her taste and greedily searching for more. Her mouth could easily become my addiction.

Her nails score my back, marking her journey as her fingers delve below the waistband of my dress pants. Tailored to my measurements, they leave little room for more than two of her slim fingers. She releases a moan of frustration as her hands move to my front and fumble with the button.

"Too…many…clothes." She whispers her words against my lips between fevered kisses.

I slide my hands from her hair and trace a path down her chest, slowing my descent as I mold my fingers around her full breasts. Releasing her mouth, I lean back focusing on the sight before me. Her tits are heavy and spill into my palms as her chest heaves, waiting for me to continue.

While her dress covers her nipples, it fails to hide their hardness. I brush my thumbs across the straining peaks watching with rapt attention as she arches her back, her body silently begging for more. I reward her with another swipe of my thumb before I lean down and capture a nipple in my teeth through the fabric, biting down with just enough pressure for her to register the pleasure of what's to come.

In my distraction, I've failed to notice she's popped the button and unzipped the fly of my pants. Her hand slides inside my boxer briefs and my dick weeps with gratitude for her perseverance. The coolness of her palm melds with the heat and hardness of my dick, setting off electrical sparks that shoot through my balls and down my thighs.

It's been too long since my cock felt the touch of someone other than me, and I'm afraid the excitement may be too much for him to handle for more than a few minutes. I lift my head, catching her eyes as she looks up at me through her lowered lashes.

"Hope. You have no idea how incredible this feels."

I watch as a triumphant smile spreads across her lips before her cocky statement rolls off her tongue. "Good to know I haven't lost my touch."

Her response throws me as she continues to smirk at me, her words hanging in the air between us.

"Huh?" I admit it's not an eloquent response, but my expectations for speech are completely severed when she continues to stroke me with the hand she has wrapped around my shaft.

"Stroked. Touched. I haven't…uh, been with… I haven't been with another man since my husband died."

Her words are shy and jumbled, though to be fair, it could be my brain struggling to process her explanation without an adequate blood supply. Her lashes fall and she releases me like she's embarrassed about her lack of sex.

If that's the case, I hope she's ready for me to blow her mind. I place my fingers below her chin and tilt it up waiting to speak until her eyes are focused on mine.

"You're telling me you haven't been with anyone since your husband?"

She gives me a slight nod and tries to break eye contact, but I keep a firm hold on her chin and tilt my head until I have her focus once again.

"Embarrassment doesn't have a place inside these walls. You are safe to ask for, tell me, or demand anything you need. Do you understand?"

She stares at me, assessing the truth of my words before she nods her head.

"The fact that you've chosen me is fascinating." I raise a brow and a smirk. "It also makes me hard as fuck to know I'm the lucky bastard who's responsible for every hardened nipple, moan of pleasure, and scream of release."

She returns a lazy grin as I drop my forehead to hers.

"In full disclosure, it's been an extremely long time since I've shared an orgasm with a woman. At first, it was a way to protect Sedona. But as time went by, I became more vigilant of the life we'd forged, and I was too greedy to risk losing it simply to fulfill my own selfish pleasures. You're the first woman who's captured my interest and hasn't let go. You're the first woman with whom I want more. This is us. You and me. No one else."

She rises on her tiptoes, placing a peck on my cheek while pushing my pants and underwear down past my butt. She brings her hands to my front and swipes a palm across the pre-cum beaded at my tip. My cock jumps at the contact bobbing in her direction in a silent request for continued attention. Her slick fingers circle my shaft in a tight grip as she strokes down to the base in a single motion.

I drop my head memorizing the vision of her hand working me toward release. She twists through her grip and pulls a prayer from my lips.

"Harder, keep going."

The friction intensifies as she works my cock, alternating between squeezing and pulling. She bends forward, my brain aware of her intentions, a split second before she sucks my tip between her pink lips. "Fuuuuuuck. Your mouth is perfection."

I nearly come from the sight of my head disappearing inside her mouth. My balls draw up, and I stumble back pulling my dick from her mouth with a pop.

"I can't let you suck my cock and still manage to keep my legs beneath me." My breathing is labored as she looks at me with innocent doe eyes.

My skin tingles, and I'm on fire. I undo the buttons on my shirt, ripping the final one clean off when it doesn't cooperate. I reach behind my neck and pull my undershirt from my heated skin. She watches me with the concentration of an Olympic judge as her eyes devour the flex of my biceps, the ridges of my abdomen, and the sharp indents at the sides of my hips. I feel the spark of fire like a physical tether as her eyes land on my nipples and the silver bars passing through their centers.

She steps into me, her eyes glazed and focused on the

jewelry attached to my chest. Her nostrils flare before her eyes dart to mine.

Her fingers trace the ridges and valleys across my stomach as I push my remaining clothing to the floor. Our gazes lock as I pull her hand to my mouth, placing a wet kiss on the inside of her wrist before sucking her index finger into my mouth.

Her eyes hold my attention as her tongue darts out and swipes across my nipple flicking the ball and sending an electric jolt shooting through my balls.

I latch on to her upper arms and push her toward the bed. My control is waning, and I need to coat my tongue in her juices before another drop of cum leaves my engorged dick.

"As much as I love your dress, I'll love it more when it's on the floor."

Her breath stutters as I turn her around my arms encircling her waist as my shaft presses between the crease of her ass. I snake my hand around to her stomach before sliding up to her ribs and across her chest until my palm is nestled between the crisscross of cotton in the center of her cleavage. The thump of her heartbeat drums against my fingertips where they explore the lace cups of her bra. I raise my other hand, pulling the tie of her dress and allowing the two pieces to open and expose her silky skin.

I cover her breasts with both of my hands, massaging them in my palms as I drop my lips to her neck and suck on her nape. Her ass pushes against my crotch and her tits fill my hands as her back bends in a perfect arch.

"This is torture. I need to feel you everywhere. Please." She begs, and my cock weeps.

She twists and falls to her back on top of the bed, shiny black heels planted flat and knees bent as she drops the straps of her bra.

"Stop."

Her hands freeze in response to the demand of my voice.

"You're like a present, and I hate when other people open my gifts."

I bend and retrieve a condom from my wallet, a precaution I've kept on hand since the last day of Hope's rotation. I toss it on the nightstand before kneeling at the end of the bed. I lift Hope's leg laying a trail of kisses from the inside of her ankle to the crease at the top of her thigh before repeating the path up the inside of her other leg.

A wet circle of arousal darkens the crotch of her lace panties. She lifts her butt as I slide my fingers to her hips and drag the scrap of lace from her body. I drink my fill of her lying bare and glistening as I crawl up the bed, stopping when my mouth is inches from her drenched pussy. Licking the length of her seam, my tongue finds her clit, and I suck it into my mouth before releasing it to blow across the sensitive bud. She bucks and drives her hands into my hair.

"Shit. Mitchell. I need more." Her whispered need threatens my control.

I balance on my knees and spread her lips, lapping at her sweet juices. I'm a desert, and she's my water.

Lick and suck.

Suck and lick.

Her wetness coats my tongue, my lips, my chin, and I can't get enough. I bring my tongue to her clit, swirling it in a circle as I push a finger inside her tight pussy.

She tightens her hold on my hair and chants my name while squeezing my head between her thighs the same way the walls of her cunt grip my finger. I give her clit a final swirl and push a second finger into her at the same time I bite down her swollen clit.

Not prepared for the crest of her orgasm, she convulses and screams. Her hands twist the bedsheets in a vice-like grip as I continue to suck and lick through her aftershocks.

"That. Was. Amazing." Her words ride her heavy breaths

as she releases her hands, and I crawl up her body stopping at her breasts which are still covered in lace.

"Seems I've neglected the rest of my present."

I slide my hands behind her to undo the clasp, but can't get it to release. I raise an eyebrow and plead for help.

"Maybe you could help me open this one?"

She smirks and contorts her arms behind her back. Seconds later, the lace slides free, and I slowly pull the fabric from her silky skin. Her nipples stand at attention as I lean forward and take one into my mouth laving it with my tongue before moving to the other one.

She runs her fingers through the waves at my temple. "I need to feel you from the inside out. Now."

I smile against a nipple, giving it a flick with my tongue while reaching for the condom. Hope pulls it from my hand.

"Allow me."

Her eyes penetrate mine as she tears the wrapper. Our gaze follows her movement as she positions the ring at the tip, and rolls it down my shaft with deft fingers. Her hands wrap around my ass urging me toward her waiting pussy.

"Don't tease. Please. And don't be gentle."

I line up with her entrance, pushing my tip between her glistening lips. Her muscles contract, sucking me into her slick heat and nearly igniting my release. I bite down on my lip focusing on the pain to keep from coming before the first stroke.

Hands on either side of her head, I release a breath and slam into her and bottom out in one thrust. She's so tight, my cock feels like it's trapped in a hot vice. Tingles shoot through my spine, and I grit my teeth as I withdraw before pounding forward.

"Yes. Just like that."

Her words spur me forward, my biceps bulging under the weight of my body as my balls slap against the crack of her ass.

Blood races through my veins like lava, raising a searing heat across my lower back as my balls draw up tight. I slam my eyes shut trying to stave off the orgasm that's barreling down my spine.

"I'm sorry. Been too long. Can't wait."

She slides her hands up my back and grips my shoulders while wrapping her legs around my hips. The tip of my cock massages the back wall of her wet channel as her heels dig into the backs of my legs. I thrust deep, and she cries out my name.

"I'm so close. Right there."

I'm mid-thrust when her scream triggers my release. My muscles tense. Pressure borders on pain as her pussy grips my cock seconds before I explode inside her. Her body trembles as her eyes squeeze shut, and I continue to slam into her, my dick pulsing until every drop of my cum has been spent. I slow my movements as her muscles relax, and her eyes open to find mine.

"That." Her eyes drop to our joined bodies, then pop back up to mine. "I don't have words. Except, when can we do it again?"

I chuckle and drop to my elbows nuzzling her neck and breathing in the scent of citrus tinged with sex.

"I wish I could claim to be superhuman and suggest a second round right *now*, but I'm going to need a few minutes." I lift my head and brush a sweaty strand of hair from her damp forehead. "You're incredible."

Her eyes sparkle before she drops her gaze and the tip of her nose turns red.

"I see your mind working. Hold that thought. Bathroom?"

She tips her head to a door on the opposite wall.

I kiss her cheek before circling a hand around my shaft to secure the condom before pulling out. Considering this is the strongest orgasm I've ever experienced, the latex is probably stretched to its limit. I make my way to the bathroom and dispose of the condom before washing my hands and returning to her bed where she waits for me, the covers flipped back in invitation.

I slide in and prop up on my side so I'm facing her.

She stares at me, quiet and assessing. I sense she wants to say something, but whatever it is requires planning. Her eyes bounce around the room, failing to land anywhere. The silence stretches, and nervousness creeps across my neck.

Her whisper is faint, and I have to strain to hear each word. "I have a confession." She peeks at me through her lush blond lashes. "You've been my closet guilty pleasure."

I lean in giving her a soft brush of my lips. "Ditto. And there's nothing guilty about desire."

"My guilt doesn't stem from my desire." Her fingers play with the hairs at the back of my neck as she stares at a spot over my shoulder. "It's because of how long I've harbored my fantasy."

I'm silent, but my brows lift in surprise.

"On the plane. When you helped the old lady and her hellish cat, and then spent the entire flight talking to a complete stranger—me—so she wouldn't have a panic attack. You *see* people Mitchell. You recognize their needs and offer help without question." Her fingertips dance along my shoulder. "Do you know how it feels to want to be first yet always falling short?" Her cerulean gaze snaps to mine. "I bet *you* don't. But…I do." My silence spurs her to continue. "I loved my husband. He was compassionate, kind, and loved me with all he had…left over. He was an amazing doctor. Spent countless hours at the hospital. When he wasn't there, he holed up in his home office, emailing and networking with medical professionals all over the world. He barely slept, and when he did, it wasn't restful. More like a battery recharge. I admired his dedication to his profession and the singular focus he had for his patients. It was the same way he took care of me after my mom died."

This is the first time Hope has mentioned anything about her life, and I'm riveted to her words knowing her story isn't going to have an ending filled with happiness.

"I was three years into medical school when my mom died. Car accident. She was my anchor, and when she died, I was devastated. I felt like I was floating in a vast ocean with no land in sight and no directions for which way to paddle."

My heart aches for the difficulties Hope has endured.

"Joe and I had started dating a few months prior. He'd just received an oncology offer in Colorado and asked me to marry him. He promised he'd take care of everything, and I could transfer to medical school out there once we got settled. It was the lifeline I needed, so I said, 'yes,' and we moved to Colorado a few weeks later."

Compelled to touch her and lend her strength, I lift a finger and trace the length of her arm as she gives me a small smile.

"To most, my life looked perfect. And it was…with a tiny exception. I was second, one step below the hospital, in Joe's life. He was my major, and I was his minor. It wasn't malicious. It wasn't calculated. It wasn't even purposeful. It was a fact, and like all facts, they never change. The hospital always held his vision, and I'd been confined to his periphery. The problem was I devoted very little effort into changing our pattern. I relied on him to make a change—putting me first—that was invisible to his eyes." She swallows. Her voice has shrunk to a whisper. "When you relieved my anxiety on the flight, you put me first. You helped me breathe without doing it for me. You gave me my fantasy…to be *seen*."

37

HOPE

I BLINK THE SLEEP FROM MY EYES AND LIFT MY ARMS OVER MY head, stretching like a cat while taking stock of muscles that haven't been sore like this in years. A quick glance at my phone tells me I've already slept half of my day away.

A satisfied smile paints my face as I recall Mitchell's goodbye *kiss*. We'd filled my bedroom with whispers and secrets for much of the night before we fell asleep just after three. Knowing he had a thirty-minute drive ahead of him, he'd set his alarm for four-thirty so he'd be home by the time Sedona woke up. He'd compared her to a bird saying her eyes pop open at first light. Considering it's daylight savings time, he'd said she'd likely be awake by five forty-five.

There's nothing quite like being woken up with a man's head between your legs, his stubble abrading the inside of your thighs, as his tongue plunges in and out of your core. I'd been unable to stifle the scream that flew from my lips as he'd licked me through an explosive orgasm. I'd coaxed him up my body and sealed my lips to his, eager to thank him for his goodbye kiss.

He'd climbed off my bed, gathering his clothing from its scattered position on my floor before retreating to my bathroom. I'd dozed while I waited until he emerged, his suit pants zipped and sitting low on his hips, his chest bare except for the glint of his piercings. His smile had been contagious as he'd licked his lips and shot me a wink before pulling his undershirt over his head and hiding his delicious torso from my sight.

He'd given me one last kiss before asking if my back door would lock behind him, which I assured him it would. Then he'd stolen out of my bedroom leaving me on an orgasm high before I'd finally managed to fall back asleep about thirty minutes later.

I climb out of bed, grab a t-shirt and shorts from the floor, and make my way to the bathroom to take care of business before going in search of caffeine. I make my way to the kitchen and start my coffee machine allowing it to warm up while I snag a cup from the cupboard. I slide my cup under the spout and press the button before gathering a loaf of bread and my favorite strawberry jam from the refrigerator. Nothing hits the spot like a cup of coffee and a jam sandwich. As I approach the table, my arms full of my makeshift lunch, my eyes catch on the mason jar of daisies before landing on a single red rose next to a sticky note.

Hope -
Last night and this morning were perfect.
I'll call you later this evening.
I want more.
Your words. Your fantasies. You.
More.
Mitchell

Mitchell's words pierce my soul. If he hadn't already

wormed his way under my skin, his note would have tipped the scales. As I walk across my kitchen to retrieve my coffee, a smirk rises across my lips. It's a good thing the red roses are on my side of the drive. Cameron would have a shit fit if he caught someone cutting one of his precious stems.

I grab my coffee cup and lift it to my lips as I walk back to the table pondering everything Mitchell shared with me last night. Tangled together under the sheets, we'd spent hours talking. He told me about his parents, who live in Chicago during the summers and Florida in the winter. He has a brother, with whom he's close, even though he doesn't see him often because he lives in California and their schedules rarely align.

He told me about Maggie and how she'd come into his life when he was at his breaking point. She'd taken over the cooking, put Sedona on a schedule, and taught Mitchell how to discipline her with a firm, but loving hand. He'd laughed and admitted to nearly crying the first couple of times he had to follow through with a timeout.

While he hadn't gone into detail, he'd vaguely mentioned a traumatic incident that had disrupted Sedona's life making it difficult for her to eat and sleep as well as given her a severe case of separation anxiety. I hadn't wanted to pry, but something in the way he'd described what happened told me the incident and his full-time custody of Sedona were woven together. He never once mentioned Sedona's mom, and I'd gathered she didn't play a part in their lives.

I'd listened intently, marveling at the talented surgeon who'd made time for tea parties, trips to the zoo, and school carpools. His daughter is his inspiration, and her happiness is his goal even if securing hers costs him his own.

He is a phenomenal doctor who loves his job, but the people in his life—his daughter, his parents, Maggie, his brother—will always be his primary focus. Just like the glimpse of the man I'd seen on the plane years ago, his contentment is interwoven in the connections he makes with people. His life had changed overnight and, by his own admission, he'd nearly buckled under the stress. Yet, he'd owned his choices and made a new song.

———

RIVULETS OF WATER sluice down my naked skin as I towel my wet hair. I hadn't planned to spend twenty minutes in the shower, but the warm water had gone a long way in relaxing muscles that held stiffness from overuse after years of neglect.

The trill of my phone hits my ears. Considering my current state, I let it go to voicemail knowing three rings won't afford me enough time to get from the shower to where my phone is plugged in on my nightstand. My toes sink into the pink fuzzy bathmat covering a piece of my bathroom floor. It's like standing on a cloud, and I congratulate myself for a splurge worth every penny I paid to the online retailer.

As I pat the wet beads from my limbs, my phone rings again. I'm off today, but considering my line of employment I drop my towel as concern floats through my consciousness. Repeated calls aren't an accident, they're an emergency. I rush to my nightstand, narrowly escaping a face plant when a pair of shorts get caught on my foot as I hurry across my bedroom floor. The ringer stops as I slide my phone into my palm.

Mitchell.

My stomach clenches and not in a good way. He's called three times in the past fifteen minutes. A voicemail notification sits at the top of my phone, but I don't waste time listening before I hit the button to return Mitchell's call.

He picks up on the first ring. "Hope. I need your help." His calm demeanor of early this morning has vanished, replaced by panic approaching hysteria.

I squeeze my phone as my mind is thrown back to another phone call that changed the course of my life. "What can I do?"

"Can you come to my house? I need you to stay here with Sedona. How soon can you get here?" His breathing is erratic, and his voice has lost all traces of restraint.

I glance at my watch. It's early evening on a Saturday. If I can leave in five minutes, I may have a chance of getting ahead of Saturday night traffic.

"I'll leave in five. Text me your address as soon as we hang up."

He exhales, his relief reaching me through the airwaves. "Thank you. Get here as soon as you can, but drive safe." He ends the call, and a text comes through a minute later.

I speed around my bedroom gathering clothes before heading into the bathroom to dress and throw my wet hair into a ponytail. He gave me no clue for the reason for his urgency, which spurs me to rush my routine. Considering his request, Sedona must be okay, and my heartbeat marginally slows its race. If not Sedona, is it Maggie? His rock. His second mother.

My heart takes off in a sprint. Mitchell and Sedona need me, and it twists my stomach because I can't offer my support until I physically see them.

I slide my cell phone in my pocket, grab my wallet from the counter, and pull my keys from the hook near my back door. Four minutes after Mitchell's phone call, my GPS is locked on his address, and I'm backing out of my driveway, pointing in the direction of the man who's magnified the sound of my heart's song.

Twenty-five minutes and a few broken speed limits later, I signal and pull to the curb of the address Mitchell texted me. I glance at my phone screen, making sure I didn't key in the wrong information, before turning into the drive and heading down a long, tree-lined path.

I know this man is successful, but this is a manor. An estate with manicured grounds, a circle drive, and an honest-to-God bubbling fountain out in front. Not wishing to disturb the idyllic picture but not wanting to waste time by asking where I should put my car, I throw my vehicle in park at the base of the stone steps, grab my phone, and exit the vehicle.

Taking in the grand porch and the enormity of the craftsman structure with a hurried eye, I run up the steps and ring the bell. I hear Mitchell's authoritative, but muted, yell at the same time distorted shadows appear in the transom to the side of the front door.

"Who is it?" A small, child-like voice filters through the wood as I hear fumbling.

"It's Hope. Your dad's friend."

Another voice, older but decidedly female, hits my ears and my brows lower in confusion. The way Mitchell described Maggie she's not a young woman, yet the muffled whispers do not belong to an older woman. Before my brain can tease out the puzzle, the lock clicks and the door swings open.

A little girl and a woman, not much older than me, stand on the other side.

The woman holds an ice pack to her right arm with a dish towel dotted in fresh blood.

Green eyes meet mine. My eyes catalog the similarities to the ones burned into my soul.

Convulsions wrack my body, one hand lifting to my mouth, the other shooting to the door frame to keep my feet beneath me.

A voice, slightly older than the last time I heard it, but still angelic, pierces my ears.

"Are you Hope?"

Heavy footsteps clap across the entryway a second before

Mitchell's face appears behind the two. A picture-perfect family of three. The similarities pull tears from my burning eyes.

Worry and grief shade Mitchell's face before he opens his mouth. "Hope, this is—"

My whisper cuts him off. Words like razor blades slice my lips as they squeeze past my shaking fingers. "EJ and Sadie."

38

MITCHELL

I GLANCE FROM THE HIGHWAY TO EMILY AS WE HEAD TO THE hospital. My brain is trying to figure out the scene we just left, and she provides no help in this messed up situation. I'd told Hope about Sedona, Maggie, and my parents, but I'd selfishly hoped I could refrain from bringing Emily into our relationship until we had more time together.

Me taking care of Emily holds the possibility of wiping away any chance at a future with Hope. It's one of the reasons I've shied away from making myself available and engaging in a relationship since the accident. I'll be tied to Emily for the rest of our lives, and not many women are strong enough to understand our relationship, much less tolerate it.

Emily's head slumps against the passenger window as she clutches her bent arm to her chest. I hated leaving Hope and Sedona without much more than an introduction, but Emily's bleeding hadn't stopped over the past hour, and I'm worried the damage may be worse than just requiring stitches.

I'd tried everything to avoid calling Hope, but I'd finally had to reach out after not being able to get in touch with my parents and knowing Maggie was two hours away visiting her son and his family as she often did on the weekends Emily visited.

Maggie didn't agree with my decision to allow Emily to stay with us once a month. She felt Emily's presence was confusing and frustrating to Sedona.

In the beginning, I'd mistakenly believed Sedona needed to see her mother as much as possible following the accident. I'd reasoned Sedona needed the familiarity after the trauma of the accident and being uprooted when I moved her back with me. It wasn't until recently, when Sedona's nightmares returned, I was forced to re-evaluate my decisions and make plans for a break.

While Emily knows she's Sedona's mother, the brain damage she suffered during the accident caused gaps in her parenting instincts and her logical reasoning, though I'd plead a convincing case she lacked parenting skills before the accident. Damage from the accident makes Emily impulsive and unpredictable to the point of being a danger to herself and those around her.

Not to mention the anger she directs toward me. She's concocted a scene in her mind where I am the villain who kept her from Joe. My ex-wife is convinced our marriage sabotaged her relationship with her long-time best friend for whom she harbored romantic feelings. Truth be known, my entire relationship with Emily had been a rebound after Joe denied her advances and eventually married and moved to Colorado.

Shit.

Colorado.

My heart accelerates. The beats are like a drum in my chest.

Pieces of this fucked up puzzle float into place.

Emily and Sedona's accident happened in Colorado.

Hope moved from Colorado.

Her husband's name was Joe.

Hope called her EJ, the nickname Emily told me Joe gave her.

Sadie. Hope had known Sedona's nickname.

We no longer used her nickname because she'd had a meltdown the first time I'd called her Sadie after the accident. It had taken me months to erase it from my vocabulary, but I'd done it to make her happy.

My hands wrap around the steering wheel, turning my knuckles white as I fight the compulsion to turn the car around and get to the bottom of this story.

"Emily, what was that back there?"

I notice the stiffening of her body, but she remains quiet. I'm not sure if it's an inability to formulate the words or her refusal to say them, but her continued silence sounds like a giant "fuck you." Anger radiates from her body, mixing with my impatience, and making the interior of the car feel like a time bomb, echoing in my ears.

"Emily?"

I was there when she saw Hope. Every muscle in Emily's body had gone rigid like she had been turned to stone. Her recognition had been as acute as the shock on Hope's face. Emily has the answers, and her refusal to engage makes me want to reach over and shake her until the explanations she's withholding fall from her tongue. Four years, I've paid for her care, dealt with her mood swings, excused her from blame, and she can't give me the fucking courtesy to answer one damn question.

I turn my head, looking at the gorgeous shell of a woman whose beauty made me blind to her manipulations years ago. Guilt slides between the cracks of my irritation. Without Emily, I wouldn't have Sedona, and I wouldn't be the man I am without my daughter.

Shit. If I hadn't ignored Emily and actually listened to her fears when she'd called me in a blind panic the night before the accident, maybe she wouldn't have been on the road, fourteen hours from home that day. Maybe I could have convinced her to talk with a professional and work through the pain of losing her best friend. Instead, I'd refused to lend an ear to her cries, and the next day I'd answered the phone and received news no one should ever have to hear.

I remember the call with crystal clarity. I'd been thirty minutes from starting a three-hour surgery, and I'd answered on a whim not recognizing the number but seeing it wasn't local. *"Mr. Anderson, your wife and daughter have been in a car accident. Your wife sustained massive injuries and has been flown to Rock Ledge Hospital in Denver. Your daughter is being treated in Boulder, and will be released to Colorado Child Services until you can get here."*

I couldn't connect the words to tell the woman Emily was my *ex* and hadn't been my wife for some time. A numbness had slithered through my veins and only became apparent when I'd dropped my phone on the toe of my shoe. While my body had been frozen, my tongue hadn't been. A "NO" had ripped from my lungs and sent two nurses running into the break room to see what had happened.

I'd bumbled my way through a disjointed explanation, their expressions telling me they didn't understand the words coming from my mouth. Ten minutes later, I'd calmed enough to find my boss and utter a half coherent form of the story. He'd canceled my surgery then called my parents. Within an hour, they'd purchased tickets, picked me up at the hospital, pushed a carry-on packed with clothes and toiletries into my hands, and helped me onto the flight.

We'd talked through options and formulated a plan while we were in the air. My dad offered to head straight to Rock Ledge in Denver, and my mom and I continued on to Boulder where Sadie was waiting with strangers and probably scared out of her mind.

I'd flown Emily and Sedona home and moved them into

my house where we lived in hell for the next six months as I fought and failed to piece a version of my once intact family back together.

It wasn't until I'd admitted I couldn't handle the stress of my fellowship, managing nurses for Emily's twenty-four-hour care, and working through Sedona's recovery that I looked for help. I'd transferred Emily from my house, where she'd received round the clock nursing care as well as physical therapy and occupational therapy, to a residential facility in Rockford, about an hour away.

I'd also found Maggie around the same time, and it was after Maggie moved in that I saw Sedona start to improve. It was three months after Emily moved out and two months after Maggie had started working for me that I'd walked into my house and heard the sound of an angel. Sedona had been standing on a chair, belly up to the counter, helping Maggie make chocolate chip cookies and laughing. At that moment, my daughter had been happy, and I clung to the first signs she had finally started to heal.

The coolness of Emily's left hand, as it touches mine, pulls me from my thoughts. I glance over to see tears streaming down her face. Her hand falls away from mine as I lift my thumb and wipe the emotion from her face. I shift my focus back to the highway. Pink tinges her cheeks showing her embarrassment. Before the accident, she'd used tears to play on my sympathies and secure the reaction she wanted from me. Since the accident, I haven't seen her cry. Not when I told her she was being transferred to a residential facility, and not when I told her, weeks ago, we all needed a break. Don't misunderstand, she has no problem releasing anger, frustration, and blips of sarcasm, but she's never cried.

Her voice, scratchy from her tears, is hesitant. "Hope. I know her." She swallows before continuing. "I knew her."

I turn my head, briefly searching her face before I nod and return my gaze to the road.

"She is the bitch who stole Joe away. He'd gotten the oncology position and asked her to go to Colorado without ever mentioning it to me. He and I had lived together for six years, and he chose her over me."

Two of those years, she'd been married to me. It was a little tidbit I'd been kept in the dark about until it showed up on a statement of marital debts during our divorce. Apparently, while we'd been married, she stayed there when I worked double shifts.

"Do you know how it feels to be pushed to the side by someone you love?"

When we'd been together, I thought for a brief time I was in love. But as we grew apart, or never really grew together depending on how one looked at it, I saw my feelings for what they were—lust.

I feel her eyes on me and shake my head. I may not know the feeling of being pushed to the side, but I know someone who does. Thinking about Hope and Emily, I have an epiphany. Both women experienced loss, from the same person, with two different results.

Hope had felt slighted by Joe's marriage to his profession. When he died, Hope had forged ahead finding strength within herself. When Joe married Hope, Emily was caught in a loop, not able to accept her perceived rejection and blaming Hope for that rejection.

To my objective eyes, Joe had a gift. Without much effort, he pulled women into his orbit. For all of his phenomenal abilities in medicine, he failed to recognize the brilliance that was his sun and moon. He didn't deserve blame for not returning Emily's romantic feelings, but he couldn't escape my condemnation for not setting her straight in her dislike for Hope. As far as I'm concerned, he should have broken off his friendship with Emily as soon as she revealed feelings he couldn't reciprocate.

"I'm sorry you felt neglected by Joe. I never realized the depth of your romantic feelings for him. Damn. That's something that may have been useful to mention to me while we were dating, and sure as shit before we were married."

The flare of my annoyance spurs my harsh response, and guilt bubbles up on its heels. Blaming Emily for shortcomings in the past means nothing at this point and won't get us anywhere except a one-way ticket on the guilt trip train.

She turns, her lips tipped in a barely-there smile, as she lifts her shoulder. "Didn't mention it because I didn't see any way to change it except for moving on with someone else. I didn't expect him to have such a hold on my heart." Turning away, she looks out the window.

I cannot imagine the chaos in her brain right now. Since the accident, she's had varying degrees of difficulty formulating her thoughts and organizing them into statements. Like a radio broadcast, sometimes her thoughts flow freely and come out clear and concise other times they are filled with static, random thoughts, and stilted sentences.

Though she stares out the window, she continues to talk. "I blamed Hope. The last time I spoke with her was about a month after Joe died. I hadn't been able to reach him, and I resorted to calling Hope, though it took a while to nail down her number." She raises her hand and runs a fingertip through the condensation her breath creates on the window. "She told me he died and apologized for forgetting to contact me. My emotions hit me hard. I was angry. She forgot me. She stole my goodbye. I screamed at her." I hear her swallow before she drops her chin to her chest. "I said she should have died. Then I hung up."

Her words knock the breath from my lungs. My heart bleeds for Hope, who had to endure those words at a time when the embers of her previous life were still smoldering, and she was trying to rise from the ashes of her own grief.

My chest twists for Emily and the poison of her guilt so tangible I feel its tentacles slithering through the cabin between us. The heat of hatred Emily's words held four years ago have turned inward and scorched her. I recognize her scars in the anger she wraps around herself.

I inhale and exhale as I grasp the final tendrils of my questions. "So, Joe was the common tie between you and Hope? Did Hope know you had been married? Did she know you had a daughter?"

She turns, and we share a tense moment before she shakes her head, her eyes falling to the space between us before I turn back to the highway.

"I didn't tell Joe about you or Sedona. I thought if I did, he wouldn't believe I'd always loved him."

I nod, not knowing if I'm flattered or irritated to have known about Joe when he knew nothing about me. I move facts and details around in my head, though there's still a piece missing. Hope called my daughter Sadie. *How did Hope know we'd once called her Sadie?* The question circles like a merry-go-round in my head before I spit it into the space between us.

"If Joe and Hope never knew about Sedona or me, how the hell does Hope know Sadie?"

39

HOPE

My eyes track the taillights of Mitchell's Tesla as they disappear down the tree-lined driveway in a streak of red. Red like the blood that invades my nightmares and has brought countless disruptions to my life over the past four years. Like a twenty-five-cent super ball from a grocery store vending machine, questions bounce through my brain while I attempt to process the shock of seeing EJ and Sadie with Mitchell.

He'd introduced his daughter, Sedona. Sedona is Sadie, the same girl I'd tethered to my heart as I talked her through her fears and attempted to shield her from the horrors of the scene where her vehicle lay twisted on the side of a mountain. I still remember the smell of strawberries as I held her to me. Her stubby finger pointing into the distance, not knowing if she would ever see her mom again.

Mitchell had taken one look at my devasted face and immediately known something was wrong, but he'd also been intent on assuring Sedona that the stranger who showed up at his door—me—was a friend and would stay with her until he returned with her mother. If he'd pushed a knife through my ribs, I don't think it would have hurt as much seeing his hand resting protectively on EJ's back.

Shit. *Were they still married? Did I have sex with a married man last night?* When the thought spears my brain, my stomach clenches and not in a good way. Running my hand over my ponytail, I sift through last night's conversation looking for words, references, and clues. When my review comes up empty, I rewind the past few months. Not a single word about having a wife or being married. I would have damn well remembered that little fact.

Warm fingers wrap around my pinky and pull me from my thoughts.

"Do you like to swing? I have one in the backyard. What about a treehouse? Daddy built me one, but I'm not allowed to climb the ladder unless an adult is with me."

Oh, Sedona, I may look like an adult, but I feel as capable as a toddler taking her first steps. My emotions are like a bubbling volcano threatening to blow at any moment, and I'm fighting to keep them from breaking free and scaring this sweet little girl.

A couple of hours, the length of an appendectomy, then Mitchell will be back with his wife, his ex, EJ, whoever she is, and I can leave and lick my wounds in private.

I grasp Sedona's fingers and smile at her, a little disappointed her cute speech impediment no longer laces her words. I hold out my hand in an invitation for her to pull us where she wants to go. She leads me through the house, and I take a quick look at the space Mitchell calls home. Considering how massive and overbearing it looks from the outside, the interior is a mix of natural light and warm colors decorated with light woods and black iron accents. The floor plan is open with wooden columns and beams dividing the massive space into specific rooms.

I feel like I've stepped into a magazine spread two hours

before the staging crew arrives. I spy a backpack slung across the back of a chair in the dining room. A pink, stuffed bunny patiently waits on the back of the couch in the living room. A pair of glitter Converse high tops sparkle from their heap against the wall of the hallway. It's endearing and real.

This isn't a house built to impress; it's a home meant for a family to create memories. If I'd tried to picture where Mitchell lived, I would have never imagined a place like this. I'm impressed, and I love his house. It's an extension of the unpretentious, relaxed man I've come to know. No matter how confused I am by the current circumstances, I can't keep the small smile from my lips.

Sedona glances over her shoulder, an annoyed look covers her face when she notices I've stopped and am gaping at the kitchen.

Six iron-backed bar stools are evenly spaced and pushed up to an island that runs the length of the room and looks to be made of reclaimed wood, stripped and varnished to a dull sheen. It's beautiful, but so is the rest of the space. A rack, full of copper bellied pots, hangs over the island, its aesthetic just as impressive as its function. A white apron sink, big enough to give a large toddler a bath, sits under a triple sash window looking over the lush green backyard. Sitting like a sentry over the kitchen is a stainless steel six-burner dual range. It's beautiful and massive and has the baker in me drooling over the number of cookies I could bake at one time.

Sedona backs up and appears at my side as I attempt to hide my excitement for this kitchen. While it has all the accouterments my kitchen in Colorado had, it lacks the sterile, cave-like atmosphere.

"Pretty sure the swing is outside and not in here."

I look down at green eyes identical to the ones I saw at four-thirty this morning. They hold the same twinkle of mischief.

"Sorry. I got distracted, won't happen again."

She huffs, then grabs my hand and pulls me to the back door, unwilling to allow me to halt our progress before reaching our destination. We step into the backyard and my eyes zero in on the biggest and cutest treehouse I've ever seen. Situated in the limbs of a massive oak tree, it has a shingled roof, a front porch, a little front door, and actual double-hung windows. I haven't even been inside, and I love it. The fact Mitchell built it makes me love it even more.

She kicks off her fuchsia flip flops and takes off at full speed to the tire swing hanging from a limb of the oak tree. I say a silent prayer this tree never dies because it will take this little girl's innocence and childhood to the ground with it. Sedona is already seated on the tire and grasping the ropes on either side of her head when I arrive in front of her.

"Give me a spin. Don't hold back. I'm almost seven. I can handle it."

Her sassiness is rooted in humor, and I know exactly who it comes from. If I didn't know better, I'd say Mitchell is sitting in front of me and taunting me for a push. I check her position and her hands to make sure she's secure before pulling back and pushing the tire forward while scooting under it. Her laughter joins her excited squeals as the ropes swing back and forth like a pendulum.

"Again, please."

Her pink-tinged cheeks and her wide gap-toothed smile have me agreeing before the second word slips between her missing teeth.

I wind up and push her again, smiling at the innocence of her joy. Thirty minutes later, my arms feel like jelly, and she's grown bored. I give her a hand as she steps off the swing and immediately pulls me to the treehouse ladder. I'm just as excited as she appears to be.

When I was a little girl, I'd read the *Magic Treehouse* books and fallen in love with the idea of a treehouse that could transport me through time and space. Our yard didn't lend itself to treehouse construction, but I'd dreamed one day I'd live in a house with trees large enough to build a place hidden by the leaves and ripe for adventures.

I send her up the ladder in front of me, making sure I follow at a close distance in case she slips or needs help. She scampers up and waits for me on the porch. It isn't until I get to the top rung that I notice the dragonfly curtains hanging in the windows. I point to them and comment on how cute they are.

"I helped my dad make them. He held the fabric stuff and did the stitches, but he let me push the pedal."

Her face beams with pride, and I wonder if there's anything thing this man can't do, or won't do, when it comes to his daughter. We crawl through the elf-sized door and each sit on one of the solid blue throw pillows situated around a round table with legs about a foot off the ground.

"Do you like to color?" The inflection in her voice tells me she loves to color and any response other than 'yes' will cost me major brownie points.

"Of course. What's your favorite? Crayons? Markers? Colored Pencils?"

She brings her finger to her temple and tips her head to the side. "Depends on the project, but I like them all." Spoken like a true diplomat.

She leans over, pulling a big basket to the table from its place near the wall. She reaches in and pulls out several coloring books and a massive box of crayons and sets them in the center of the table. She taps the pile of books.

"These are my favorites right now, but I've got two unicorn ones on my birthday list."

We each choose a page from one of the books and start work on our masterpieces. After the strenuous activity of pushing the swing, my arms are happy for a little relief. We color in silence until my runaway thoughts intrude on the companionable quiet. I glance at her every once in a while, smirking when I see her tongue peeking out of the corner of her mouth as she concentrates on coloring within the lines.

Knowing it's wrong to speak with Sedona when I should take my questions to Mitchell, I can't contain the words that pop out of my mouth. "I'm sorry your mommy got hurt."

Her focus stays glued on her paper as she casually lifts a shoulder. "Emily does stuff like that a lot. She uses more band-aids than me."

Her eyes go wide, but she doesn't lift them from her paper. I find it strange Sedona refers to her mom by her first name. She does it like she's stating a fact.

My curiosity is piqued, and I continue down my path ignoring the posted *Do Not Enter* sign. "Does she get hurt a lot?"

Sedona throws her crayon in the box and chooses another one. "When she's here, she does." She turns the paper at a different angle and continues coloring. "It's because she doesn't listen to the rules. I've tried to help her, but she just yells at me, so I quit trying to be nice."

Her little nose scrunches up like she's smelled something bad, most likely the stench of her mom's atrocious manners.

My mouth falls open, and I quickly drop my chin and randomly start coloring as I try to hide the shock stamped across my face. *Who yells at their child for trying to help?* I bite my tongue and continue coloring wishing I'd had the good sense to avoid the topic of her mom before I found out the stark difficulties of their relationship.

Sedona picks up her paper and lifts it toward me. "What do you think?"

I tilt my head from one side to the other pretending to assess her work. "I think it's brilliant. I love the colors you used and how you stayed in the lines all the way around the box. You should win a prize for how good it is."

Her smile is so big I can see nearly every tooth in her mouth. "Is it good enough to win me a snack?" Her eyes sparkle with humor.

"You know what? I have an idea. Let's clean up in here and make a trip to the kitchen."

"Does your idea involve chocolate?" Her eyebrows lift as she finishes her question, and I have to stifle a giggle since she reminds me so much of her dad at this moment.

40

MITCHELL

EMILY JUMPS OUT OF MY CAR AND RUNS TO THE BACK DOOR AS
soon as I put the vehicle in park. She's barely uttered a word
since we walked into the hospital. I'd called the attending
physician in the emergency room before I'd left the house so
he'd known what to expect when we got there. Forty stitches
and a gauze wrap later, we're home, and Emily is bolting from
my presence.

I let her go without calling after her. Today registers "shitstorm" on the stress meter. I can't fault her for wanting to carve
out time so she can process her thoughts about seeing Hope as
well as come to terms with today being the last day she'll spend
with us for a while.

I check my watch. We'll need to leave in a little over an
hour if I want to have her back by check-in at nine p.m. I walk
up the front steps like my feet are made of the cement. I'd had
no time to talk with Hope before I'd left Sedona in her care,
and I can't imagine the types of questions burning through her
brain.

The smell of chocolate and vanilla hits my nose when I
step through the front door. I toe my shoes off, leaving them in

the tray in the foyer before walking toward the kitchen. I study Hope and Sedona as I approach, seated on the stools at the kitchen island, backs to me, heads tilted together as their shoulders shake with the vibrations of the giggles coming from their mouths.

I take a step and stop, suddenly assaulted by an overwhelming desire to snap a picture so I can have a physical depiction of my dream as a father. Me walking through the door, my girls messing around in the kitchen, their words and laughter echoing throughout the house and seeping into the walls.

The scene I'm looking at is joy in its purest form, and I want to bottle it so I never have to go without.

It's family.

It's a connection.

It's what I've wanted since I took full custody of Sedona. More than anything, my heart wants this, and my heart wants Hope.

I clear my throat and take the final steps into the kitchen. Both of them hear me and turn around. Sedona has half of a cookie sticking out of her mouth, and Hope has a spot of chocolate at the corner of her lips. I have an urge to step forward and remove it with my tongue, but it's probably not a good plan considering Sedona just met her, and my ex-wife is currently under the same roof.

"This is the closest I've ever come to actually finding someone's hand in a cookie jar."

Sedona stuffs the final bite of the cookie into her mouth and narrows her eyes. "We don't have a cookie jar."

My chuckle is rusty when I answer. "It's an expression, princess. It means I caught you doing something you shouldn't be doing."

Hope smiles and cocks her head. "What shouldn't we be doing?"

I can't tell where her mind's at, and I need to get a sense of how she's feeling. "Sedona, why don't you run up to your room and grab the book we've been reading so you can show it to Hope. I bet she'd like to see it."

Sedona's off her chair and halfway to the stairs before I finish my suggestion. I slide onto her vacated stool and steal a cookie from the small plate sitting in the middle of the island. I fold it and stuff the entire thing in my mouth. Damn. I love Hope's sweets.

I lean sideways my arm skimming hers as I whisper into her ear. "She'll be busy searching for a bit. She doesn't know I brought the book into my room so I could read ahead."

"Seriously, you're cheating on your shared reading experience?" The tease in her voice negates the seriousness of her accusation.

"I had hoped to read much longer last night. But, if you'll recall, I had a previous engagement." I smirk and give her a wink.

We sit, touching but not talking, as I eat another cookie. The silence is deafening and filled with unanswered questions suspended between us.

"So, everything alright with EJ?"

I dissect her question looking for censure, but find nothing other than neutral fact-finding.

I rub the back of my neck. "Yeah, she'll be okay. She sliced herself pretty good. Took forty stitches to close. She's lucky Sedona was concerned and found me upstairs quickly. If Emily would have been by herself, I don't know if she would have recognized how serious the injury was."

Hope's eyebrows dip in confusion. "How could she not realize it was serious?"

"It's a result of the accident. She doesn't always feel pain like you or me, and her reasoning is impaired. I once found her in my bathroom putting a band-aid on a second-degree burn she got from trying to make macaroni and cheese on the stove unsupervised." Hope's mouth drops open, but she says nothing, so I continue. "Looking at her, you'd never know she has the difficulties she does. It's why she can't live on her own, and… it's why she can't live here either."

Some of the tension Hope is holding seeps out of her after she processes my statement. "So EJ doesn't live here?"

I turn toward her, wanting her to see my face and hear my words. "No. She hasn't lived here full-time since right before Sedona was three. I had to transfer her to a residential facility in Rockford because I couldn't handle the stress of her living here. I've tried to foster a relationship between Sedona and Emily by having Emily stay with us one weekend a month since she transferred, but even once a month has taken a toll on Sedona. In fact, today is the last day Emily will be with us for a while. It's been a long time coming, but I've been too scared to separate Sedona from her mom. Turns out Sedona is happy about the split. At least for now."

Hope lays her hand on top of mine. "I cannot imagine what your lives have been like. You're an amazing man and an amazing father, but…" Her 'but' has my eyes darting to her face, and I watch as a single tear rolls down her cheek. "But, I will not be in a relationship with a married man. It's not fair to anyone involved, no matter the circumstances. I'm sorry."

Her tears flow freely after she finishes, and I hang my head, silently berating myself for not starting the conversation from the beginning.

I turn and cradle her head in my hands as I lean towards her, removing her tears with the pads of my thumbs. "Hope, Emily and I aren't married. We divorced before the accident."

Her entire body freezes as I continue to wipe her tears. Her chest rises and falls, and I glimpse relief in her glassy eyes. "EJ is your ex-wife?"

My lips brush hers in a soft caress. "No matter the circumstances, I never, nor would I ever, cheat on my wife."

She sniffs. "For future reference, lead with the ex-wife part. Always lead with that."

I bring her mouth to mine sealing my lips to hers. I still have questions, and I pray Hope is willing to answer them so we can move forward.

Her body follows mine as I break the kiss and brush a wisp of hair behind her ear.

"There's still something I need you to clear up for me." She nods, and I ask. "Emily said she never told Joe about Sedona, so how did you know we used to call her Sadie?"

41

HOPE

MITCHELL'S FACE IS A MASK OF CONFUSION AND SUSPICION when he asks me how I know Sadie. I'd irrationally hoped he'd figure it out so I wouldn't have to dredge my memories, but he wasn't there, and he has no way of knowing how interwoven our lives became four years ago.

I lick my lips, stalling so I can collect my thoughts and approach this conversation with the least amount of discomfort. A creak on the stairs startles me, and I turn to see EJ cautiously making her way down the back stairway. I twist my neck to look at her. Blues meet blues as she freezes on the final step unsure if she should intrude, but appearing as though she needs to speak with me as badly as I want to avoid her.

Mitchell sees my conflict and flicks his fingers to warn EJ away from the pending discussion. She turns to retreat, but not before I see the pain of isolation flash through her eyes. I take a breath, placing my hand on Mitchell's before hitting the wall of her back with my offer.

"EJ, I think you may want to hear this, too."

Her body relaxes, and her shoulders hunch forward, and I know I've made the right decision.

For all of her hateful words and distrust for me, she's hurting and suffering alone. Sequestered by fate, she's living a life for which she had no say or control. She lost everything: a normal relationship with her daughter, her best friend, and worst of all, herself, yet she's had no one to share the burden of her loss with.

Fate swooped in and shit on her life, then took off leaving her to sort through the mess on her own. Sympathy for her bleeds from my soul. She may see me as a villain, but I'm her last true connection to her best friend and the life she lived before our paths intersected.

She's quiet as she walks into the kitchen, grabs a glass from the counter, and fills it from the tap at the sink. She crosses to the island choosing to lean against the side opposite the two stools Mitchell and I occupy. Her body language promises she'll be a listener, but not an active participant in what I have to say.

Mitchell squeezes my hand, and my eyes leave EJ's to connect with his.

"Thank you." His gaze shines with unshed tears like he'd wanted EJ to be a part of this, but he'd refused to disrupt the story that was mine to tell.

My eyes bounce around the kitchen, steeling myself for the onslaught of emotion.

"I, uh, had a job while I lived in Colorado. Joe wasn't thrilled considering he thought it was beneath someone who had completed three years of medical school." I glance at EJ and see her intense focus lacks any specific emotion. "But, I was slowly losing myself in the monotony of days that held no purpose outside of working out, grocery shopping, and cleaning the house. My mom had died just before I moved to Colorado, and I'd been having difficulty handling my grief. I needed a purpose, so I got a job as an EMT."

I'm looking directly at Mitchell, and I notice the moment

his thoughts leap ahead to the gut-wrenching part of the story. EJ stands like a statue, her only movements are the increased rise and fall of her chest. Her brain is also putting together pieces, though it's a slower process for her, and she may not remember enough to paint the gruesome picture.

"Finding the EMT position was a decision I made at the urging of my psychiatrist, Dr. Johansen, who was helping me work through my grief. That job ultimately saved me following my mom's death and later, Joe's."

A cough bubbles up from EJ's lungs, and she drops her eyes to the countertop to hide the emotions covering her face.

"Being an EMT was completely different than working in the hospital. Faster paced. Scary. Raw. And a hell of a lot more real. The decisions my partner and I made truly rode the line between life and death. It was as exhilarating as it was frightening. The crew I worked with was phenomenal. I was the only female in a pack of loud, rowdy guys who would do anything for me."

I slide my gaze to the left as a smile tips my lips. Those men may not have physically saved my life, but emotionally they'd kept me from vanishing into a sea of darkness.

"When Joe died, they looked after me. They stopped by my house, brought me meals, and texted to see if I needed anything. Chief Matthews went above and beyond his job as a boss by getting me some paid time off and hooking me up with a support group where I met people like me who had lost their spouses in tragic accidents. After about two weeks, I felt strong enough to go back to work. It was shortly after I went back that EJ called, and I realized I had failed Joe. The one person outside of me and his dad who should have been at his funeral was EJ, and I'd not even remembered to contact her and relay what had happened."

My stare, which had been focused on the countertop, lifts

to EJ's, and I see her flinch as I admit my truth. EJ and I didn't get along, but we both cared for Joe. She should have been there, and it was my fault she wasn't.

"EJ, I'm so sorry. I know my words can never replace my neglect, but I'm sorry you weren't there. My guilt has eaten away at me for the past four years. The problem with guilt is it's an infinite emotion because the action that causes it can never be undone."

Tears create silent rivers down EJ's cheeks, and she raises her hands to wipe them away before she gives me a slight nod of acceptance. A chain, I hadn't realized was wrapped around my heart, snaps, and I instantly feel the balm of forgiveness.

I release my hand from Mitchell's and slide it toward EJ, though she makes no move to touch my hand or acknowledge my olive branch. I slowly pull my hand back and Mitchell intertwines his with mine before I continue my story.

"About two weeks after I returned to work, my partner, Shawn, and I were dispatched to a car accident. We were first on the scene."

I close my eyes and take a breath through my nose trying to eradicate the stench of the burned rubber that will never leave my memory.

"It was the worst I'd ever seen. A mass of twisted metal was wrapped around the guardrail on one of the most dangerous roads in the area. The car was obliterated, and I remember thinking *how could anyone walk away?* My partner, McNair, and I checked the perimeter confirming there were two occupants. The driver appeared to be female, due to her clothing, and a toddler who was strapped into a child seat in the back. The toddler was screaming and flailing her little arms knowing something was terribly wrong. McNair assigned me to the small child, and he did what he could with the driver until the rest of the team showed up a few minutes later."

Mitchell bows his head and wipes at the corners of his eyes. I cannot imagine the turmoil he's in listening to the day he almost lost his daughter and her mother.

My throat is parched from trying to hold back the onslaught of emotion clawing at my heart to break free. I slip from my chair and fill a glass with water, taking greedy sips as I return to my seat beside Mitchell.

"I focused on the little girl, her screams telling me her condition was far better than the driver. I wracked my brain trying to think of anything I could do to keep her attention away from the horror of the blood and twisted metal scattered across the front seat just a foot from her."

I raise my hand and splay my fingers as I recall her gesture and how she tried to reach me when her little body was confined to the seat behind the glass.

"I needed to find out what her name was so I made my mission a game. It wasn't until she started yelling answers through the window that I recognized she mixed up her speech sounds."

Mitchell nods his head, and I glance at him. The faintest of smiles sits on his lips, and his eyes are focused on a memory outside of the kitchen we're sitting in.

"Her little face had screwed up in frustration when I'd failed to understand her name. She was on the verge of tears, and I wanted to scream because of my failure. It wasn't until I recalled a lecture during medical school where we'd received basic information about speech development that I remembered a trick we'd been instructed to try. I finally figured out she had been trying to tell me her name was Sadie. My heart soared when she gifted me with a huge, satisfied smile." My mouth smiles in response to my memory. "By the time I'd figured out her name and she'd told me she was two, the team had arrived and started prepping the tools to cut the driver out of the car. Knowing it would be loud, I tried to prepare Sadie and make sure she kept her attention on me. She was so good at following directions, but what truly stole my heart was the innocent trust she gave freely without question. I think it's one of the most precious gifts I've ever received."

My eyes well with tears, and I look to the ceiling to keep them at bay.

Mitchell's head shakes back and forth, his eyes glued to the countertop.

"I used to tease her about her speech, but there wasn't a dollar amount too extreme I wouldn't have paid to hear her utter just one word in the six months after the accident. She didn't talk for six months. You were the last person to hear her two-year-old words."

He runs his hand through his hair as he fights the tide of his emotions.

I lift my gaze to EJ. Her hands are braced on the island, and she's hunched over like her arms are the only reason she's still upright. She senses my attention and raises her eyes to meet mine.

"EJ, you were her singular thought that day. She called for you and fought against my hold as the ambulance rushed you to the waiting helicopter. You're her mom. She loves you."

Like a dam breaking with little warning, EJ's mouth opens and a torrent of sobs filters out. She lifts her hand to her lips in an effort to hold them back, though the flood cannot be contained. Mitchell stands and rounds the island wrapping her in an embrace, careful of her bandaged arm, as moans rip from her chest.

"That was the last day she called me mommy. She hasn't called mommy for four years. Mitchell, I did this. Why did I do this?" Her chants are low and loop between her sobs.

His voice drips with honey like he's soothing the cries of an ill child. "I can't tell you why. It was a freak accident. A horrible blip in time."

Her palms connect with his chest and push him back, effectively breaking his embrace. Her eyes are red, and her face is painted with regret as she wipes the wetness from her cheeks.

"I was so angry. At life. At you, for not listening when I'd called the night before. At Joe, for leaving me here and not loving me. I held no control over my life. I wanted to scream, '*Look at me. See me. I'm suffering right in front of your eyes.*' I'd failed in my marriage. I'd failed in my relationships. I'd failed in life. When I hung up with you, I made a plan. I hadn't been to Joe's house, but I knew where it was. I was on my way there. I wanted something of Joe's. Anything, so I could always have him with me. I'd just come around a curve and passed a sign for another ahead. As I focused on the wavy line on the sign, I realized I didn't need something that *belonged* to Joe. I needed *him*. I couldn't, and wouldn't, fail again. I pushed the gas pedal to the floor. At the last second, Sadie's voice sang, 'Mommy, I lub you.' I hadn't failed *her*. Her love wasn't conditional. If I followed Joe, I'd leave her. She'd be my final failure. I slammed on the brakes and twisted the wheel, but it was a heartbeat too late."

EJ's knees buckle, but Mitchell lunges forward and flattens her to his chest. His face is ghostly white and scattered with tears.

EJ has just admitted to attempting suicide, yet she'd pulled back in a final moment of clarity. Sedona's little voice had changed the course of people's lives. I knew EJ's words would never be uttered outside of this kitchen. The past couldn't be changed, and the future wouldn't benefit from the truth of her words.

Sadie is an angel who will never know the gift she gave her mother on Baxter Bend.

I'm reminded everyone traverses an uncharted path. Each

is given a map made up of invisible pathways appearing and disappearing in response to the choices made along the way. Like the uniqueness of a fingerprint, no two maps are the same and no two outcomes are identical. It's not my place, or anyone else's, to point out the imperfections in the road already traveled.

42

HOPE

THE WIND BLOWS ACROSS THE GRASS, COOLING MY BARE ANKLES and reminding me how quickly summer will transition into fall in the coming month. I pull my cardigan against my torso and hope my coming here unannounced doesn't upset EJ, I mean Emily.

She had asked me about a month ago to call her Emily since EJ belonged to Joe and his memory. She hadn't done it as a malicious gesture. It was her way of saying she was trying to move on, and she needed my help in the process of doing so.

My eyes drift across her as she approaches the bench along the walking path. An assistant shadows her but trails a few steps behind giving Emily independence, even if it's just an illusion. Emily is not tall, but her posture and the way she walks reminds me of a willow tree, quiet and graceful. Her full dark hair has grown over the summer, and I make a mental note to ask Mitchell if her monthly allowance includes trips to the salon on the premises.

Her physical beauty is intimidating, but it isn't until she lifts her eyes, blue like broken sea glass, to mine that my mouth goes dry. Emily's face, her body, the way she walks is model perfect, and I have to stifle the thread of jealousy threatening to flood my veins.

Once upon a time, she'd held Mitchell in the palm of her hand. Yet, she'd released him. If she hadn't, he and I would have never been more than friends. I feel like I should buy her a huge gift and thank her, which, in a way, is the reason for my visit.

I've seen Emily twice, though we haven't spoken since the day she sliced open her arm and ended up lancing open my heart in the process. I've accompanied Mitchell, at his request, and Sedona both times they've come here to visit. I've lent them my support silently from the car while they've spent an hour with her during family days.

Mitchell says he's finally starting to heal now that he knows what truly happened on the mountain. He's been seeing a counselor, a choice he shared with me two weeks after he started going, and dealing with the emotions he's allowed to fester for four years.

Emily stops in front of the bench. Her eyes pierce me with curiosity, which is much better than the contempt I figured would greet me.

I brush invisible dust from the seat beside me. "Good afternoon, Emily. How are you?"

She stares at me as her brows pull down over her blue gaze. "What are you doing here?" While her voice isn't gruff, it's not welcoming either.

"I thought we could talk. Would you like to have a seat?"

I paste a smile on my face hoping it looks non-threatening instead of nervous. I bounce my heels on the cement beneath the bench, thankful I'm wearing rubber-soled shoes that make no sound. Emily squares her stance and crosses her arms across her chest. Goosebumps rise across my skin in response to her threatening posture as I wait for her to volley the ball back to my court. I raise my brows and tilt my head to the right, hoping the surprise of my visit is enticing enough for her to sit down.

She lets me sweat for another minute or two before she steps forward and drops onto the bench. "So, what are you here to talk about?"

"Joe."

My single word is like a cattle prod. She jumps up from her seat, her breath coming in short bursts as she stares at me with nothing short of contempt. We wage a silent staring contest as I wait for her curiosity and her feelings for Joe to outweigh her disdain. When she makes no move to sit back down, but she doesn't turn to leave, I start talking knowing she's listening by the sway of her body.

"Joe was a good man. He was caring and charismatic and passionate. The problem was while he loved me, he loved his job more. He was always at the hospital, talking with patients, networking with other doctors, developing treatment plans. He worked an insane number of hours, and it affected other parts of his life. There were many nights where he would sleep on a cot instead of coming home."

Emily nods and slowly takes a seat the bench. Her eyes tilt to the ground, and her posture tenses. I look over at her and smile, though she can't see me do it.

"He missed dinners and date nights, and often ditched hospital functions so he could stay with his patients. He became obsessed with his job and with his fixation came apathy for our relationship. Over time the Joe I'd met and grown to love became harder to see under the stranger I didn't know. While he continued to meet my immediate needs, he neglected to see we were failing miserably as a couple."

I glance over and catch the flinch that crosses her face. She turns, and her eyes meet mine. "His lack of contact? His failure to return my calls? That wasn't because of you?"

My lips turn down, and I shake my head slowly. "No. I may not have enjoyed being the third wheel at your get-togethers, but I never discouraged him from spending time with you. You were his best friend, and I was fine with your title."

Emily raises her thumb biting at an already ravaged cuticle. From the look of her fingers, they take the brunt of her stress.

"Were you thinking about leaving him? Getting divorced?"

Her expectant glare is ice. I imagine she's thinking about her life and how it may have been different had I not been in the picture. Though I'll never be sure, I tend to think she would've been pushed to the back burner just the same as me.

I shake my head, embarrassed to answer her question and reveal the insecurities of my younger self. "I was unhappy, but I didn't see it for what it was until after Joe died. I believed my unhappiness stemmed from losing my mom, moving halfway across the county, leaving medical school, and just plain boredom. I'd been a medical student. I'd been around doctors and their schedules. I convinced myself Joe's hours were normal, and his drive was due to his new job. It wasn't until much later that I discovered the root of my discontent."

She turns her head and studies me. "Sounds like you're pushing your problems on someone who's no longer here to defend himself."

Emily doesn't pull any punches. I wonder if she's been like this her whole life or if this is a side effect of the accident.

I chuckle. "Uh, no. I wish I could say I was projecting, but it took me many hours in therapy before I could recognize and acknowledge what I just told you." I fill my lungs with cool air before broaching the true reason for my visit. "I didn't come here to upset you or try to change your mind about Joe. I came here because I have something I'd like to give you, as a gift from Joe."

She drops her chin and focuses on her finger as she traces an invisible path in the chipped paint of the bench seat.

"For all of Joe's faults, he was a caretaker. He did it for his mom when she was sick, he did it for me when my mom passed, and now I'd like him to do it for you."

Her finger stops moving, her head tips up, and her eyes are like lasers hyper-focused on mine.

"When Joe took the job in Colorado, he took out a life insurance policy. He wanted to make sure I would be okay, financially, in case anything ever happened to him. He paid the bill every year, and I had no idea he'd done such a thing until I found the policy while I was clearing out his office. It was like he'd somehow known something would happen to him. Maybe that is why he was so obsessed with getting ahead at the hospital and treating more patients than he could comfortably manage. But I guess there are some things we'll never have the opportunity to know."

I drop my hand on top of Emily's, and she stiffens, though she doesn't pull away like I thought she might.

"This place you live in, it's nice. I know it costs money, and I don't want you to ever worry about being able to pay for your care, which is why I've set up a trust in your name with Mitchell as your trustee. I've talked to Mitchell, and the interest from investments should be more than enough to pay for your care as well as have some extra spending money for clothes and incidentals."

She stares at me, a blank look covering her face.

"I know our conversation is a lot to process, but hold on to this truth. Whether he said the words or not, Joe loved you. Maybe not in the way you loved him, but he still loved you. Honor his love by letting him take care of you even though he can't be here physically."

We sit in silence as I let her process everything I've said. Ten minutes later, she shifts and stands up turning toward her assistant who's waiting about ten feet away. She starts to walk away but turns back after she's taken a few steps.

"Hope. You didn't have to do this. Why did you?"

I give her a sad smile and lift my shoulder in a shrug. "Because once upon a time, I knew what it was like to be cared for by Joe Roberts. Now it's time for you to know how it feels."

43

MITCHELL

I FLIP THE BOOK CLOSED AND GLANCE AT SEDONA. LONG, DARK
lashes brush her cheeks hiding the emerald green beneath her
closed lids. Her hair, wavy like mine and the color of her mother's, fans across my chest where she leans against me. This time
of day is my favorite, and I'm already dreading the days she
starts declining my offer to read her a bedtime story. I slide the
book onto her nightstand and slowly roll out of her embrace.

She'd been exhausted and had barely made it half-way
through a chapter before her lids started to flicker. I guess I
can't complain considering a glittery unicorn hell-bent on
saving the world doesn't capture my interest either.

After she'd spent the majority of her day swimming at her
friend's house, I'd picked Sedona up after I'd gotten off work,
and we'd gone to dinner followed by a full round of mini-golf.
She is a natural on the putting green, and I hate to admit she
beat me without the handicap I'd volunteered to give her.

I stand up and stretch the kinks out of my back and eye her
bed with a healthy dose of disdain. A twin mattress hasn't fit
my body since senior year of high school let alone accommo-

dated two bodies—mine and my daughter's—even if the second body is the size of a snack pack of Cracker Jacks.

With the stress of changing Emily's routine and the excitement of the budding relationship I've developed with Hope, Sedona's summer break is quickly approaching its end. I've been extra vigilant of our time together, making sure to cram our nights full of fun before she heads back to a school routine and the weather turns too chilly to do anything outside other than freeze our butts off.

I shut off her light and go downstairs interested to hear about Hope's meeting with Emily. Knowing Emily and Hope like I do, I'm thinking I should have sent a neutral third party to act as referee and bodyguard to make sure their conversation didn't turn into an exchange of fists.

My foot has just hit the bottom stair when I see headlights from Hope's vehicle creeping up the drive. I smile knowing she's drinking in the excitement of driving through the tunnel formed by nature. She'd been embarrassed to admit such a thing to me until I'd casually asked why it always takes her so long to get from the end of my driveway to my front door.

I'm secretly pleased my home brings her pleasure since I'm hoping she'll agree to move in with Sedona and me when her lease is up. I unlock the front door and walk out to lean against one of the wooden columns that support the front porch.

She exits her car, and I scan her face and body for any signs of trauma. Other than a few wayward wisps of hair that have fallen from her ponytail, she looks like the Hope I've come to adore.

She trudges up the steps as my eyes linger on the tease of bare leg she's sporting beneath her knee-length skirt. She stops a foot away and looks up at me through her eyelashes. Not able to resist touching her, I reach forward and pull her flush with my front before brushing a kiss across her forehead.

"How did it go?"

I place my hands on her upper arms holding her away from me so I can see her face. Her smile pops the balloon of my tension, and I pull her back into a tight hug.

When Hope had proposed setting up a trust for Emily's care, I'd initially balked and flat-out refused. She'd explained the hospital had offered her a settlement since Joe was technically injured while on the job. She'd admitted suing the hospital had never crossed her mind, but she'd agreed to take the settlement money they adamantly pushed on her.

She'd invested the life insurance money, telling me she'd felt like she'd know when the time was right to use it. Using the hospital settlement and profits from the sale of her house, she had finished medical school and moved to Illinois to make a fresh start.

It wasn't until she explained the details that I'd been willing to mull her proposal over and see it for the gift it was. Emily had loved Joe. It didn't matter that I could continue to provide for her care, it was the fact that Emily could feel protected and taken care of by the one person she'd always loved. Once I thought about it in that way, it was easy for me to agree to help Hope set up the trust.

"I think she's going to take it." The uptick in her voice tells me she's happy, and that's all I wish for her.

I move my hand down over her short skirt, stopping when my fingers contact the first sliver of her exposed thigh. "Want to have a slumber party tonight?"

She lifts an eyebrow and blows her wisps away from her face. "A slumber party? What are we, five?"

I chuckle and waggle my brows. "You've obviously never been to a Mitchell Anderson slumber party. Why don't you come in and let me give you sneak preview?"

I lean down, wrap her ponytail around my fist, and pull her neck to my lips before laying a trail of kisses from her jaw to her ear. She's breathtaking when she wears her hair in waves that cascade down her back, but she's a damn goddess when she sweeps it into a ponytail.

She follows me into the house, and I pull her down the hallway and into my bedroom. Before Hope, I'd never really liked having my master bedroom situated on the main floor where Sedona seemed so far away on the second level. With Hope's vocal range in the bedroom, I'm overjoyed for the increased distance. I've even tossed around the idea of sound-proofing the master before Sedona grows older or loses her ability to sleep like the dead.

I push her to the edge of the bed and fall to my knees, eye level with her full lips. I lean forward and wrap a hand in her hair. She moans, and my dick punches against my zipper with the force of a heavyweight boxer. I crush my lips to hers running my tongue across the seam enticing her to open, so I can delve into her warm, sweet mouth. Her hands tug at my hair raising goosebumps across my entire body. Hope can take me from zero to sixty with a single kiss.

I explore her mouth while trailing my other hand up the back of her naked thigh, stopping to appreciate the soft lace that falls across the curve of her tight ass. My fingertips slide beneath the delicate fabric inching slowly toward the heat of her core.

"Why are you going so slow? Previews are meant to tease and give you the down and dirty details in under two minutes. Get on with it."

I smile, knowing as soon as I slide my body into hers, she'll go off like a firework within seconds. I figure I have a good sixty seconds, and I don't plan to waste them. I squeeze her ass, dropping my fingertips between her crack while grinding my chest against her clit. Her back bows and I know she's seconds from detonation.

I stand and push her back, following her down as she hits the soft mattress.

She grabs the waistband of my sweatpants and tugs them down with rough fingers. My cock springs free and her whole body freezes, momentarily stunned by my lack of underwear. She takes my dick between her hands pulling and twisting the way I've shown her. I grab a condom off the pile on my pillow —a little detail I attended to earlier this evening—and rip it open with my teeth.

Hope's hands greedily move over my body as she sucks on my nipple and takes a barbell into her mouth. Fuck. The sensation is utterly delicious and totally worth the pain and embarrassment I went through when I got them.

Overtaken by sensation, I almost drop the condom on the bed before I get it rolled down my shaft. I shake my head and smile as I reach beneath her skirt and push her panties to the side. I use a hand to line up with her dripping pussy, rear back, and push all the way to the hilt as I rock forward.

"Holy shit, Mitchell. Yes."

I pump a few more times, finding a rhythm before her walls start to contract. I lift my hand and dip my thumb inside her mouth. "Lick it."

Her eyes flair with heat as she pulls it to the back of her throat and sucks.

"Shit. That feels fucking fantastic." I squeeze my eyes closed before pulling my thumb from her mouth and moving it to her clit and circling it with her moisture. Her walls clench and her ass lifts off the bed a second before her scream fills the room. She moans and bucks as I slam into her two more times before I follow her over the edge.

It's not until our breathing has returned to normal and her ability to speak returns that I hear her sarcasm.

"Characters were solid. Plot could use a little work. Sex was off the charts hot. I think I'd like to see the main attraction. I'll stay."

I bark out a laugh at her cheekiness. This woman is everything I could wish for and more.

EPILOGUE

ONE YEAR LATER...

Sedona and Mitchell zig-zag between the crowd of adults and children who are wandering between the animal exhibits. The pair smile and laugh like loons as I follow at a wide distance. Wisps of hair, not confined to my ponytail, stick like glue to my neck, and beads of sweat run down my chest and fall between my cleavage. I'm the definition of a hot mess, and I've never been happier.

The heat of the sun has sucked the energy from every visitor except for the crazy dad and his equally silly daughter who are practically running through the zoo leaving me to plod along behind them like a human pack mule.

An umbrella hangs from my wrist, a jacket is tied around my waist, and a backpack filled with snacks, water bottles, hand sanitizer, and a first aid kit is slung over one of my shoulders. I'm positive I've over-prepped, but one can never be too prepared for a trip to the zoo on what seems like the hottest day of the year.

Noticing Mitchell and Sedona have stopped to watch the

lions, I take a seat and fall into an entertaining session of people-watching. My rapt attention is riveted on a dad who walks by leading seven children, the oldest doesn't look any older than twelve, in a single file line with the mom and the eighth, yes eighth, child bringing up the rear. The baby—I assume it's a baby and not a kangaroo—is strapped to the mom in one of those baby slings. The kind that makes a parent look like they're hauling a sack of potatoes. The crazy-looking sling looks the opposite of comfortable, though I've heard my patient's parents rave about them.

An older man and woman walk by, the woman's hand tucked into the crook of the man's arm. The man is dressed in a short-sleeve button-down shirt and dress pants with a black fedora perched on the top of his head. The woman, who's wearing a floral pattern dress that looks like a post-World War II original, has the most serene smile on her face. I can't help but wonder how long they've been married considering she looks at him with stars in her eyes.

My gaze bounces between people, and I realize I've lost track of Sedona and Mitchell. Since I lack the energy to leave my seat, I figure I'll stay where I am and wait for them to find me. *Aren't those the instructions they give hikers?* Stay in one place, so you're easier to find.

"Where did you go? We turned around, and you were gone."

My eyes snap open as Sedona's voice startles me out of my catnap. I hadn't realized I'd let my eyes close. Sedona snuggles in tight to my side, and I put my arm around her. At almost eight-years-old, I don't know how much longer she'll seek the comforts of hugs and kisses.

I stroke my fingers through her hair. "Where's your dad?"

"He said he needs to check on something and use the bathroom. He sent me over here so I wouldn't wander off."

I nod. That sounds about right. She is constantly giving me

heart palpitations by wandering off when we are in stores or at the park.

I stare off into space wondering what's keeping Mitchell.

Sedona's hand taps on my thigh, her index finger raises just a fraction to point at someone while she talks. "See that guy over there? He's a member of the Traveling Fliers, a family of trapeze artists. It explains why he's wearing tight spandex pants."

My eyes dart to hers, and she waggles her brows.

"What made you say that?" My heart pounds against my ribs as I wait for her answer.

"Dad did. He and I play this game all the time. Hasn't he ever played it with you?"

My eyes jump around zeroing in on the wavy hair, strong jaw, and tall frame of my husband as his long strides erase the distance between our present and our past. His green eyes land on mine, and he smiles.

Like blinders falling away, my heart finally sees what years and distance have tried to bury. It may have taken almost twenty years but my music returned, and he's standing right in front of me offering me his hand.

———

I WALK into the Sedona's room and approach her bed. She turns her head, and I see her dad's eyes as she looks up at me. Reaching out her hand, fingernails painted her favorite shade of pink, she pats the spot next to her.

"I got your place all ready."

I look to the area where her hand rests and see a name tag. Scrolling lettering in pink marker, outlined in glitter, proudly displays *Mommy Hope*. Moisture coats my lids as I quickly shift my eyes from hers.

I pull a box from behind my back giving myself a few

minutes to gather my composure. Her eyes land on my surprise and light the same as they do when I take her to the book store.

"Is that for me?" Dimples frame her toothy grin as she leans toward me, finger pointing to the small, silver gift clasped between my fingers.

I nod.

"Oooo, what is it? Can I open it?"

She pops up on her knees, and the bed begins to jiggle as she bounces in an effort to contain her excitement.

"Well?"

She tilts her head, and her dark mop of hair falls to the side. I hand her the box, and she pulls the top off. "Oh, I love it. It's shiny and sparkly."

I carefully trace the musical note in the middle of the heart. "This is a magic necklace. It was given to me when I was about the same age you are now."

"Magic? Really?" I see the conflict in her face. Her youth wants to believe what her eight years have trained her not to.

"It's magic to me. A stranger gave it to me—a boy. He said the heart could transport me anywhere I wanted to go. And you know what? He was right. It took me away but brought me right back to where I needed to be. That's what makes it magic." I run my fingers over her dark hair. "Would you like to hear the story?"

Her eyes grow wide, and she nods her head, crossing her hands in front of her as she waits for me to begin. I let my thoughts linger on the long-buried memory before letting the words fall from my lips.

"I tugged at the waistband of the tights my mother forced me to pack when I left for the trip. Not only was I roasting in them, but I'd obviously grown a bit since I wore them last, and they were cutting into my belly button. Plus, every time I took a step, it felt like they were going to fall to my knees. I'd spent most of the day trying to secretly pull them up when the other students weren't paying attention.

Not that any of them paid me a minute of their time anyway. Every kid on the trip was with a friend. No single riders in the whole group, except for me. I was mad at my mom for thinking that going on a trip with a bunch of kids I didn't know would help me meet more friends. The fatal flaw in her plan was thinking I wanted to be friends with any of the superficial, boy-crazy girls or rude, mean boys.

I followed the orange flag Ms. Raymond carried like it was an American flag. She never put it down, nor did she let it touch the ground. I wouldn't have been a bit surprised if she had a little light on her visor that illuminated it when the sun went down.

I'd ridden alone through the darkness of the haunted house, nearly peeing myself when one of the cast members stepped behind me and boomed, 'Step to the dead center of the room,' as I entered the ride.

On the spinning teacups, I was an Asian family's 'extra one' where I narrowly escaped puking my breakfast omelet on their little girl's glittery silver shoes.

My ears were still recovering from riding the runaway train through the mountains with Ms. Raymond who swore the train was her favorite ride, then screamed the whole way when she realized the train we were riding was not the same train that went to the front of the park. I was miserable, and I had the chafe marks and ringing ears to prove it.

Ms. Raymond, or Screaming Eagle as I'd dubbed her, stopped abruptly.

After taking roll call she declared, 'You have thirty minutes for a bathroom and snack break. Meet back here.' She looked at her digital watch secured around her wrist, 'No later than two o-clock. Does everyone hear me?'

A chorus of 'yeahs' filtered through our twenty-person group.

'Excellent. You've been great so far. Don't disappoint me by being late. Off you go.'

She gave us a flick of her wrist reminding me of someone trying to shoo flies away. Who knows? Maybe that's what she considered us. Pesky flies.

Thankful for the reprieve, I stepped toward a nearby bench, sat down, and watched the backs of the students as they hurried away in their little groups of twos and threes. The day had been nothing short of horrible. I should have amped up my protests when my mom told me she was booking the trip. She'd had to work double shifts for an entire month to pay for a trip I'd had no desire to go on.

Staring off into space, I was totally unprepared when a voice deeper than my own said, 'I think that guy in the yellow shirt over there is a lemon salesman. It's the only explanation for his sour face.'

A snort fell from my mouth, and I belatedly raised my hand to catch it, mortified a noise so offensive had come from my body. I glanced to my side, trying not to move my head, and saw long, hairy, skinny legs attached to well-worn sneakers splayed out in front of the bench. I felt his shoulders touch mine as he leaned in, offering his apologies for startling me.

I turned and angled my body toward him catching his green gaze that reminded me of the lush moss on the base of the tree that grew outside my bedroom window. Deep and bright. Almost too green to be real. He was kinda cute, not that I was into looking at boys. But if I was, he would have been okay to stare at."

Sedona's snort tells me she's listening, but her reaction says she hasn't reached the "boys are cute" stage yet. *Thank God.*

"He'd surprised me. Not only had he talked to me—a stranger— but he'd made up the most ridiculous story about another stranger, and then shared it. He had guts, that was for sure.

Unable to hold my curiosity, I blurted, 'How do you do that?' My outburst confused him, so I clarified. 'How do you make up stories about other people?'

His answer was concise and uncomplicated. 'They just come to me, and it beats being bored.'

He told me a crazy tale about a woman and her look-alike dog before he prompted me to try his game. I ended up picking a baby and giving him superhuman powers. Lame, but not horrible considering it had been my first attempt.

We traded stories until someone called to him. He looked across the courtyard, and I followed his gaze to three people I assumed were his mom, dad, and brother. Our time was almost up, and my pulse started to climb as I realized he was the first, and only, person I'd ever felt comfortable talking to right from the start. I'd had a few friends at school, but those relationships were because of the teachers.

He stood and held out his hand like he intended to give me something. I looked down and saw a sparkling necklace with a small heart.

He urged me to take it and told me, 'Hope is the music of life. It can take you anywhere.' I thanked him and took the necklace.

I watched him walk away marveling at my luck. If I hadn't taken a seat on that very bench when I did, I would have never met the boy of my dreams."

I blink away the remnants of the memory and look at Sedona. Her hands are hidden behind her head, her eyes squinting as the pink tip of her tongue peeks out of the corner of her flattened lips. A frustrated growl slips from her mouth as she unsuccessfully tries to secure the clasp.

She holds up both ends, "Mommy Hope, you're right. It is magic. Can you help me?"

My heart melts as I hold out my hands and smile at my

sweet girl. She is the balm to my bruised soul, and I love her with every piece of my being.

She transfers the ends of the necklace to my waiting fingers and turns, lifting her long hair out of the way so I can fasten the jewelry around her neck. I run my hands through her hair before she turns around and throws her arms around me.

I turn, angling my lips so her ears can catch my whispered words. "I'm passing its magic on to you since I don't need it anymore."

She pulls back and looks straight into my eyes. "Why not?"

"Because, sweetheart, I hoped one day it would bring me back to the boy of my dreams, and it did."

THANK YOU

Of all of the fabulous books available worldwide, I thank you for choosing *Heartbeat*, and I hope you enjoyed your reading experience. If you have a few minutes to leave a review on your favorite platform, please e-mail me through my website, www.alipierce.com, and let me know where I may send my personal note of thanks to you.

ACKNOWLEDGMENTS

Typing "The End" is nowhere near the finish line when bringing a book baby into the world. *Heartbeat* is covered in the fingerprints of so many fabulous people. Whether a suggestion, a comment, a review, or words of encouragement, you have each helped me introduce my baby to the world. Thank you.

Readers: *Heartbeat's* journey to your hands is precisely what its title reflects. This story burrowed into my heart until its song could no longer be ignored. It started with a single scene: two strangers meet on an airplane. From there, it blossomed into the story you've just finished reading. I love opening a book and escaping the reality of life for a few hours. My hope is *Heartbeat* gave you the same type of escape.

Karen Gill: If I could "build" my dream writing partner, I wouldn't come close to reaching the perfection you are for me. You are the best damn alpha reader and editor any writer could hope for as well as my best friend. Thank you. Those two words seem paltry in comparison to everything you are to me, but I'll continue to say them. Yes, I did sneak in an inside joke from Cancun. I knew you'd find it.

Lucy Frieders and Norm Jannisch: You are both

extraordinary beta readers. Your quick turnaround time helped keep me on deadline. Your attention to detail and your insightful comments elevated *Heartbeat* to its final, shinier version.

Mom and Dad: In the past year, you've heard more about writing and publishing than you'll ever care to know, but you still listen patiently and give great advice. Your support is unwavering. Thank you.

Scott: You are the guy who gives his all, so I can follow this dream. Whether it's providing tech support, emotional encouragement, or marketing to your colleagues, you're always in my corner. I'm so lucky you chose me as your Euchre partner all those years ago. I don't know what I would do without you.

Little P: You are a killer PR agent, and you've always got my back. I'm lucky you're still willing to accept cuddles and kisses as payment.

Middle P: You're my DJ. You match songs to my words and find the tunes I need to keep me focused.

Big P: Our word count competitions are becoming fierce. You keep me on my toes.

I love you all.

ABOUT THE AUTHOR

Ali Pierce is a speech language pathologist, turned storyteller, whose passion is creating stories that weave hope and love into everyday life. Ali lives in Illinois with her husband and three children. When not writing, Ali can be found shuttling children to and from school, trying to figure out the formula for a perfect Instagram feed, or buried face first in a book.